BOOKS BY HELEN~

Helena Newbury is the *New York Times* and *USA Today* bestselling author of sixteen romantic suspenses, all available where you bought this book. Find out more at helenanewbury.com.

Lying and Kissing

Punching and Kissing

Texas Kissing

Kissing My Killer

Bad For Me

Saving Liberty

Kissing the Enemy

Outlaw's Promise

Alaska Wild

Brothers

Captain Rourke

Royal Guard

Mount Mercy

The Double

Hold Me in the Dark

Deep Woods

MOUNT MERCY

HELENA NEWBURY

DEDICATION

To my high school English teachers, Ms. Collinge and Mr. Roberts. Without you two, this wouldn't be possible.

1

AMY

S OMETIMES, I wonder: what if I'd never left the operating
theater? I could have stayed safe. Stayed warm. But I'd never
have met Doctor Dominic Corrigan. I'd never have fallen headfirst
into those blue Irish eyes. I'd never have known what it took to love a
man like him, or what it was like to be loved by one.

And we'd be dead. We'd all be dead.

On the morning I met him, I was in the zone. The hospital, the
operating theater... all of it had melted away and I was only aware of
the soft violins of Bach's double concerto, the reassuring weight of the
scalpel in my hand and the steady rhythm of the patient's heart.
When I spoke, even my voice was a little slow and dreamy. "You can
tell Mrs. Barlow her husband's going to be okay." I began to close up
the incision. "Good job, everyone."

Krista, my head nurse, grabbed the phone and passed on the
good news. She'd barely put it down, and I'd only just finished
suturing, when it rang again. "They want you downstairs for a
consult," she told me.

Downstairs. I came out of the zone in a split second. I kept my
voice calm, but my stomach was already knotting. "Ask Patel to do it."

"He's in the middle of a heart bypass," said Krista apologetically.

I pulled off my surgical mask. "Weisler, then." Now my voice was pleading.

"He's working on a head injury. Some teenager came off her dirt bike."

That only left me. I had to go *down there.* I nodded and walked out into the hallway. When I hit the elevator button for *1, Emergency Room,* my chest went tight.

Surgery, where I manage to hide most of the time, is on the very top floor of the Mount Mercy hospital, furthest from the outside world. It's a secure little burrow: no one comes up there unless they're scheduled for a procedure. The ER? That's the polar opposite. It's where hundreds of strangers pour in every day. I could hear it before the elevator even reached the first floor. Yells and screams and running footsteps. Shouts and pleas and anger and above all, *people.*

I don't do so well with people.

When the doors rumbled open, I caught my breath and took an unconscious step back. Gurneys rattling past, nurses running back and forth with supplies, the ear-splitting whistle of defibrillator paddles rising in charge and the dull thud as they fired. A babble of voices: doctors and patients and relatives and cops, all demanding answers, *now, this instant.* Surgery is about planning and precision, sometimes hurried but never panicked. The ER is one continuous panic. You want to know what it's like? Get four or five mechanics, huddle them around a freshly-wrecked car and then push the whole thing out of a plane and tell them they have to get it working again before it hits the ground.

The doctors in the ER cursed and bitched and joked and somehow it *worked,* they formed a noisy, close-knit team, like a rowdy group of football jocks who win every game. They communicated non-stop. I'm painfully shy. They made split-second decisions. I'm all about thinking things through. They were heroes who lived for the adrenaline rush. Confident, grinning lions, hungry for the next patient.

I'm more of a dormouse. My dad once told me, *people like us do better in a lab.* And he was right: I'm a scientist who somehow landed in a hospital. I thrive on order and the ER was chaos. I really, *really* didn't want to go out there.

And then I saw him, across the room: the case I'd been called downstairs for. A biker in a sleeveless leather jacket lay on a gurney, a knife buried in his chest right up to the hilt. Definitely a surgical case. My mind was instantly spinning with a diagram of the man's anatomy, visualizing all the damage the blade would have done. We had to get him upstairs *now*.

Except... an ER doc, a big guy I didn't recognize, was leaning over the man. He'd just finished re-inflating the man's lung—so far, so good—but now he was preparing to do the worst thing possible: pull out the knife.

I felt my eyes bug out. I darted out of the elevator and right into my own personal hell. "Stop!" I yelled. But my voice is moderated for the quiet calm of the OR. I was a mouse squeaking next to a busy freeway.

And crossing the ER felt like scuttling across that freeway. I'm not that small, about 5'5", but everything felt huge and fast and loud. Carts and gurneys racing across my path, cops tussling with drunks, nurses running between patients... all the people who belonged down there and then *me*, trying to thread my way between them.

I'm used to people not noticing me. It's deliberate. I tend to... hide. But it means no one moves aside for me. And as I struggled and dodged, I could see the doctor flexing his arms, preparing to pull the knife.... "*Stop!*" But just as I yelled, paramedics burst through the doors with another patient, drowning me out.

I ducked under a cop's upraised arm, turned sideways to slip between two nurses and slammed against the biker's gurney. My hands wrapped around the doctor's hands on the handle of the knife and I pushed *down* just as he pulled *up*. "STOP!" I yelled.

And the doctor stopped.

Everything stopped.

I stood there panting with relief, staring down at the knife. The hands under my fingers were huge and tanned. God, and so *warm*.

The ER is a freezing, drafty barn of a room, but he throbbed with heat.

My gaze tracked slowly up his arms. They were... *wrong*. Surgeons, we're quick and deft with long fingers like pianists. Doctors might carry a little more muscle from all that heaving patients onto gurneys but this guy looked more like a Marine. His forearms were as thick around as my thigh and chiseled with muscle, tanned to a light caramel and dusted with glossy black hair. But what really made me stare were the tattoos. The tail of what looked like a serpent began just above his elbow and went upwards, looping and twisting. The black ink gleamed as the design stretched over the curve of his bicep... and then his blue scrubs cut off my view.

As I looked up, I had to twist awkwardly to face him. There was a gossamer touch as the little hairs on his arm brushed my elbow and then our forearms were bumping up together, the warm solid bulk of him pressing against my cool skin.

I swallowed and lifted my chin. He was big: his chest filled my vision, glorious slabs of hard muscle that pushed out the front of his blue scrub top, the scoop neck just low enough to catch a glimpse of tan flesh.

I lifted my chin even more. He was tall, too. I was eye-level with his pecs. My lips were just the right height to kiss his nipples.

I flushed and craned my head *right back.*

And I was captured.

His eyes were like the sky, but not a sky you'd see over Colorado or Texas or anywhere in America. They were chips of the sky in some other land, an ancient sky that hung low, clinging to dark rocks with its mists, bathing the landscape with its tears. They were breathtakingly beautiful... and *sad.* Just for a second, they were the saddest thing I'd ever seen in my life.

But just for a second. I'd caught him off guard, but he put that right immediately. His back straightened, his lips pressed together and those eyes turned bright and diamond-hard, like the sky itself had frozen. The feeling was totally different. Before, I'd been captured. Now I was pinned.

He had high, almost graceful cheekbones that made me think of somewhere cold, but his skin had been warmed to a deep tan. A hard jaw with just a dusting of careless, *I don't give a fuck* stubble. That jaw would have made him look too brutal if it hadn't been set off by a gloriously full, soft lower lip that pouted out, arrogant and knowing. I learned soon that no matter where you tried to look on that face, you'd always be drawn back to those eyes and that lip. He was dangerously good looking and he dripped with confidence. If the doctors in the ER were lions, this guy was the leader of the pride. I didn't recognize him: was he new?

His dark brows arced down just a little as he studied me. I could feel his gaze on every freckle, every loose strand of copper hair that had spilled out beneath my surgical cap. I could feel it on the line of my jaw and on my lips. It set off a lashing, twisting streamer of energy inside me that connected straight to my core and made me crush my thighs together.

The corners of his mouth rose lazily up.

A cocky smile.

An *oh, it's on* smile.

"Who the fuck are you?" he asked. The *fuck* wasn't aggressive. It was amused. Intrigued. Which made no sense, I've never intrigued anyone.

I nearly said *Amy* but I was suddenly aware of the nurses, the other doctors, the whole rest of the ER. How long had we been staring at each other? Two seconds? Seven hours? "Beckett," I said. "Surgery."

"Beckett." His accent was like brutally hard, rain soaked rock, each surface turning silver as lightning lit it up. Musical and violent. My name was transformed into a two-syllable slap, intimate and playful. I felt my cheeks flare. "I've put a tube into his lung to re-inflate it, but the knife has to come out," he told me.

For a split-second, I thought: *what knife?*

Then I looked down at our hands, my fingers still wrapped over his on the knife's handle like we were the betrothed at some ancient wedding ceremony. Appropriate: his accent sounded old. Not *old man.*

Old country. And then I got it. *Irish.* And not the soft lilt of the south. This was darkly sexy, untamed, a rumble that resonated right down my body. *Northern* Irish.

"You pull it," I said, forbidding my voice to shake, "and he'll bleed out. It hit a main artery. The pressure of the blade's all that's keeping him alive."

He looked down at our hands. "Blood's filling up his chest cavity and squeezing his heart. If I don't pull it out to relieve the pressure, he's dead."

I focused on the pulse monitor. He was right: each *beep* came with just a little more difficulty. I could hear the man dying. But I could imagine the frantic, terrifying nightmare that would ensue if that blade came out in the ER: instead of a slow leak we'd have a gushing firehose. "I'll do it upstairs," I told him.

"We don't have time."

Another *beep* from the monitor. This one was agonizing: everyone around the gurney felt it. I could visualize the heart being crushed, fighting against the pressure. I could feel myself wavering... but it was just too risky. "You can't do this down here!" I snapped.

"I'm his doctor." He was as calm as I was panicked. But he was running out of patience.

"Why even call for a surgical consult if you're not going to listen to me?" I asked desperately.

"I didn't."

My heart flip-flopped. *What?!* Was I in the wrong place?

"I did," said a voice from behind us.

Both of us craned over our shoulders. Dr. Henry Bartell, administrator of the hospital. He still goes by *Doctor,* even though it's ten years since he traded the ER for spreadsheets and meetings.

"My first day and already you're second-guessing me?" said the Irish doctor.

"Don't push it, Corrigan," Bartell told him. "You're not in LA now. You set a foot wrong here, I'll bounce you out the door. Beckett's our best surgeon. If she says it stays in, it stays in."

I felt myself flush down to my roots. Bartell and I get on, mainly because I'm the only person who gets their paperwork in on time. I'm not trying to be the teacher's pet: following the rules is just the way I'm wired.

The doctor moved his hands off the knife, taking mine with them. I sighed in relief. But then Corrigan turned to face me, leaned in and *loomed*. Face-on, he seemed even bigger: those shoulders seemed to block out the whole ER until it was just him and me. "You think it's too risky?" He was still calm, still controlled, but I could hear the frustration boiling away under the surface. He was sure he was right, just as I was.

I nodded. "Mm-hmm." I crossed my arms, glared, and tried to look assertive. Then uncrossed them. *Dammit!*

"Thing is, Beckett, slow and certain might be the way to go when you surgeons are upstairs in Mount fucking Olympus but down here in the trenches we need to take some chances." His voice was fast and hard, the accent like being caressed by silver-veined granite. "You're the cautious type? I get that. It's kind of adorable. And if I ever come upstairs, I'll sit with you and fill in every form in triplicate before we so much as cut a toenail. But down here, in the ER, with my patient, my word is God and if we need to take chances, we'll take them. Are you really a good surgeon?"

"What?" My head was spinning and my face was hot. I was being dressed down, but it didn't feel cruel. Not when, with every word, those eyes were burning down into mine, melting me just when I needed to be made of iron.

"Are you really a good surgeon?" he repeated.

"Yes!" I'd never admit that, normally, but I was flustered.

"Good."

And with one quick move, he pulled out the knife.

2

AMY

F OR A SECOND, I just stood there staring. *He didn't just do that. He did* not *just do that.* Then Corrigan extended his arm with a flourish and let the knife go. It fell and *thunked* into the floor, the tip buried in the linoleum. Blood gushed in red rivers from the wound. I could feel panic spread through the people around the gurney as the numbers on the blood pressure monitor went into freefall. A nurse met my eyes across the table: *is he crazy?!*

Behind me, Bartell got the words out before I could. "What the hell do you think you're doing?" he bellowed.

But Corrigan was utterly calm. He reached down and grabbed my hands. A jolt went through me, right down to my toes. There was something about his touch, strong and warm....

He guided my hands into the wound. "Keep pressure there," he told me. I pressed hard and the bleeding slowed. But we still only had seconds to save this guy.

Corrigan started probing the wound, searching for the severed artery. He had to move in close and his hip pressed against mine. Two paper-thin layers of scrub material separated naked me from naked him. I was close enough that I could catch the scent of him and it was addictive, sweet vanilla with a heady kick of sandalwood. Part of me was mad at him. Part of me just wanted to bury my nose between his pecs.

He looked away from the wound as his fingers moved. I do that, too: when you can't really see what you're doing, it helps to look at something else and go by feel alone. Except... he looked at *me*. At the little slice of pale shoulder blade above the neckline of my scrubs. At the copper hair that had slipped free at the side of my cap, a whole lock of it hanging down and grazing my cheek. I felt myself flush.

"There," said Corrigan. "Got you, you bugger. Clamp." A nurse handed him a clamp, and he clamped the artery.

Everyone held their breath for a few seconds. Then a nurse said, "Blood pressure's stabilizing. Rhythm's healthier, too." There was a kind of awe in her voice.

"He's still got a hole in his chest!" My voice was tight with panic.

"Well, *feck*," said Corrigan. Not *fuck*, like before. *Feck*. It was lighter, gentler and very, very Irish. "If only we had a top surgeon on hand who could fix it."

As he slid his hands out, his fingers brushed mine. That jolt again, like teenagers holding hands. *Get it together, Amy!* The guy was still going to die if I didn't work fast.

I grabbed a suture kit and went to work. But this was nothing like working in the OR. I reached for some gauze but my fingers closed on thin air: I was used to everything being in its place. Then a nurse leaned against the gurney and the patient moved sickeningly under my hands, nearly dislodging a clamp. A supply trolley sped past me, missing me by an inch. An ambulance siren started to wail, just outside, and then there was a blast of freezing wind and loose paperwork blew across the room as the doors opened.

I couldn't hear, couldn't think. I could feel the panic rising up inside. I take patients' lives in my hands every day, but it's calm and controlled. Every step is planned. This was the opposite: a mad, confusing scramble with a guy's life on the line. *This is why I stay upstairs!*

But out of all the eyes watching me, there was one pair that felt gentle. Sympathetic. I glanced up for a split second.

It was Corrigan. Watching, willing me to succeed.

And as I looked down at the wound again, feeling his eyes on me... somehow, I managed to slip into the zone. Everything else fell away and my fingers seemed to move on their own, sure and certain and quick. I heard one of the nurses mutter a curse, impressed.

I sutured the last bleeder and stepped back. "There."

Corrigan's gorgeous lips curved into a grin. "I knew you could do it."

And beneath the teasing, cocky tone, there was genuine admiration. For once, instead of flushing, I stared right back at him, trying to figure him out.

He wasn't prepared for that. And for an instant, I thought I saw it again: something beneath all that confidence and charm, something painful and deep. Something real.

I was still staring when Krista ran up to us. She looked at me. She looked at Corrigan. "Okay. What did I miss?"

I dropped my gaze. "Nothing. We're taking this guy upstairs." I kicked off the gurney's brakes and heaved it into the elevator. I managed to do it without looking Corrigan in the eye again.

But it didn't matter. I could feel his gaze following me until the elevator doors closed.

Upstairs in the sanctuary of my operating theater, with the knife wound guy on the table and Brahms playing on the speakers, I hoped life could get back to normal. But no.

"Corrigan's been to Libya," said Krista. "And the Congo. And Uganda. *Doctors Without Borders.*"

I met Krista two years ago, the day I arrived at Mount Mercy hospital. She's a frizzy-haired firework of a person, my head theater nurse and my best friend. Normally, I love hearing all the hospital gossip, especially because, as we both agree, I have no life of my own. But today she was talking about Corrigan, the one guy I was trying to forget.

I tried to focus on the lung I was repairing but I couldn't get into the zone. Playing in a loop in my head was the way he'd dressed me down...and the way he'd smiled at me. I couldn't work out if I was mad at him or melting at him. *Both?*

"He's been shot," said Krista, awe in her voice. "He has bullet scars. Three of them. And a scar from a machete, right across his chest."

I tried not to think of hard pecs or the way his body had felt when it pressed against mine. "How would you even know that?" I mumbled.

"Someone saw him in the locker room this morning." Krista grinned. "The word they used was *lickable.*"

"Anesthesia still okay?" I asked. I was desperate now to change the subject. Every time I thought of those Irish eyes, a hot ripple went right down my body. If Krista noticed, it would start a conversation I did *not* want to have.

But Lina, our anesthesiologist, was no help. She just solemnly nodded from behind her monitor. A six-foot, imposing blonde from Austria, she almost never speaks during operations, just sits there watching over the patient, a silent guardian.

And now Adele, our junior nurse, joined in. "A nurse from pediatrics knows a nurse who knows a doctor who knows *another* nurse who worked with Corrigan in LA." She dropped her voice to a whisper. *"They had a thing."*

"I don't want to know," I lied.

"I do," said Krista quickly.

Adele's eyes went big. She's so young and innocent, sometimes she looks half kitten. "They have this swimming pool in the basement, for physiotherapy, and someone came in and they were—"

"No—" said Krista.

"Yes! In the shallow end, with her legs wrapped around him."

Krista squealed with delight.

"Can we just focus on the patient?" I pleaded. I knew it was useless. They were like a couple of teenage girls *squee*-ing over the hot new exchange student. Who was also the star quarterback *and* was in a band. The more they talked, the more I could feel Corrigan's muscled hip pressing against mine. I started to think about that stubbled jaw and how it would rasp gently against my cheek as he moved in for a kiss. *This is crazy!* I never got like this about a guy. And guys never look at me the way he had.

"Dominic. Even his first name's sexy," said Krista.

I shook my head. "No it isn't." *Yes it is.*

"He's like some muscley, Irish doctor of *lurvvv*," said Krista with relish.

"No nurse can resist him?" I asked sarcastically.

"Not just nurses," said Krista. "Doctors. Surgeons...." She looked at me. I appeared completely disinterested... I hoped. "Anyone female," Krista continued. "The man gets around. I heard that when he was in Detroit, someone walked into an office, looking for the hospital's head of legal, but Corrigan was sitting in her chair. And then they see her heels, sticking out from under the desk."

Blood was welling up in the wound. "Could I get some suction, please?" I asked.

Krista dutifully vacuumed the blood away. But then, "That's what *he* said."

She and Adele doubled over, giggling uncontrollably behind their masks. I swear I even heard a snort from Lina. *Goddamn that man!* He was three floors away and he was still managing to disrupt my neat, ordered little world.

I closed the hole in his chest, then started stitching him up. *There. Finished.* The guy would heal up just fine.

And staring at the wound, I had to admit something. The bleeding had been bad, but, with some fast work downstairs, I'd handled it. His heart, though, *had* been about to stop. If we'd left the knife in as I'd wanted, this guy probably wouldn't have made it.

Corrigan was a cocky, risk-taking womanizer. But he'd been right.

When I'd closed up and finished, I went out into the hallway and leaned my head against the window that looks out over the town. It was March and so far it had been a mild winter with only an inch of snow on the ground.

Mount Mercy, named for the mountain that rises above it, is really too small to need a hospital, but they had to build one somewhere to serve all the villages around the area. Most of the staff don't even live here. They commute from one of the other towns, where there are movie theaters and more than one restaurant. But I love this place. I love the way it looks in the summer, with wildflowers turning the fields into a blaze of color and—even though I hate the cold—I love how it looks now, in winter, with the snow dusting the rooftops.

I love that most of the buildings date back to the Gold Rush, and that a lot of the locals have roots here going back that far. Even the police feel old-fashioned. Looking down Main Street, I could pick out the well-cushioned body of Earl, the head of our tiny police force, as he patrolled on foot, the sun glinting off his silver walrus mustache. Beside him was Lloyd, the young cop he was training. The hospital was a regular stop for them on their beat. In fact, Earl seemed to hang around the hospital much more than he needed to, as if he liked spending time here. None of us could figure out why. But he brought in boxes of his homemade apple and caramel donuts, so no one argued. It's a cozy nest of a town.

The mountain freaks a lot of people out. It's beautiful, with thick pine forests and a gorgeous white snowcap, but on the side closest to the town there's a huge outcropping that looms over us. It literally casts a shadow over the town each morning. If all that rock ever broke loose, it'd slide straight down the mountain and bury us, but nature has smiled on us ever since the town was formed a hundred years ago: hence *Mount Mercy*. And I like it. It's a reassuring sign that nothing ever changes here.

Until today.

Now Corrigan was here, prowling around my cozy burrow. It made no sense: he couldn't be interested in me. If he was the new quarterback, I was the weird, geeky girl who hid away in the library. But whenever I closed my eyes, I saw that cocky, lust-filled gaze.

He wanted the geek girl.

And—I flushed—I had a crush on the quarterback.

I didn't understand it. He was my complete opposite: confident where I'm shy, loud where I'm quiet, risky and quick where I'm cautious and slow. He was everything I shied away from and nothing like the men I'd been into before. And yet I was drawn to him. I couldn't stop thinking about his eyes or the way his body had felt when he pressed up against me. And that brief second of vulnerability I'd seen, that hint of something deeper underneath his cockiness, that only made it worse. I knew he was totally unsuitable, a womanizer who was only after one thing. I knew he couldn't *really* be interested in me. And yet I was fascinated.

Goddamn him. Why did he have to come here?

3

DOMINIC

WHY DID I have to come here?

I was in the ER break room, pouring coffee into someone else's *World's Best Dad* mug. The acrid smell made my nostrils prickle: it must have been sitting on the hotplate since dawn. But I needed the caffeine. Last night, my first in the apartment I'd rented, I hadn't slept at all. Even after going for a run. Even after hitting the town's one bar and sinking some late-night beers. This place was just too damn quiet.

In LA, I'd had three locks on my door, bars on the windows and a siren wailing past every few minutes. In the Congo and Libya, it wasn't a normal night unless you were jolted awake by the crackle of gunfire or the thump of an explosion. But in Mount Mercy, I could hear myself breathing. I wasn't sure if people even locked their doors, here.

And the quiet gave me space to remember. I'd laid awake staring up at the ceiling, feeling the void where their voices and footsteps should have been.

I drained the coffee, wincing. At least hospital coffee was the same the world over. And when I slammed the mug down, I had a plan.

If Mount Mercy was too quiet to distract me, I'd find something else. I'd go back to that bar and get wasted. Or I'd borrow some skis and find a black run, something that would get the adrenaline pumping. Or....

The break room had a window that looked out into the hallway. I could see a couple of the nurses out there, chatting away at the nurse's station. I'd seen their eyes go big when they first saw my tattoos and heard my accent. I'd give one of them the silver-tongued Irish charm and take her back to my place. Or maybe both of them. Yeah, sex was the answer.

Except....

My gaze had drifted to a sign that pointed the way to different departments. An angled arrow led upstairs. *Surgery,*

Amy Beckett.

Smart. Annoying. Sheltered. She'd last about five minutes, down here in the real world. But she hadn't backed down when I'd gotten in her face. She might be shy, but she had a spine. And she hadn't gone all doe-eyed and melty over me but...there'd been something. Something a lot more interesting.

Stupid. Why make it hard on myself? This place was packed with women. I looked back to the nurses. One of them caught my eye and gave me a smile. I smiled back.

But....

It was a weird feeling, like when your tongue keeps wiggling a loose tooth even though it hurts. There was something about Beckett. She was all buttoned-up and smart and efficient and her body was hidden under those shapeless green surgery scrubs. But there were these little things... like the blue eyes that had gone from frosty to steaming hot when we'd glared at each other just right. Or her creamy skin, that pale throat leading down into the neckline of her scrubs, tempting me with thoughts of what she might be wearing underneath. I imagined a black, lacy bra and sexy little black panties, silky fabric stretched over firm ass cheeks. My fingers sliding under the material at the front and *down* and *in* and her letting out a high, shocked little squeal of pleasure as I parted her slickened folds.

And that red hair. The hair most of all. Not fake, cherry red, not auburn like fall leaves. Full-on glossy copper, bright as a flame. I'd only seen a single lock that had escaped from under that tight surgical cap: just a hint that under all that cool formality there was something scalding. All I could think about was pulling it free and letting it spill down her back in a shimmering wave. I'd roll the strands over her breasts with my palms until her nipples jutted out, hard and perfect, and my kiss swallowed up her moans.

I turned away from the window. *Feck.* Now I was rock hard in my pants.

Well, fine. The cock wants what the cock wants. I'd find her, work my magic on her, and get her into bed like all the rest.

As I headed towards the door, though, I had this itching, nagging sensation. *She's trouble.* I didn't just want to fuck her. I was... *fascinated* by her. Despite the fact she was so different to the others. Maybe because of it. And that felt dangerous.

Nah. It'll be fine. I flung open the door.

And walked right into a teenager.

"Hi!" she said, far too brightly for a Monday morning.

I rubbed a hand over my face, feeling my stubble scratch. "Who are you and why are you so perky?" I frowned. "Where did you steal the scrubs from?"

"Bethany Taylor!" she said, no less perkily. "I'm your medical student."

Were students really that young these days? I knew she must be early twenties, but she looked like she was barely in college. Was *I* really that young, once? "*My* student?"

"Mr. Bartell paired me up with you. He said it'd be good for you."

Bartell. I always hated administrators and this one already had it in for me. I wanted out. I needed to get back to a city, to the bustle and noise. But Bartell was right, I was beyond my last chance. Being fired three times in a year will do that.

I studied Taylor suspiciously. She had long, golden hair straight out of a shampoo commercial, bubblegum pink lipstick and she was looking at me excitedly...and just a little cautiously. "What else did Bartell say about me?" I asked tiredly.

"Nothing, Doctor Corrigan."

"Taylor...."

She bit her lip and looked at the floor. "He said don't let you rub off on me because he doesn't need another loose cannon."

I waited. "... and?"

Her cheeks colored. "He said not to let you chat me up."

I sighed. Come on, like I'd fuck a MED student! Then I frowned. Okay, there was that *one* time.... But not now. Now, I had my sights firmly on Beckett. "We'll get on just fine, Taylor," I told her. "What have we got?"

She led the way to Exam One and pulled back the curtain. A white-haired guy sat on the edge of the bed and a much younger guy sat on the visitor's chair. "William Jackson, possible arrhythmia, history of coronary heart disease...." She ran through his vitals while I studied the guy.

He was in his sixties with a deep tan that he sure as hell hadn't gotten in Colorado and a thin coat that said he wasn't used to the weather here. Two of the local cops strolled past the open curtain. Instantly, my patient was on his feet. "I don't need to be here," he said.

"You do," said the young guy in the chair. "You're having palpitations."

Now *he* looked like a local. He was in a heavy plaid shirt and he had a thick jacket hung over the back of his chair. He couldn't have been much older than Taylor, with thick, unruly black hair and big blue eyes. He'd rolled up his shirt sleeves and his arms were loaded with muscle. Probably had all the girls after him. But his eyes were following the cops, too. Both of these guys were mixed up in something shady.

I got the old guy to open his shirt and listened to his heart. The faded prison tattoos weren't a total surprise. And... *yep*. "You *are* having palpitations," I told him. I turned to the young guy. "Good catch."

He flushed. "I... uh... did a few years of medical school."

Taylor stepped forward, interested. "No kidding? Where'd you study?"

The young guy looked at her and their eyes *locked.*

"I'm Seth," said the young guy.

Taylor grinned and bit her lip. "Bethany."

I rolled my eyes. *Ah, young love.* "Nice tan," I told the old guy. "Florida?"

He looked at me suspiciously, then nodded. "Flew in last night."

"You have altitude sickness," I told him. "Florida to Colorado is a ten thousand foot difference. It can cause palpitations if you already have heart disease. It'll pass in a day or two. But I want to do an ultrasound of your heart, just to be sure there's nothing else going on."

Both of them jumped up. "No need," said the old guy. "I'll be fine. Thanks, doc."

I narrowed my eyes. This was more than just a couple of criminals being antsy around cops. They were scared of something else. I put my hand on Seth's chest, blocking him. "What's going on?" I asked.

He wasn't going to tell me. But when Taylor cocked her head to the side and made *it's okay* eyes at him, that did the trick. "My dad," Seth blurted at last. "He doesn't know we're here. He'll be mad."

And he rubbed at something on his forearm. A tattoo, still angry red with freshness. I've been around the world, but I'd never seen anything like it: two crossed rifles beneath a clenched fist.

I looked at the old guy. The sudden fear I saw in his eyes, just at the mention of Seth's dad, made me go cold inside. They hadn't been nervous about being caught by the cops. They'd been nervous about what Seth's dad would do if they got themselves arrested. Who the hell *was* this guy?

"A half hour," I told them. "Let us do the ultrasound and you can get out of here."

"*I can do it!*" said Taylor, so fast it was almost one word. She and Seth looked at each other and grinned again and she blushed. Seth reluctantly nodded and the two men sat down.

As I walked away and grabbed the chart for my next case, I

couldn't shake my uneasiness. The instant that ultrasound was done, I wanted those guys the hell out of the ER. They seemed harmless enough themselves, but they were mixed up in something bad. Bad enough that I didn't want them bringing it here.

4

AMY

THE HOSPITAL CAFETERIA is a lot like a high school cafeteria. Bartell and the other suits are the teachers and they stick strictly to their own table, if they deign to eat in the cafeteria at all. The ER staff are the jocks, loud and confident, fist-bumping and back-slapping. The medical students are the new kids, big-eyed and anxious. And surgeons sit at the geeks' table in the corner. That's where I was, on my own, *American Journal of Surgery* propped up between my coffee and my tray so I could hide behind it.

I was always going to be an introvert. From the time I was toddling around our apartment, my parents could tell I was taking after my dad, a biologist who studied insect anatomy. I preferred books to playing ball, went quiet and big-eyed around other kids and had my dad's unnatural focus, happy to sit on his knee and peer through a microscope for hours.

But it was okay because my mom was this glittering, sparkly sunbeam of a woman who dragged me to other kids' birthday parties and forced me out into the sunshine to hula-hoop with her. At first, I couldn't understand how she and my dad could be in love when they were so very different. As I got older, I realized she was the puzzle piece that fit with him exactly, balancing him out. With both of them together, I had a hope of turning out something like normal.

And then, when I was six, she started to get this pain in her side. A pain that made our doctor look worried and send her for tests. And then she went to the hospital...and didn't come home.

For two months, my dad and I visited her every day as the cancer destroyed her one organ at a time. The doctors fighting to save her were heroes, in my eyes. When she kept getting worse, I wasn't angry at them. I just wanted to help.

At her funeral, squeezing my dad's hand as they lowered the casket, I said, *I want to be a doctor.*

And, tears running down his face, he said *okay.*

He probably forgot about it within a few days, but I didn't. Studying was a way to cope with the pain and without my mom to coax me away from the books, I became a recluse, spending every break and lunch hour in the school library memorizing anatomy. My dad reacted the same way: devastated at losing her, he buried himself in his work. When I ran out of textbooks, I'd help him. While other girls were braiding each other's hair and talking about boys, I was preparing microscope slides. It turned out I'd inherited my dad's steady hands. We loved each other, supported each other, but we were two introverts holed up in a house with no one to drag us outside. Each day, I became a little more isolated, a little more shy.

The other kids bullied me mercilessly: I was so awkward, so weird, it was easy for the girls to make fun of me and for the boys to make me blush. So I learned not to draw attention. I got smaller and smaller until I could walk into a room and no one would even notice I was there.

When it came time for college and I told my dad I wanted to go to med school, he tried to talk me out of it. *People like us do better in a lab,* he said. But I was stubbornly determined and, eventually, he nodded. The day I went off to med school was the happiest day of my life.

But medicine was nothing like I expected. I soaked up the science like a sponge, but when we started to do rounds and had to take histories and present cases, I mumbled and flushed. When a question was asked, I didn't have the confidence to speak up. Worse, school had taught me to be invisible, so no one noticed me or realized I needed help. The residents teaching us just plain forgot about me.

It turned out, medicine was all about people and I couldn't *do* people. My ER rotation was the worst. Drunk people, violent people, relatives who needed comforting, husbands and wives and kids who I had to deliver bad news to. I had to figure out which patients were drug-seeking liars and which women were silent abuse victims. I needed to be assertive and intuitive and I was neither. And when traumas came in, making frantic, split-second decisions went completely against all my instincts. I went home every night and cried. My dad was right. People like us belonged in a lab. I was on the verge of quitting and going into research.

And then I started my final rotation: surgery.

It was a revelation. Suddenly, everything just felt *right*. My knack for anatomy made me the perfect fit: I knew every branch of every artery, could feel a patient and visualize what was happening beneath the skin. The steady hands and intense focus I'd inherited from my dad finally came to the fore. The surgeons teaching me said I was a natural and I loved the quiet calm of the OR. *I can do this!* I specialized in surgery, graduated with honors and came to Mount Mercy. I'd found my place.

I'd been here two years, safe and warm in my little burrow.

Safe and warm. And quietly, stoically, unimaginably lonely.

The cafeteria doors banged open and Corrigan strolled in. Spaces suddenly appeared at three different tables as women scooched aside to make room.

I tried not to stare at those thick forearms as he filled his tray. I started thinking about how mad Bartell had looked that morning. Krista was running a book on how many days it would be before Corrigan got fired and it didn't seem fair. However cocky and arrogant he was, he'd been right about the knife.

Corrigan turned and swaggered towards—

Where is he...wait—

By the time I realized, the blue of his scrubs filled my vision. "This seat taken?" he asked.

His voice was different, now. Away from the breathless urgency of the ER, it was slower, almost lazy. And that Irish accent... a low rumble that spilled silver dust down the length of my spine and ended in a hot throb between my thighs.

I shook my head.

Climbing into the cafeteria's bench seats *never* looks cool but he somehow pulled it off, casually hooking one leg over and then swinging himself in. For a second, his crotch was right at my eye level and wherever I looked, my eyes kept winding up there.

He dropped into the seat and gave me a cocky, knowing grin. I could feel the confidence rolling off him and slapping up against me in big, intimidating waves.

Say something cool and funny. "People are betting on when you're going to get fired," I blurted. *Yeah. Not that.*

But he just laughed. "They always do."

I shook my head at him. "How can that be a joke? Don't you care?"

He glanced across the cafeteria at Bartell. "About getting fired by that prick? Not particularly."

Anyone sensible would have just nodded and smiled. But this is me. I just sort of say things, especially when I'm nervous. "Isn't this your last chance? What if nowhere will take you? What if you can't practice?"

For a second, his grin fractured. I'd hit a nerve. So he felt the same way I did: he couldn't imagine doing anything other than medicine. So why was he so relaxed about it?

He shrugged. "There's always somewhere that needs doctors. Britain. France. Back to the Congo, if I have to."

I stared at him, trying to imagine being rootless like that. I'm a nester.

He stretched his shoulders, spreading his arms out wide like he owned the whole table, the whole *room*. His scrub sleeves rose up his arms, revealing more tanned bicep, more dark ink. Then he laid those sculpted forearms on the table and leaned in to me. I started to lean in to meet him... then caught myself. He couldn't be interested in me so he must just be teasing me. I wasn't going to fall for it. I sat bolt upright.

He smirked.

Dammit! Why was he doing this? Why flirt with *me?* I glanced to the side and saw four different women glaring at me. *I didn't ask him to come over here!*

"Why do you wear that all the time?" he asked, nodding upwards.

"What?" And then, before I could stop him, he'd plucked the surgical cap from my head. "Oh! I just kind of... forget I have it on."

He nodded thoughtfully. "Yeah, I bet you do. You never stop being a surgeon, do you?"

What? What did that mean? I was flustered and blushing and every time I looked in his eyes, I got lost again.

He spun my cap around his finger. "You need to get out of the OR and have some fun, Amy. Can I call you Amy?"

I blinked at him. *How did he know—*

"I asked around," he said.

I tried to imagine someone asking people about me, pursuing me like that, and couldn't. *This must be a trick.* Some way to tease the shy girl, like the jocks had in high school. And even if he was serious, no way was I going to become one of his one-night stands and have the whole hospital talking about me. I shook my head. "I don't think that's a very good idea."

"Fine." He slapped the table hard enough to make the whole room jump. "Beckett it is."

Beckett. The way he formed the *B,* like his lips were blowing a kiss, the way that hard *k* sounded in his accent, like *fuck...* it sounded way more intimate than *Amy.*

He gazed at me and, however much I looked away and looked back, he was *still* looking at me. Watching me as if I was the only one in the room who mattered. A twisting, crackling energy began, arcing down inside me. It lashed at my groin until I wanted to circle my ass against the bench. I could actually feel myself heating and moistening. But it didn't stop there, low down and base and sexual. It changed. It rose up, filling me, making my heart race. "Stop that," I told him.

"Stop what?"

My heart was thumping in my chest, now. Something was happening. Heady and scary, like standing with your toes over the edge of a cliff. Looking into those Irish eyes was like drinking from a firehose. But every time I looked away, I immediately looked right back. "*That. This.*"

"I'm not doing anything, Beckett."

And underneath the heat, underneath that diamond hard, cocky exterior, I glimpsed something. He was telling the truth. This wasn't just him.

This was us.

But then I flushed and dropped my eyes. I could suddenly feel everyone looking at us, laughing at how ridiculous the idea was. The quarterback and the geek girl. "You're not really interested in me," I mumbled.

His brow crinkled in a frown. He leaned in towards me. "Don't tell me who I'm interested in, Beckett."

The doors at the back of the cafeteria slammed open. "*Corrigan!*"

We both looked round. An ER nurse stood in the doorway.

"Paramedics are bringing in an eight year-old girl," she said. "Bus crash. It's bad."

Corrigan's face changed in a heartbeat. He was up out of his seat and running before the nurse had finished speaking. The doors banged closed behind them.

I hesitated. I hate the ER. And I'm not even meant to be down there unless I'm called. But there'd been something in the nurse's voice. If the kid was really that bad....

I jumped up and sprinted after them.

5

DOMINIC

W E REACHED THE ER just as the paramedics crashed through the door. "What have we got?" I yelled.

"Eight year-old girl, crush injuries. Open tib/fib reduced at scene. No sign of bleeding, but blood pressure's dropping. She's been in and out of consciousness." The paramedic started reeling off her vitals. All of them were lousy and getting worse.

"Let's move her!" Everyone grabbed hold of the backboard she was lying on. I counted three, we heaved her onto a gurney and I got my first proper look at her.

Tousled blonde curls. A button nose. Big, blue, terrified eyes. She could have been Rachel, grown up. She'd be exactly the right age. *Fuck.* I drew in a shuddering breath to help hold it together and listened to her chest, looking off to the side to help me focus—

And saw Beckett. She was standing back from the huddle, eyes wide at the noise and the chaos. *She really isn't used to this, is she?* But weirdly, I was glad she was there.

"Decreased breath sounds bilaterally," I said, my voice tight. "Can you tell me your name, sweetheart?"

"Rebecca." She sobbed it out and the pain in her voice nearly broke my heart.

"Rebecca, I'm Doctor Corrigan, we're going to make you all better, okay?"

"Pressure's falling, 95 over 40," a nurse said. She kept her voice carefully level, but I could see the fear in her eyes. This kid was heading south, fast.

"Two units O neg on the rapid infuser, *stat!* IV wide open," I snapped. "She's bleeding from *somewhere:* let's roll her." We carefully rolled her, but there was no blood anywhere. "*Fuck.* The bleeding must be internal."

"Pressure 88 over 38," said the nurse. This time, she couldn't keep her voice level.

I cut open Rebecca's clothes and started checking her abdomen. She was a mess of bruises. And all the time, her blood pressure was dropping, dropping.... We had to figure out where she was bleeding from, fast. "What happened?" I yelled over my shoulder as I worked.

"Truck plowed into a school bus," said the paramedic.

I glanced towards the door, but there were no other gurneys being wheeled in, no sirens outside. "Where are the rest of the kids? The teachers?"

"Crash was between here and Denver. The other kids weren't badly hurt so the Denver paramedics got them out first and took them back with them. But she was trapped in the wreckage, it took an hour to get her out."

"And you brought her *here?*" I snapped, exasperated. The fact she looked like Rachel was getting to me. "She's here *by herself?*" No one to ask about her medical history, no one to get consent from.

"Her pressure was dropping," the paramedic said defensively. "Mount Mercy was closer!"

I fumed and brooded on it for a few seconds, but he was right. "Yeah," I muttered. "Yeah, okay. You probably saved her life." I just wished there was someone else we could ask about what happened. "Rebecca?" *Fuck.* Her eyes were going glassy. "Rebecca? Honey?"

"I feel funny," she said groggily.

"I know, honey." I was fighting to stay calm, now. I could feel the sweat breaking out on my forehead despite the cold of the room and there was a sick churning in my stomach. The nurses around the table were glancing at each other, the fear spreading between them. *We're going to lose this one.* I caught Beckett's eye again across the room. She had a hand over her mouth, her eyes huge. "Can you tell me how you were hurt, when the truck hit?" I asked Rebecca. "Was something pressing on you?"

She nodded. "The bus all folded up. My leg got trapped.. And my tummy got squashed." She pointed weakly from chest to groin.

"Something must be damaged inside." I said. "Ultrasound, now!"

"80 over 30," said the nurse, her voice quavering. She put a hand on the kid's shoulder, willing her to hold on. Everyone around the table knew how she felt.

A nurse ran over with the ultrasound trolley and I held my hand out for the probe, my other hand crushing the gurney's rail, knuckles white. Five seconds went by. Ten, but the nurse was still flipping switches. "What's the problem?" I snapped. I knew I was losing my cool, but I couldn't help it, not with a kid on the table.

"I don't know! It won't switch on!" She kept working at it. "It was fine this morning!"

Rebecca tensed in pain and then her eyes closed. Her vitals suddenly fell off a cliff. "No palpable pulse." called a nurse. Then, in a quieter voice, "We're losing her."

"No we're not," I spat, pointing an accusing finger at her. "No, we're fucking not! Get me the spare ultrasound!"

Everyone looked blank.

I lost it. "*Get me the spare!*" I roared. "*The spare fucking ultrasound! Get me the spare!*"

Three different nurses ran in three different directions, clucking about whether it would be in Pediatrics or OB/GYN. The kid's pulse missed a beat. Slowed. Missed another one. I felt my chest close up.

She was going to die because we couldn't find out what was wrong with her.

6

AMY

I WASN'T CONSCIOUS of moving. One moment, I was pressed up against the wall, watching and cursing and praying.

The next, I was sliding under Corrigan's arm and stepping in front of him, right next to the little girl. *Oh Jesus,* she looked so small.

"What—" started Corrigan but I ignored him. I ignored the voice in my head that asked what the hell I was doing, that told me I couldn't do this. I shut out the noise and the people jostling me and I pretended I was upstairs, where it's calm.

I put my hands on Rebecca's chest and started gently pressing. My eyes defocused.

The skin was just a distraction. After years of surgery, I know internal anatomy like you know the layout of your house. I could see it in my head, a multi-colored textbook diagram overlaid on her body, how she *should* be. And I could feel where it was different, where her ribs had cracked and bent, where organs had been squeezed and damaged.

"Something's ruptured." The poor kid was a wreck. All I wanted to do was to rush her upstairs to surgery so I could start fixing her. But I couldn't do that until we'd stabilized her. I closed my eyes completely and used just the very tips of my fingers, where they're most sensitive. "Feels like the blood's concentrated... *here.*" I pressed on her left abdomen. "I can feel a broken rib. It must have sliced into her spleen."

For the first time, I turned around... and looked straight into Corrigan's eyes. There was none of that cocky hardness, now. He was desperate. In pain. "We can't get to it," he said. "If we open her here, with all that damage, she'll bleed out in a couple of seconds."

He was right. I thought fast. "Maybe we can stop it somewhere else. Have you ever done a Reboa?"

"I've seen one, I've never done one. You?"

"Only once." My chest contracted. But if I let the panic win, this kid was going to die.

I turned back to Rebecca. It must have looked like I was staring blankly at her abdomen. But in my mind, I was seeing arteries as they crisscrossed and arced, following the one that fed the spleen back along its length to—"Scalpel," I said and bent low over Rebecca's bed.

Corrigan didn't argue, just laid the scalpel in my hand. I made an incision in Rebecca's groin. Corrigan handed me the catheter and I started to ease the tube into her artery, threading it up into her. It suddenly jammed and I froze, my heart in my mouth. God, she was so *small!* The only other time I'd done this, it had been on an adult. If I went too fast, I could tear her—

Corrigan's hand landed on my shoulder, huge and warm. I didn't look round but I could feel my heart slowing down, my body relaxing just a bit. I didn't know him but, for some reason, his touch calmed me. I took a deep breath and kept going, easing the catheter a little deeper. "Inflate the balloon," I told Corrigan. "*Slowly.*"

Corrigan depressed the syringe's plunger, his thumb moving just a fraction of an inch at a time. I pictured the balloon inflating, deep inside Rebecca's body, sealing the artery and stopping the bleeding. I stared at the blood pressure monitor and prayed. Everyone else around the gurney did the same.

The numbers fell... and then slowly stabilized and started to reverse course. The nurse watching the monitor sucked in a huge, relieved breath. "Pressure's coming back up!"

I straightened up, my legs shaky from how close we'd come. That's when I felt Corrigan's eyes on me. *"Good job,"* he said, and there was genuine admiration in his voice.

I flushed and looked away, pretending to focus on stripping off my gloves. But I could still feel his gaze on me and it felt really, really good.

Krista gently touched my shoulder. "OR's prepped," she whispered.

I hadn't even realized she was down here. She'd figured out the kid would need surgery and got stuff ready, all without being asked. I squeezed her hand. "I don't know what I'd do without you," I told her.

"She's waking up," called a nurse.

Corrigan and I looked down as Rebecca's eyes opened. "It hurts!" she whimpered. Corrigan nodded to a nurse and she pushed some pain meds into the IV.

"Rebecca, this is Doctor Beckett," Corrigan told her, grabbing me by the upper arms and pulling me forward. "She's going to put you to sleep so she can fix what's wrong with you, okay?"

Rebecca looked up at me. "What *is* wrong with me?"

I opened my mouth... and closed it again. I'm bad with people, but I'm even worse with kids. My dad always talked to me like an adult, distant and scientific. I had no clue how to be comforting to an eight year-old. I stared down into her scared little face. "Well your leg was fractured, and your spleen and other organs have been—"

Rebecca's face crumpled. "Am I gonna *die?!*"

I froze, horrified. *This is why they keep me in the OR,* I thought helplessly.

Corrigan stepped forward. *"No."* He perched on the edge of her bed and took her tiny hand in his big one. "See, it's like you have a baby elephant." He put his hand waist-high. "About *so* big. And this elephant, he thinks he's a puppy. So he tears around the house, trunk in the air, chasing after you, knocking stuff over..."

The Irish in his voice made the story magical. Despite her fear, Rebecca gave a little giggle.

"And one day, he jumps into your arms. And you go down on your butt and he knocks all the air out of you: *oof!*"

"Because he's so heavy," said Rebecca.

"Because he's so heavy. And all that stuff inside your tummy, it gets bruised, just like when you fall over and get a big black bruise on your leg. So we need to go inside you and patch everything up so it doesn't hurt." He pushed a lock of hair back from her forehead. "But you won't feel a thing because you're going to be asleep the whole time."

I gazed in wonder at him. He looked utterly different. He looked like a father.

"So she can fix me?" asked Rebecca, looking doubtfully up at me.

"*Yes,*" Corrigan told her firmly. He looked over his shoulder at me. "Because she's a fantastic surgeon." And what made my heart melt was, his eyes matched his voice. He believed it.

I gave Rebecca what I hoped was a reassuring nod. And then I nodded thanks to him for stepping in. "Rebecca, where are your parents? Do they live in Denver?"

She shook her head. "Wichita."

What?! "Your folks are in Kansas?!"

"We're on a trip. Our Mathlete team is taking on a school in Denver tomorrow."

Krista had already gotten Rebecca's folks' phone number from the paramedic and had the hospital phone to her ear. After a few seconds she shook her head. "Voice mail."

"Rebecca," I told her, "We're going to reach them so they can fly in and be here when you wake up. But we're going to have to put you to sleep now so I can fix you up."

The poor kid's eyes went huge and scared. "Can't you wait?! I don't want to—" She looked around desperately and I realized she was looking for something, *anything* familiar. But she was hundreds of miles from a friend, a parent, a teacher.

And something happened inside me. Before I knew what I was doing, I'd grabbed her hand. Through a sudden flood of emotion, I said, "You're not on your own. Okay? Because until someone else gets here, *I'm* going to take care of you."

Rebecca pressed her lips together tight... and squeezed my hand and nodded.

I squeezed back, shocked at myself. I was the most awkward, least motherly person in existence. But somehow it felt right.

Krista cleared a path and I wheeled the gurney to the elevator. Just as we got inside, a big, warm hand on my hip stopped me. A stubbled chin rasped against my ear and then there was a hot, Irish whisper. "Take care of her. Okay?"

I looked round... and saw that same vulnerability in his eyes again. In that second, Dominic Corrigan was the most torn-apart soul on earth. *What the hell happened to this man?*

I nodded, not trusting my voice.

The elevator doors closed and he was gone.

7

AMY

FOUR HOURS LATER, I closed the last stitch and staggered back from the table. "Done," I managed.

Lina, on anesthesia, and Krista and Adele, my nurses, all gave me exhausted nods and we shared a sigh of relief. "Good job, everybody," I said, leaning back against the wall. I couldn't straighten up properly. My whole back had gone into spasm from hunching over the operating table and my fingers were cramped and numb. But we'd saved Rebecca.

I'd repaired the damage to her left lung and removed her ruptured spleen; luckily, spleens aren't vital and she could live a normal life without it. She'd lost so much blood that it had been too dangerous to try to fix her leg. I'd have to do a second operation tomorrow and she'd be worryingly fragile until then. And I was worried about her kidney function: we'd have to keep an eye on that until she was stable enough to transport to a bigger facility with a specialist renal surgeon. But if all went well, she'd be fine.

I wanted to be there when she woke up, so I sat by her bedside in the intensive care unit while I called her parents in Kansas. They were terrified. I couldn't imagine what it must be like, to know your kid is sick so far away. "What time does your flight get in?" I asked.

"We can't fly in!" Rebecca's mother sounded near-hysterical. "Denver airport's closed by a blizzard. No flights are getting through. We're going to try to make it by road, but the roads are bad too."

I checked out of the window. Nothing but blue skies in Mount Mercy. But then Denver was two hours' drive away. "Try not to worry, we're taking good care of her. Just get here when you can."

I hung up and looked at the slumbering Rebecca. "Looks like it's just you and me, kid," I whispered. And I sat there as the daylight faded, watching her sleep.

The room was almost dark and I was half-dozing myself when she stirred. I quickly turned on a lamp so that she didn't panic. "Hey!" I gave her a big smile. "Hey! It's all over! You did great. You're going to be fine."

She gave me a tired smile, but then looked around. "Where's my mom?"

A big, tight swell of worry filled my chest. "They're coming, but there's a lot of snow coming down between us and them. So it may take a little while."

Tears welled up in her eyes. I grabbed her hand. *What do I do?* I knew I needed to distract her, but I had no idea what eight year-old girls liked. All I remembered about being eight was memorizing all the types of butterfly because reciting them was the only way to make my dad smile again. And I'd really wanted a cat—"Do you have any pets?" I blurted.

"J—Jupiter," she croaked. "My hamster."

"Why did you call him Jupiter?"

"'Cos he's big and round, like a planet."

I grinned. "I always wanted a pet," I told her. "Tell me about him."

We wound up talking for over an hour and the longer I stayed, the less awkward I became. She was a really sweet little thing, smart as hell and really into science and math but confident, too. She was a glimpse at what I could have maybe turned out like, if I'd had my mom's influence to balance me out.

When the anesthesia had faded and she'd slipped into healthy, normal sleep, I stumbled downstairs, blinking in the bright hallway lights, to find Corrigan. He'd want to know she was okay.

Thankfully, the ER had quietened down. I figured all the doctors must be with patients because the hallways were empty. I started making my way past the exam areas, shivering: why did the ER have to be so *drafty?* I was hoping I'd hear Corrigan's Irish accent. Instead, I heard cursing and then a hard, heavy *thump,* as if someone had been slammed up against the wall. I stopped, right outside the curtained entrance to Exam One.

"Did I tell you you could leave, Seth?" I'd never heard a voice like it: a low rasp, like a cold wind blowing through jagged, rusty metal. It was the opposite of Corrigan's accent: it set every one of my nerves on edge. I froze, staring at the curtain, afraid to move.

"No Sir." A younger voice. Was the *Sir* military? Or was it a kid speaking to his dad? It sounded like a little of both. "I just—"

"So you disobeyed me." It was a Colorado accent but stripped bare and hardened by hate. The hairs on the back of my neck prickled. I'd never heard such raw, poisonous anger.

"He was just trying to look after me, Colt." A third voice, older but more gentle. "You know I got a problem with my heart."

"*IF* my men need medical attention, *I* will decide when and where." For all its fury, the voice hadn't risen above that low rasp, which made it all the more chilling. "Do you understand me, boy?"

The younger guy wheezed, as if he was being choked. "*Yes, sir.*"

But that wasn't enough. "*Do you understand me?*"

I had to get help. But as I took a step, my sneaker squeaked on the linoleum.

The curtain was whipped aside and I froze, staring right at the man they called *Colt.*

He wasn't a big man. He wasn't much taller than me and he didn't have Corrigan's wide shoulders or strong chest. But he was the most frightening man I'd ever seen.

It was as if he used to be a normal, average guy and then something had happened to him, over many years. Something that had boiled away every gram of fat, leaving only sinew and gristly muscle. Something that had dug the trust and kindness and humanity from him, leaving only rage and iron-hard resolve. Beneath the rolled-up sleeves of his plaid shirt, his skin was stretched drumskin-tight over veins and muscles, every inch covered in faded tattoos. His eyes, above his long, salt-and-pepper beard, were like two points of cold light at the bottom of a mineshaft.

He'd had the younger guy pinned up against the wall by his throat, but now he released him and turned to face me. Both the younger guy and older guy backed away, terrified.

His eyes never leaving me, Colt pushed back his shirt and drew a wicked-looking knife from his belt. "You hear something, doc?" he rasped.

And he stepped towards me.

8
___

DOMINIC

I'D JUST FINISHED examining an old lady with a sprained wrist when I heard the voice. I pushed back the curtain of our exam room and looked across the hallway, straight into Exam One.

I recognized Seth and the old guy I'd examined that morning. As soon as I saw the guy with the knife, I had no doubt he was Seth's father. The family resemblance was unmistakable, but it was the fear in Seth's eyes that sealed the deal. *This* is what he'd been scared of, that morning. And I could see why. His father looked as if all he'd done for twenty years was work out and drink whiskey. He was stripped-down and wiry, like a dog that's gone feral.

And then I saw who he was walking towards: Beckett. Ice rose up inside me and grabbed hold of my heart. I was between them before I was even aware I was moving, blocking the man's path, shielding Beckett's body with mine. The fear turned to protective rage as it reached my lips. *"Back the fuck off!"* I roared. *"Right now!"*

His face was two feet from mine but he didn't so much as blink. He either had the self control of a saint or he was full on batshit crazy. His arm tensed, ready to stab with the knife. It was one of those big hunting knives and it wasn't just for show: the thing was worn and scarred with use. *Shit.* I've been around and I know how to fight, but

I've also seen up-close what a blade can do to people. And once he stabbed me, Beckett might be next.

There was a patter of feet at the far end of the hallway. Seth's dad and I both looked up to see a pair of cops racing toward us. I'd seen them a few times around the hospital: Earl, old and overweight, and his protégé Lloyd, dark-haired and gangly and barely old enough to wear the uniform. They must have heard my yell. I had no idea why they hung around the hospital so much, but right now, I was very glad they did.

Seth's dad looked back to me and hesitated... then put the knife away just before the cops got close enough to see it. My eyes caught on a weird tattoo on his forearm: two crossed rifles beneath a clenched fist. Seth had the same one.

Earl came to a stop beside us, panting. "What's going on?"

Now it was my turn to hesitate. I could tell Earl what had happened and try to get the guy arrested but.... I glanced at Seth and he was shaking his head. He'd had the same thought I had: his dad wouldn't go quietly. And I wasn't sure our local cops could handle him. Earl was out-of-shape and old while Lloyd was too young and twitchy. If it turned into a fight, Beckett would be right in the middle of it and could wind up as a hostage... or dead.

And then Taylor came around the corner. *Shit!* She and Seth had a real thing for each other: they'd been flirting with each other all morning, every time she passed Exam One. And I'd let them because... well, I can be a soppy fucker, when I see two people so obviously smitten. But now it was coming back to bite me. When Taylor saw Seth facing off against the cops, she ran right into the middle of everything and put a hand on his shoulder, looking up at him for answers. Seth's dad scowled and I saw the hand closest to his knife twitch.

"Everything's fine," I told Earl tightly. "These guys were just leaving." I glared at Seth's dad and prayed he'd take the easy way out.

For a long second, he just glared at me. I saw Earl finger his gun and wondered how many years it was since he'd had to shoot it. And Lloyd...had he *ever* fired his?

"Don't interfere in my shit again," muttered Seth's dad. And he turned and stalked away, the old guy falling in behind him.

Seth turned to me. "Thank you," he said in a low voice.

"Seth!" barked his dad.

Seth winced. He looked at Taylor and I saw his shoulders slump with guilt and humiliation. The poor kid really liked her and now she'd seen a part of his life he'd never wanted her to see. "Sorry," he told her. And he hurried after his dad.

I frowned. Why had Seth and the old guy still been here? They should have left hours ago. Then I winced. The broken ultrasound! With only one working unit, the whole hospital was backed up.

I spun around to check Beckett. She was standing there white-faced, her arms clasping herself as if she was cold. I felt that chill inside me again, imagining the blade shoved between her ribs. *She could have died!* And suddenly, I had my hands on her shoulders. "You okay?"

She nodded as if she didn't trust her voice.

"You're not okay," I snapped. "You're shaking." I pushed her into the nearest exam room, put my hands on her waist, and lifted her onto the edge of the bed. And then... I just stared at her. And she stared back at me.

She was panting with fear, but I was panting just as hard, overwhelmed by a sudden protective fury. *Someone tried to hurt her.* "They're gone," I told her. "No reason we've ever got to see them again." Without thinking, I brushed a lock of copper hair back from her cheek. I hadn't felt this way about anyone since Chrissy and Rachel.

I blinked, trying to clear my head, but I couldn't. I knew that my defenses were down, that she was looking right inside me. But she was open, too: I stared into those shining blue eyes, beyond all the awkwardness and shyness, and I saw someone who was alone. Just like me.

I swallowed and looked down at my feet. I had no idea how to deal with this.

She broke the silence first. "Thank you."

I nodded, still unable to speak.

"Rebecca's going to be okay," she told me.

Relief washed over me, so much that I had to fight the urge to hug her. I let out a long breath. "Thank you." But with the relief came thoughts of Rachel, her grin like sunshine, the brightness of her lighting up the dark space inside me for an instant, showing me its vastness. *Fuck.* It was all too much, at once: I was going to lose it and fucking cry or something.

Earl came to my rescue, poking his head around the corner to check we were okay. "You get a name on that guy?" he asked.

"The old guy called him Colt," said Beckett.

Earl mouthed the name, frowning. "I swear I've seen him somewhere before." He shook his head and waddled off, Lloyd following behind him.

The interruption bought me just enough time to get myself together. To bring that other me back. I pushed the past down deep where it belonged and by the time Beckett looked at me again, I'd clawed that cocky, I-don't-give-a-shit attitude back into place. It was a layer of armor that would ward off questions.

If they think you're shallow, no one tries to dig deep.

I saw Beckett cock her head to one side, confused. She knew something had changed. I'd just have to convince her that the cocky me was the real me. The only me. No more slips.

But now that I'd buried those deeper feelings, the raw attraction took over. I looked at her and I *couldn't stop,* my breathing coming quicker and my heart starting to race.

I leaned infinitesimally towards her, close enough that I could smell the clean, warm scent of her. My breath caught as I looked down at her soft lower lip, already dreaming about how it would feel as I crushed my lips against hers. My eyes flicked to the little semicircle of pale skin at the neckline of her scrubs. That mystery, almost nothing showing...she was sexier, to me, than some stripper in a G-string. God, I wanted to know what her breasts looked like. Wanted to ram that top up to her neck and fill my hands with them. Wanted to jerk down the pants and cup her pussy in my hand, let her rock against me as my fingers explored her. Then I'd spin her around and bend her over the bed....

The blood was thundering in my ears. One hand was still on her waist and the press of her against my palm was the best thing I'd ever felt.

I was getting addicted to this woman.

Our eyes were locked on each other. Our breathing had fallen into time. She gave the tiniest shake of her head: not a *no,* a disbelieving *why?*

I frowned. *Are you serious?* Didn't she know how gorgeous she was? Then I remembered a doctor's reaction, when I'd asked about her. *Beckett?* he'd asked me, mystified. *The surgeon, Beckett?* As if no one would ever be interested in her. I wanted to punch the guy. It wasn't right, that everyone overlooked her.

I stared right back at her and let her see how certain I was.

And those blue eyes slowly filled with heat. That was what really drove me crazy about her, I realized. Not the pale skin or the copper hair, but the hint that deep down, underneath all that shyness, there was a woman with a lust to match mine, who'd grab my ass to urge me deeper, who'd claw my back and scream my name until her throat was raw. All I had to do was free her.

I could still hear that warning voice in the back of my mind. She was different. We had something together, something that would make it hard to say goodbye in the morning.

But I drowned the voice out. I couldn't fight this: it was too strong. I had to have her.

I put my hands on her shoulders. "I'm taking everyone out for drinks tonight," I told her. "New guy buys the beers, and all that."

She immediately shook her head. I could see her trying to retreat back into her safe little burrow. "I don't really...."

"*Beckett.*" She froze, when I said it like that. Interesting. "I already told you, you need to get out more. You saved a little girl's life and you survived nearly getting stabbed. That deserves a drink."

She looked away. Looked back. Looked away again. But every time her eyes came back to me, I was waiting for her. Challenging her to deny what was building between us.

"One drink," she said at last in a small voice. I hadn't picked up on her Colorado accent before because it was so soft and somehow shy. You know how big and confident a Texas accent is, herding all the syllables into line? This was the opposite of that. It suited her perfectly.

"One drink," I agreed. And stepped back. She hopped off the table and hurried off and I watched her until she was out of sight. I could feel that cocky attitude hardening, strengthening into a protective shell around me. I told myself that I'd get her into bed and that would be the end of it.

9

AMY

F OR A FULL half hour after work, the doctors' locker room was packed out. Every woman in the hospital was preparing to head to the town's one bar to drink with Corrigan.

Almost every woman. I waited in the hallway, pretending to study the notice board, until they all flooded out in a clatter of heels and confidence. Only then did I creep in. The place was a battlezone: hair dryers dangling from tangled cables, lipsticks rolling across the tiles, the air acrid with hairspray and clashing perfumes. They weren't taking any prisoners. And I was going to walk into that same bar? *Me?*

I changed into the street clothes I'd arrived in that morning: my favorite blue jeans, ragged on one ankle, a thick green roll-neck sweater I wore because it kept the wind out and a black leather biker jacket I'd picked up on a whim from a yard sale. My hair was still pinned up and I was wearing barely any makeup. Unlike most of the women, I didn't keep a pair of heels at work for nights out. On the rare occasions Krista managed to drag me out to be sociable, I went like this and then hid in the corner.

At high school, without a mom to talk me through teen romance and heartbreak, I'd just stayed away from guys. So I hadn't learned the flirting that seems to come so effortlessly to all the other women.

I was clunky and awkward. I'd only had two brief relationships since I'd come to Mount Mercy, one with a guy from the mining company, one with a guy who planned to open a hardware store here. Both had fizzled out after a few weeks. I was shy, sexually, and they hadn't known how to bring me out of myself so they'd thought I was cold.

With Corrigan, it was different. I only had to hear that accent or look into those eyes and it was like a switch had been thrown inside me. He said my name and I got wet.

But I knew his reputation. All he wanted was a one-night stand and I didn't want that. I couldn't think of anything worse than going to bed with him and then seeing him move onto the next woman. And the hospital gossip machine would go crazy. Everyone would be talking about me. The thought was terrifying: it took me straight back to high school and everyone teasing me. The only safe thing to do was to stay away from him.

But he'd protected me—maybe even saved my life. And he'd helped me when I was trying to reassure Rebecca.

I was going to have to work with him. I couldn't just blank him.

One drink. I'd have one drink.

I headed for the exit. Just as I was about to step outside, a blast of heat warmed the side of my face. I turned to see Maggie emerging from the door that led down to the basement, wiping her hands on a rag. "Been working on the furnace," she explained. "There might be some bad weather heading our way and I don't want it dying on us."

Maggie is our maintenance chief and she's been with the hospital so long, she's almost part of the building. She can fix *anything,* from a worn-out ECG machine to a leaking oxygen pipe, and without her the whole place would have fallen down years ago. She's in her fifties, with a close-cropped afro dyed golden blonde. She can come across as sort of gruff, especially when someone breaks something, and I was intimidated by her for about a year, until I realized she's just fiercely protective of the hospital. She lost her husband some years back and it's almost like looking after the hospital is a replacement.

"I'm heading to the tavern," I told her. "Want to come along?"

"Nope," she said, and walked past me without breaking her stride.

But a few feet further on, she stopped. "... thanks," she said, without turning around. "But I've got a fuse box up on the third floor to rewire."

At nine in the evening? I bit my lip, staring at her back. I could hear the pain in her voice. Staying here, working late into the night, was *safe.* Safer than being around people, and remembering how lonely she was. "Some other time?" I asked.

"Yeah," said Maggie. "Sure." And she set off down the hallway. *She needs to find someone,* I thought sadly.

Outside, the air was gloriously fresh and just cold enough to make me catch my breath, and there was still only an inch of snow on the ground. Krista, who was a local girl, had told me stories about the blizzards that sometimes hit the area but it looked like my second winter here was going to be as mild as my first.

Mount Mercy's main street looks incredible at night. There are very few street lights: the town preservation committee doesn't like them and so instead we have ball-shaped lanterns and strings of fairy lights bathing the sidewalks in a soft, warm light. A lot of the buildings are over a hundred years old, so it still feels like a frontier town. And the fact we're so isolated, with so few lights, means the sky at night is amazing, deep blue with a billion points of shining light. We'd get star gazers here, if we weren't so far from a highway.

I'd always loved living there, but that night, it felt different. I kept thinking about Corrigan, traveling the world on a whim. I'd never even been anywhere hot: not proper, soak-it-up, warm-your-bones hot. I could feel my life ticking away, each day spent in the same room of the same hospital in the same town. I'd found a cozy burrow, but was I sheltered... or hiding?

Midway down Main Street is Krüger's Tavern, our one bar. For a while, we didn't even have one: the bar closed down and fell into disrepair for about six months. Then a guy from Germany passed through the town, fell in love with a local and bought the place. He'd modeled it on German beer cellars, combined with a bit of alpine hunting lodge: there were thick furs on the wooden benches and a huge open fire, and they specialized in oversize tankards of cold beer and bowls of fries dripping with melted cheese.

I hauled open the door and was hit by a solid wall of warmth, light and noise: clinking glasses and laughter and, above it all, a silver-edged accent. I slipped inside.

Corrigan was at the very center of the room, his chair rocked back and teetering on two legs, a frosty beer in his hand. The whole bar was listening to him tell a story, the crowd three deep around his table. I was in awe. *How does he have so many friends, so fast?* I'd been in Mount Mercy two years and I still only knew a handful of people well.

I moved closer, listening to him talk about Africa and the time he and two other doctors had hidden on a farm to escape a local warlord. "So I'm crouching there, eye-to-eye with this goat...." He was a natural speaker: confident but disarmingly friendly, infectiously fun and with just the right amount of cursing. And that glorious accent, all lilting silver vowels and hard, rumbly consonants... I could have listened to him for hours. It was warm in the tavern and he'd stripped down to a white t-shirt that set off his tan, tight enough that it hugged his biceps and those magnificent pecs. Suddenly, I was imagining running my hand over that firm slab of muscle, feeling the cotton rasp against my palm, the warmth of him soaking into me....

I flushed and looked away. And when I looked again, I saw who'd secured the best seats in the house, right at his table. Five women from the hospital, effortlessly sexy and seductive. Two were throwing back their heads, laughing at his joke. Another was leaning forward to touch his hand. Two more were just gazing at him, lashes heavy with mascara, each trying to pretend the other didn't exist. No way could I go over there.

I stepped back. And at that second, Corrigan glanced up and looked right at me.

I froze for a second and then took a step towards the door. He frowned, confused. Then he cocked his head as if to say, *you should know better, Beckett.*

I hurried away, slipping through the crowd towards the door.

Behind me, the story suddenly stopped. There was a disappointed chorus of female voices: *Aw*....

Panicking now, I reached the door, wrenched it open—

A foot slammed it closed. An arm hooked around my waist and spun me around. I looked up—

Our faces were less than a foot apart. My chest, rising and falling as I panted, was a hair's breadth from brushing his. Those blue eyes burned down into me, frustrated and lusty and just a little amused. "You can run, Beckett," he told me. "But I'll chase you."

10

DOMINIC

S HE JUST STOOD THERE, astonished, glancing down at my
hand on her waist... but not asking me to move it. *Has no one ever
chased her before?* Not fucking possible. God, she looked even better,
out of those scrubs. I'd been dreaming about her body and now I
could fill in all of the details the shapeless scrubs had hidden. Tight,
dark denim clung to long legs and a ripe peach of an ass that I
wanted to grab with both hands. Her cute little biker jacket hung
open over a soft sweater that showed the outline of her breasts and
God, they were glorious. Full and heavy, two perfect mounds I
needed to lift in my palms and bring my tongue to. I was already
imagining what they looked like. Given her creamy skin, I was
guessing at delicate pink nipples that would crinkle and strain as I
rubbed them.

All of the other women had put on little strappy tops and skirts. A
few had even changed into dresses. I like cleavage and sequins as
much as the next guy but the weird thing was, the combination of
tight jeans or leggings on the bottom half, outlining a woman's ass
and hips, and the softness of a sweater covering her breasts...it's my
favorite thing for a woman to wear.

It's not a seduction outfit. It's a relationship outfit, for when you're crazy about someone and can't keep your hands off them. You can run your hands over the denim and feel the woman's thighs and ass, squeezing and pressing in just the right places to make her gasp and buck. You can stand behind her, her head twisted around as you kiss, and smooth your palms over the soft wool, working it over the smoothness of her breasts. You can dive underneath it with your hands, skin on skin, and feel her up even though everything's hidden.

I caught myself. *A relationship outfit.* I hadn't thought that way since—

I pushed the idea away before it could form. *Back to the plan.*

I grabbed Beckett's wrist and led her through the bar, looking for a place quiet enough to talk. It was rammed: it's amazing how many people show up when they hear *drinks on me.* But I didn't care how many of them came or how many of the women were now glaring at me, pissed that I'd abandoned them. All I cared about was her.

She was hanging back as I led her, but not actually trying to break free. And every time I checked over my shoulder and caught her eye, I could see that heat flaring for a second before she looked away. *She wants to. But she doesn't want to want to.* The idea of that had me rock-hard in my jeans.

I grabbed a couple of bottles of beer from the bartender and then turned and pressed the cool glass into her hand as we reached a dark corner. Before she could argue, I clinked our bottles together and glugged some of mine back. She lifted her bottle too and suddenly I was *lost,* my eyes locked on her soft lips as they nuzzled the hard mouth of the bottle. *Fuck!* What was it about her? Every other woman here was trying to get me to look at her and I couldn't take my eyes off this one.

I moved closer, our bodies almost touching.

I wanted to know everything about her. I wanted to know whether anyone had ever massaged warm oil into those amazing breasts and what noises she made when she came. I especially wanted to know whether, under that dark denim, there was a little patch of that copper hair waiting for me between her thighs or if she was more of a dark brown. But I had to be patient. I had to start slow. "So why surgery?" I asked.

She blinked at me, confused for a second, but that was an answer in itself. *She can't imagine doing anything else.* She loved it, the way I love the chaos of the ER. "Medical family?" I asked. Medicine runs in families *a lot*. My dad and granddad were both docs in Belfast. Hell, I would have been, if I hadn't met Chrissy and come to the US.

Beckett shook her head, her pinned-up copper hair catching the light. "But my dad was a biologist. He discovered all kinds of stuff about the internal anatomy of insects." She did one of those adorable blushes. "He was... like me."

"Smart?"

She blushed again, even though I'd meant it sincerely. "Weird."

I frowned. If she was weird, it was a weird I liked. Maybe because she was so utterly different to anyone else I'd known. "You're wasted up in the OR. You could save a lot of lives downstairs."

"The ER scares the hell out of me," she muttered, looking at the floor.

I leaned forward and put my lips to her ear. "But when you had to, you got in there and did it anyway. Rachel would be dead if not for you."

She jerked her head up and I got the full effect of those glittering, pale blue eyes. *What? What'd I say?* I reran my words in my head. *Rachel? Shit.* How the hell had that happened? I *never* slipped up like that. I quickly changed the subject. "You should let your hair down."

She touched her pinned up hair. "Oh. No, I don't think—"

"I bet it'd look amazing down." I'd started this as a way to change the subject but I was serious, I really *did* want to see it down. I came even closer and reached out a hand to grab her hair clip. She twisted her head. I reached from the other side. She twisted again. "*Beckett!*"

I was only playing but it didn't come out like playing at all. I was too fucking horny. It came out as a growl with a warning spank on the end as I hit that final *t*. She went utterly still, looking up at me with huge eyes. I gazed down at her, both of us breathing faster, and suddenly the mood changed completely. I'd been trying to get things back on track, to make this into a simple one-night stand. But I'd forgotten how strong this thing was. She only had to look at me like that and I was completely out of control.

I opened the hair clip. Her hair cascaded down in copper waves, spilling over her shoulders and midway down her back. It changed her whole look: she was wilder, more sexual. *Freed.* I'd never wanted to see a woman naked more.

Without thinking, I put my hand on her cheek. She was soft against me, her skin still cool from the night air but heating as she flushed. Her mouth worked as she tried to say something. My gaze locked on her lips again and I felt my eyes narrow. I was imagining the feel of those lips under mine, how it would feel to open and spread her, plunge my tongue between them and own her mouth. But I had just enough rational thought left to know that'd send her running. So I settled for running my thumb over her lips instead, both of us catching our breath as I touched that silken flesh for the first time.

"Why are you interested in me?" Her voice was pleading.

"Why wouldn't I be?" I frowned. I got that she was shy and awkward, but how had all the other guys in this place missed her? I thought about how she'd looked a few moments ago when I'd chased her through the crowd to the door. She'd slipped between people and they'd barely noticed she was there....

Something twisted in my chest. She *hid.* She was so used to hiding, she was almost invisible.

She looked at the floor again.

I put two fingers under her chin and pressed it back up. *No you don't.* As soon as her eyes met mine, I saw the pain there. She was as alone as I was and too shy to reach out to anyone, and these idiots couldn't see what was right in front of them. That protective urge rose up in me again. I didn't just want to fuck her, I wanted to wrap her up in my arms and protect her, make her happy. But that was crazy. I couldn't have that with anyone, not anymore. All I was good for was—

I faltered. *Shit!* I suddenly saw what it would do to her, if I talked her into bed and then moved on the next day.

I dropped my hand from her chin as if burned.

"I have to go," she muttered.

I was thinking fast. "Beckett, wait—"

But she was gone, slipping through the crowd towards the door.

I looked down at the hand that had held her chin. It suddenly looked so big and clumsy. I'd thought getting her into bed would be fun for both of us: just some hot, casual sex. But now...no way could I do that to her. If I strolled out in the morning and moved on to someone else, like I always did, it would tear her apart.

I couldn't just fuck her. But I couldn't forget her, either. *What the hell am I going to do?*

11

AMY

I STUMBLED out of the tavern and the night engulfed me, cold air and darkness bathing my cheeks, hiding my blushes. My whole body was throbbing with heat. *How does he do that to me?*

By the time I'd walked the length of the street, I was pulling my leather jacket tight around myself. The temperature was definitely dropping. Maybe the bad weather in Denver was heading our way. But that heat was still strumming inside me. The memory of his hands on me, the way his eyes had focused on my lips....

I live in a basement apartment: some people hate the idea of being below ground but to me, it's snug. And the building is old enough that it has a real fireplace where I can have a log fire. It's cozy, especially sitting beside it sewing—

Yes, I do embroidery. Look, I know, okay? Krista finds it hilarious too. But I got into it a few years ago as a way to relax and I couldn't stop. It suits me: dexterity and focus. I've done cushions and throws and a huge, king-size comforter for my bed...there's something nice about lining my nest with soft things. I just sometimes wish I wasn't there alone.

Stupid. Like anyone would seek domestic bliss with me. Certainly not Corrigan. He'd been to the Congo, Libya...the man lived for danger. Even here in the US, they said he always chose hospitals right in the worst areas of big cities. His life was gunshot wounds and gang violence. The quiet of Mount Mercy must be killing him.

Tonight, because I hadn't been home to set a fire, the place was freezing. I hit the bathroom, stripped off everything but my panties, pulled on a nightshirt, and dived into bed. I *hate* being cold, especially in bed, so I have three blankets on top of the comforter. Even so, I sometimes wake up in the early hours, unable to really get warm. My dad used to say that some people, like us, just run cold. Of course, he had my mom to keep him warm.

Tonight, the sheets were freezing. Every time I shifted position, a new part of me touched icy cotton and made me wince. I wound up lying perfectly still, staring up at the ceiling with just my eyes and nose showing above the blankets.

Dominic. Corrigan.

His name was an incantation, some Irish folk magic full of hard *m*s and rolling *r*s. It rippled down my spine and made me twist and buck, despite the touch of the cold sheets. The room was dark and that made it easier to imagine him there, standing over the bed. Those incredible eyes just a glint in the darkness, those arrogant lips twisting into a smirk....

There was absolutely no way I could get involved with him. But now, alone in the darkness, with no one watching, all the heat that had been building between us all day could finally come out. The brief blast of cold as he lifted the covers and slid into bed with me and sealed them back around us, trapping us in a warm little cavern.

With the other men I'd been with, sex hadn't been great. I'd been too shy to ask for what I wanted and they'd assumed someone timid like me would want it slow and gentle. In reality, that wasn't what I fantasized about at all. Corrigan, though...he was different. He'd be utterly ruthless in seeking out what made me come. He'd command me to tell him.

Command. I kept thinking about the way he said *Beckett.*

My ass began to grind against the sheets as I imagined big, warm hands gliding up and down my inner thighs.

Before I was really aware of what I was doing, my panties were tangling around my ankles and then they were lost in the bed.

I could almost feel the weight of him, pressing the mattress down between my legs. His knees spreading mine. His hand cupping my pussy—

I drew in my breath. I had my hand down between my thighs but it was *his* fingers I felt teasing me, stroking me, his fingertips that started to nudge inside, finding me hot and shamefully wet. I stared up into the darkness and saw *him,* eyes gleaming down at me, the light from the window catching the edges of his broad shoulders and the hard slabs of his chest.

And then he was leaning down to kiss me, burying his fingers in my hair as his lips sought me out and claimed me, spreading me and exploring me, his thumbs stroking my cheeks. And I felt the first touch of his cock on my inner thigh, throbbing and ready and *God*, so thick and hot. I panted through the kiss, my ass grinding in circles on the bed in anticipation, and I felt him smile.

He lowered himself atop me, his hips sliding up between my thighs to open me more, his big body pinning mine. I felt the touch of the arrow-shaped head of his cock against my slickened lips and my breathing sped up.

He nudged against me, teasing me, once, twice...and then—

My head rocked back against the pillow at the glorious, silken stretch of him entering me. Hot and thick and unstoppable, plunging deep and God, I was soaked, he'd be able to feel how wet I was for him. He went *deep*, right up to the hilt, and I clawed at the muscles of his back as he filled me completely. He stopped for a second, and I panted, looking down the length of our bodies as the covers slid down his back. The hard cheeks of his ass were just visible in the room's dim light, my pale thighs spread wide around them. The proof that he was buried inside me.

He began to move, a slow drumbeat under the music he whispered in my ear. Irish silver that told me to let go, that took away all the shyness and set me free. Each silken *push* sent pleasure spiraling out through my body until I was twisting and gasping, grabbing at the sheets. As he started to thrust faster, it all started to spill out: all the need I'd been bottling up, all the fantasies I thought I should be ashamed of. My knees rose either side of him and I started to claw at his back, then his ass, pulling him in deeper and grinding up against him.

I panted as we kissed, our mouths open and urgent. God, he was as out of control as me, his whole body hard with lust, his hips slamming between my thighs. The pleasure built and built, hot ripples spreading out from my groin, crashing together and filling me up. *Come for me,* he panted, his lips just touching my ear.

And I did, the climax a wave that lifted and carried me. My back arched, my heels dug into the mattress and I shuddered and rocked against him, calling out his name.

When the pleasure finally died away, I came back to myself. I was lying in my bed, knees wide, my fingers sticky with my juices, my whole body gleaming with sweat. I could feel my cheeks flush red in the darkness.

I rolled onto my side and burrowed down into the now-warm bed. *How the hell did that get so out of control?* But I knew the answer to that: *Corrigan.* He woke something in me, something I couldn't fight. *How am I going to look him in the eye tomorrow?*

And what would happen when I did?

12

DOMINIC

THE NEXT MORNING, the sky was still blue, but the temperature had dropped by a full ten degrees and my rented pickup grumbled before finally rumbling into life. I was a little slow to get going, too. I'd had another restless night, this time thinking about Beckett.

I liked her more than I wanted to admit. I'd never thought I'd meet another woman who I liked in that way, after Chrissy, but I liked Amy Beckett. It wasn't that they were the same: they couldn't be more different and maybe that's why she'd blindsided me. I hadn't known I wanted someone like that.

I wanted to get her the hell out of that OR and show her the world. It wasn't fair that she was hiding away. She deserved a life. She needed to be fed ice cream in a park on a really hot day, my arms wrapped around her from behind as we sat on a blanket. She needed to go swimming in the sea, both of us riding the waves as we kicked around in the surf. She needed to go walking in the forest early on a misty morning, freezing in silence as we saw a deer. She needed... *me*.

Except I couldn't give her any of that. There's a reason I keep it shallow, keep it simple. I can't have anything else. Not without Chrissy and Rachel.

I couldn't just sleep with her and I couldn't have a relationship with her. Around four in the morning, I'd finally reached a conclusion. The only thing to do from now on was to avoid Beckett completely.

When I pulled into the cafe on Main Street to grab breakfast, the locals were shaking their heads and muttering about the bad weather in Denver...and that it might head our way. "Could be a long day at the hospital," the old lady behind the counter warned me. "I recommend the *Behemoth*. In case you don't get to eat again for a while."

I shrugged. I'll try anything once. "Hit me."

The *Behemoth* turned out to be a foot-long hot sandwich. The cafe started with a French baguette, brown and crunchy on the outside, soft and white inside. They flattened it out, then sliced it open and filled it with sliced sausage, fried onions and diced potato, all dripping in gravy. Then they wrapped the whole thing in waxed paper and served it with a super-size takeout cup of coffee. I ate it one-handed as I drove the rest of the way to the hospital and it was wonderful: rich, spicy sausage, the tang of golden fried onion, piping hot chunks of potato and that amazing gravy soaking the bread.

I was still sipping my coffee when I walked into the ER. Taylor, my med student, was already there, taking off a woolly hat and combing her long, blonde hair out with her fingers while she watched a wall-mounted TV. I still couldn't get over how young she was. "Could get bad, if that comes our way," she said, nodding at the screen. A forlorn reporter stood in front of an intersection in Denver, hugging her coat around her as a howling wind plastered her with snow. The caption said it was ten degrees. *That doesn't sound so bad.* Then I remembered this was America, and they used Fahrenheit. *Christ, that's minus twelve!*

"Nice coat," said Taylor.

I'd forgotten I was wearing it. It was a big orange parka I'd bought years ago in Chicago when we had a really cold winter. It was kind of ridiculous, hugely thick with a furry hood and way too many zippers and toggles. But Chrissy had loved it. She'd kept stealing it on weekends: she'd sit on our house's little balcony, curled up on the chair with my coat wrapped around her like a blanket and her hands warmed by a hot cup of coffee and she'd look so damn cute....

I took a deep breath and pushed the memories back down inside. "What have we got?" I grunted.

"Ten year-old with a broken arm," said Taylor. She led the way to an exam room.

The kid—Alex—was dressed for school. Just from the amount of pain he was in as I gingerly examined his arm, I could tell it was a messy break from twisting or bending, not a clean snap. "How'd you do it?" I asked.

His dad answered for him. "Running in the house." He was in a fancy suit and his eyes kept gravitating back to the screen of his phone.

I looked at the kid again. I couldn't see much more than blond curls because his eyes stayed permanently on the floor, avoiding confrontation. I'd seen a lot of kids like that. A suspicion started to grow in my mind, sickening and cold.

"500 miligrams acetaminophen IV for the pain," I told Taylor. Then I turned to Alex's dad and shook my head. "X-Ray's backed up," I lied. "Could be two, three hours."

"Oh, fucking great," the dad snapped. "I'm late for work already!"

"Ms. Taylor can show you a quieter place, if you need to make some calls," I said helpfully.

He sighed and nodded, then followed Taylor without even a backward glance at Alex. As soon as he was gone, I turned to the kid. "That true?" I asked gently. "Were you running in the house?"

He hesitated. Nodded. But he still wouldn't look at me. And there was something about the way he was sitting, hunched forward as if he didn't want the chair to press into his back. The suspicion was growing and spreading, chilling me... but at its center was a hot pulse of anger. "You hurt your back when you fall?" I asked.

He shook his head.

I struggled to keep my voice casual. "Let me take a look, just in case."

For the first time, he looked up and his eyes were wide with fear.

The suspicion became a certainty. "Just in case," I said again.

13

AMY

I HAD TO walk to work because I'd left my car at the hospital the night before, but it meant I could stop at the bakery on the way. I grabbed croissants, Danishes and coffee for the OR staff. I just wished I'd put on a thicker coat: it was much, much colder today and I was shivering by the time I reached work.

Upstairs, Krista pounced on me as soon as I came out of the elevator. "Bless you, Amy." She grabbed a Danish and a coffee. "*Sooo?*"

I flushed. "So what?"

"So *what happened?* Everyone saw you and Corrigan in Krüger's."

"Nothing! We were just talking!"

Krista cupped my cheek in one hand, stared intently into my eyes and brushed her thumb across my lips.

"*What are you doing?!*" I squeaked, trying not to drop the rest of the coffees.

"Nothing. Just talking. This is how people *just talk,* isn't it?"

I huffed and knocked her hand away. "Okay, okay! He's...interested. He *says* he's interested."

"Of course he's interested! So what happened?"

"Nothing! I went home!" Then, quickly, "Alone!"

"And jilled off."

"*Krista!*" I went crimson.

"Oh, like you didn't."

I hurried into the OR and started lining up my surgical instruments with exacting precision. When I trusted my voice again, I said, "I'm not getting involved with him."

"I don't think anyone gets *involved* with him. They just get under him. Maybe you should, too."

"Krista!"

"Look: okay, he's just about the sex. The man's about as deep as a puddle. But a night of rolling around with a smokin' hot Irishman between your thighs—would that be so bad?"

"Yes! I'm not being the next Corrigan conquest." And I marched out before she could argue. But as I hurried over to intensive care to check on Rebecca, I couldn't figure out which bothered me more: her encouraging me to sleep with Corrigan or her writing him off as shallow. I was sure there was more to him than people saw.

Rebecca was still very fragile, but well enough that I'd be able to do the second stage of her operation that afternoon. "Then I'll be all fixed?" she asked.

"Yes. There are a few things we'll need to keep an eye on, but you should be fine." I was still a little concerned about her kidney function: if it went south, she'd need a specialist center. But it was looking okay for now.

I called her parents to see what time they'd be arriving. But when I got through, they told me Denver airport was still closed and now some of the roads were being closed, too. They were holed up in a motel just outside Colorado, worried out of their minds. Rebecca's lip quivered and something surged up inside me, fierce and primal.

"Don't worry," I heard myself say into the phone. "I'll keep her safe."

And Rebecca blinked back the tears that had been about to spill. I put Rebecca on the phone and sat there watching her talk to her folks, shocked at the feelings that were tightening my chest. Growing up without my mom and with a dad who was so geeky and practical, I'd always thought I'd missed out on developing any sort of maternal instincts. I certainly couldn't imagine ever being a mom. But for the first time, those instincts were waking up. I really liked this kid. I wasn't going to let anything happen to her. It was incredible... and scary.

As I got into the elevator to head up to Surgery, my mind slid back to Corrigan. *Of course* I couldn't sleep with him. But...as the doors closed and I zoned out for a moment, I was suddenly back in the fantasy from the night before. His hard body spreading my thighs, his cock driving up into me as he whispered in Irish silver all the things he was going to do to me....

The elevator doors opened...onto the ER. *Wait, what?* Why had I gone *down* instead of *up*? I was sure I'd pressed the button for Surgery.

Almost sure. *God, I pressed* ER, *didn't I?* Subconsciously, I wanted to see him. So strongly that I'd even come down here, to the place that drove me crazy. I shook my head and mashed the button for Surgery. My subconscious could go hang. I wasn't going to sleep with him so the less I saw of him the—

Corrigan flung aside the curtain of an exam room and stalked across the room.

I took a step back. *Everyone* took a step back. Corrigan's face was twisted with rage and every muscle was straining with tension. Each step he took seemed to shake the floor and when an empty gurney got in his way, he shoved it halfway across the room. "*YOU!*" he thundered, pointing.

Everyone followed his finger to a guy in a suit. The guy's face went pale.

"*You did that!*" Corrigan bellowed. The Irish in his voice was sharp and hard as an axe blade. "You twisted his arm until it snapped. *Because he was late for school?!*"

The elevator doors started to close. I shoved them open again.

"That's bullshit!" said the guy. He took a step back, then another, but Corrigan was coming too fast. "I told you, he fell. He was running—"

Corrigan reached him. "I saw the burns on his back," he spat. "Did he *fall* onto two dozen lit cigarettes?"

And he slammed his fist into the guy's face.

14

AMY

THE PUNCH had all of Corrigan's fury behind it. The guy in the suit staggered backwards, hit a gurney and tumbled over it, tipping it over with an almighty crash. For maybe the first time ever, Mount Mercy's ER went utterly silent. I stumbled out of the elevator and stood panting in shock.

Corrigan stood over the felled man, his breath shaky with anger, his chest heaving. I'd never known he was capable of this. He wasn't a violent man, he was gentle. But this came from somewhere down deep, something he couldn't fight. It was a father's protective rage.

I thought of the night before, in the bar, when he'd called Rebecca *Rachel*. What if it hadn't been just a random slip? What if he had a daughter? It would explain why Rebecca's injuries got to him so much. There was definitely no ring on his finger, so...*he must be divorced. I wonder how often he sees them?*

The guy in the suit slowly got to his feet. Blood was dripping down his face from a broken nose. At the same moment, Bartell rushed into the room along with a security guard. "*What the hell is going on?*" he bawled, already glaring at Corrigan.

"This son of a bitch hit me." The guy in the suit stabbed his finger at Corrigan. "I'll sue!"

Corrigan's breathing slowed. He looked around and then his shoulders fell. He knew he'd screwed up. He'd likely wind up with an assault charge which could lead to him losing his license, plus the hospital would be sued. Worst of all, the assault would be used to make the father look like the victim in court and he might get away with the child abuse. Unless.... "He hit me first," said Corrigan, his voice loud in the silent room.

"Bullshit!" snapped the guy in the suit, his hand to his nose to try to staunch the bleeding.

Bartell looked around the room. "Did anyone see what happened?"

Everyone had seen what happened. And most of the people standing there had been in the Krüger's the night before, drinking on Corrigan's tab. But... I watched, horrified, as one by one they all looked at the ground. No one was prepared to lie for him and put their own career on the line, even if it meant a child abuser went free. Now I knew how he'd made so many friends so easily: he hadn't. Just a load of hangers-on who were happy to drink and laugh with him but turned tail when he needed them. And Corrigan didn't look surprised. *This is how he likes things*, I realized. At each new hospital, he'd build a reputation as a party animal, a fun guy to know... but he'd make no real friends.

He was as lonely as me.

"You're through, Corrigan!" Bartell snapped. "Clear your locker!"

Corrigan drew in a deep, shuddering breath and for a moment I thought he was going to yell. Then he just nodded. I saw a few people glance at each other, upset but not surprised. I remembered Krista's book on how many days he'd last. *But this isn't right! He's a great doctor!*

"I saw it!" I blurted.

For once, it was quiet enough that I could be heard in the ER. Bartell slowly turned to stare at me.

I swallowed. I'm a terrible liar. Even for dumb little things like Krista's surprise birthday party. This was huge. "That guy hit Doctor Corrigan first," I said.

Bartell's eyes seared into me. He *knew*. I felt like a kid being stared down by the principal. I'd never been in trouble with him before, not *once,* in two years—

I glanced at Corrigan. Then I looked back to Bartell and nodded stubbornly.

Bartell ran a hand over his face tiredly. And then, just for a second, I thought I saw him soften. He pointed the security guard towards the guy in a suit. "Watch him," he ordered. "And call Child Services and the police." He glared at the rest of us. "Everyone get back to work!"

Everyone made themselves scarce. And suddenly it was just Corrigan... and me.

15

DOMINIC

I STOOD THERE for a second just gaping at her. Then, without willing it, I was crossing the room, eating up the distance between us in huge strides. I had to force myself to pull up when there was still space between us or I would have grabbed her right then.

My eyes searched her face. *What did you do?* I wanted to rage at her. She shouldn't have put her neck on the line for me!

But she just lifted her chin and stared back at me, resolute. The woman everyone overlooked, the one everyone underestimated. A few strands of copper hair hung down out of the front of her surgical cap, her soft lips pouted up at me in stubborn defiance and... *fuck*. I've never wanted to kiss someone so bad. My fingers actually throbbed: I knew now what her skin would feel like in my hand, knew how easy it would be to whip that cap off her head, unpin her hair and set her free. Tilt that chin up just a little and bring my lips down on hers....

But I couldn't. I couldn't do that to Chrissy and Rachel.

I shook my head at her. "You didn't have to do that."

She crossed her arms. Her slender forearm accidentally brushed my abs and we both pretended it hadn't happened but I could feel my muscles tingling from the contact. "You saved *me* from that Colt guy," she said.

Just the mention of her in danger made me come over all protective again. Someone wheeled a gurney in through the doors and the blast of cold air made her gasp. I wanted to grab her, pull her against me and shelter her with my warmth.

But I couldn't. For her sake, I had to do the opposite. "Well, Beckett, I guess that makes us even," I said, fighting to keep my voice level.

She looked up at me, confused. She could hear the finality in my voice.

I forced myself to stare back at her, stony-faced.

She nodded, turned and hurried off to the elevator without looking back.

When the doors closed, I watched the indicator climb all the way up to Surgery, my chest tight. This whole time, I'd been desperate to get her out of there, thinking she was wasted in the OR. Now I was glad she was up there where it was safe, where no one would pull a knife on her or make her lie and jeopardize her career.

She was back where she belonged, far away from me.

16

AMY

B ACK UPSTAIRS, I got started on the first operation of the day, a routine appendectomy. Head down, Brahms plays over the speakers, I tried to get into the zone. But I kept snapping back to Corrigan telling me we were even. He'd said it like he was slamming a door shut. Why? Because I'd walked away the night before? Because he'd realized I didn't want a one-night stand? It felt like more than that. There'd been real conflict in his eyes. And the way he'd punched that guy, to protect a child... there was more to him than anyone else was seeing.

But it didn't matter. He'd made it clear that we were done.

"You okay?" muttered Krista.

I looked up, then looked at Adele and Lina. All of them were watching me. I realized my hands had slowed to a stop and I was just staring at the wound without seeing it. "Just figuring out my next move," I lied.

But like I said, I'm a terrible liar. Krista caught my eye, worried.

I pushed all thoughts of Irish doctors out of my head and finally managed to get into the zone. An hour later, I finished and closed. "Good job," I told everyone. Lina wheeled out the patient and—

An electronic scream split the air, so loud and so sudden it jolted right the way up my spine. Thank God I hadn't been working on a patient. Adele, Krista and I stared at each other. *What the hell's that?!*

It rose and fell: a klaxon. After ten seconds or so, it mercifully stopped. Then a woman's voice, recorded and tinny. "*All staff, report to the ER. This is not a drill.*"

The three of us stared at each other, then joined the flood of people running down the stairs. "Have you ever—" I began.

Krista shook her head. "I never heard that before."

We burst into the ER to find it rapidly filling up with people. Save for a few nurses who stayed behind to monitor critical patients, everyone who worked in the hospital was there.

Bartell started to speak, then paused and climbed up onto a table so his voice would reach the back of the crowd. I could see sweat beading on his forehead despite the cold. "A few minutes ago, the state issued a critical weather warning for this area. The blizzard that's been hitting Denver is heading right for us. The road between us and Denver is already impassable."

That was bad. We got most of our supplies from Denver. But that was only the beginning.

"With the amount of snow the storm's bringing," said Bartell, "*all* the roads out of Mount Mercy are going to be blocked within the next few hours. We're going to be totally cut off. And the blizzard could last for days."

The crowd erupted into worried chatter. The town was no stranger to snow, but we'd never been cut off before. Only a handful of staff lived here in Mount Mercy. Most people commuted in from one of the bigger towns. Some were already grabbing their coats. Unless they left now, they'd be cut off from their families, their kids.

"We have no choice," said Bartell. "We have to shut down."

I blinked. "*What?!*" I looked around, confused. It seemed crazy: the snow wasn't even here, yet. "OK, so some people need to leave early but we don't need to—"

Bartell shook his head. "*The next shift can't get in!*"

Oh *crap.* I hadn't thought of that. We'd have no staff!

"Here's what's going to happen," said Bartell. "All surgeries and procedures that aren't actually in progress are cancelled. All non-critical patients are to be sent home immediately. Anyone who's critical gets put in an ambulance and transported to Colorado Springs: that's the nearest hospital we can still reach." He raised his arms. "*Go!*" He climbed down off the table.

The crowd started to move around me, but I stood frozen, disbelieving. "You think it can really be *that* bad?" I asked Krista.

She nodded. "Back in 2003, they got three feet of snow in Denver. Up here, with the wind blowing it around, we got drifts *seven feet deep.* It can get down to ten degrees: colder, with wind chill. Complete white-out. You won't be able to go outside, never mind get to another town!"

I nodded slowly. I suddenly wished I'd paid more attention to the news over the last few days. The blue skies here had fooled me. The bad weather had seemed so far away...I knew that Denver had already been brought to a standstill, that's why Rebecca's parents—

Rebecca!

I launched myself through the crowd towards Bartell. "*Wait!*" I yelled. He was already talking to a cluster of doctors, trying to organize twenty things at once. "We can't shut down!"

He reluctantly turned to look at me. "We have to. We can't function without staff."

"But there's a little girl, Rebecca Kemple! She had a splenectomy yesterday, and she's still in the ICU with an open Tib fib fracture. I need to finish what I started before we can risk moving her."

He winced. "She'll have to go in an ambulance to Colorado Springs—"

"That's a *three hour drive!* She won't make it!"

Bartell opened his mouth to speak, but he couldn't offer me anything. He spread his arms wide, helpless. "I'm...I'm sorry, Beckett. I have to do the best I can with what I have. If we don't evacuate the patients, they'll have no care at all. More will die."

My shoulders slumped. It wasn't his fault. He was doing everything he could. I turned and stumbled away from him, feeling sick. I was remembering the promise I'd made to Rebecca's parents. *I'll keep her safe.*

For a second, the room blurred behind tears. As I tried to blink them back, I saw Corrigan watching me, looking as agonized as me. *We're going to lose her.*

And then I remembered something I'd read when I first came to Mount Mercy. That *might* work. But to have a chance of making it happen, I'd have to—

I looked around at the massive crowd. I'd never felt so small, so shy, in my whole life. *I can't!*

But if I didn't, Rebecca was going to die.

On shaking legs, I climbed up onto the table where Bartell had stood. "We can keep the ER open!" I said in a strained, hesitant voice.

No one heard me.

I took a deep breath and yelled. *"We can keep the ER open!"*

Everyone stopped and stared. I think it was the surprise of me raising my voice as much as anything else.

"Beckett, what the hell are you doing?" snapped Bartell.

I stared down at all the faces looking up at me... and froze. *I don't know how to do this!* I needed to not just talk to them, I needed to convince them to join me and I was the world's least suitable person to give a speech.

"Well?" Bartell's voice was strained. Not unkind, but he was trying to get the evacuation going and I was holding everything up.

I felt my face go hot. I opened my mouth, but nothing came out...

And then I saw Corrigan, at the back of the crowd. He nodded and mouthed something to me: *Go on, Beckett!*

"It's in the emergency handbook," I said in a rush. "If the hospital is shut down, we can keep just the ER running for emergencies and critical care. It needs *way* fewer staff. Rebecca could be moved down here."

Bartell gawped at me and then put his hand to his face and shook his head. "Trust *you* to have read the emergency handbook. But we'd still need doctors."

"I'll stay," I said immediately.

"You're a surgeon, not an ER doc!"

"I did my ER rotation when I trained, the same as everyone else."

"Years ago! And you hate it down here!"

"I can handle it," I said. And prayed that was true. That ER rotation had been the worst six months of my life and this would be way worse, an ER with a skeleton staff. But if I wanted to save Rebecca, I had no choice.

"That's one doctor," Bartell said grudgingly. "You need more."

"I'll do it."

I caught my breath. The voice was a low rumble, shining with Irish silver. I looked to the back of the room and found Corrigan gazing straight at me.

"You've been here *one day!*" said Bartell in disbelief. "You barely know your way around!"

"Beckett can show me," said Corrigan, gazing steadily at me.

"Me too," said a young, blonde-haired woman.

Bartell sighed. "Taylor, you're a med student!"

"She's a quick study," said Corrigan. And I saw Taylor's face light up with pride.

"This is crazy," said Bartell. "You'd need nurses—"

"Right here," said Krista, pushing her way to the front. Adele and Lina were right behind her and a handful of other nurses joined them.

"I'm staying too," said Maggie. "Got to keep things running."

Bartell opened his mouth to protest... and then let out a long sigh instead. "You're all crazy," he muttered. Then he shook his head ruefully. "Guess I'd better call my wife and tell her I won't be home for a few days."

I blinked in disbelief. "You're staying?!"

He looked embarrassed that he'd been caught being nice. "Someone has to make sure you don't burn the place down." He did his best to scowl.

I wanted to hug him. But he saw the look in my eyes and put his hands up defensively. "Yeah, yeah, okay," he said. "We still need to evacuate everyone who can make the journey. We've got less than two hours before the blizzard hits."

I nodded gratefully... and ran.

The next two hours passed in a blur as we discharged all the patients we could and transferred all the ones we couldn't to ambulances for the long trip to Colorado Springs. I made sure to check in on Rebecca and it was a good thing I did: she was watching all the other patients being wheeled out. "Everyone's leaving," she said as soon as she saw me.

"Not me," I told her. "I'm staying right here with you. And I'm even going to move you downstairs, so I can keep an eye on you."

"Back to the ER?" She actually sounded excited.

"Back to the ER," I said. I was operating on adrenaline and the reality of what I'd signed up for hadn't fully sunk in yet but the fear was already starting to churn in my stomach.

I moved her bed downstairs to the temporary intensive care area we'd set up in one corner of the ER, then ran to help with the other patients. It was a frantic, breathless panic: all of us could feel the blizzard breathing down our necks. We had to work so fast, in the final half hour that it turned into a production line: gurneys flowed out of the elevator and kept moving all the way to the ambulance bay with doctors running alongside to check charts and nurses loading supplies and hanging fresh IV bags. At last, we were down to just four patients who needed to be evacuated.

"*Come on!*" yelled Bartell. "The blizzard'll be here any minute!"

Krista and Adele grabbed the first patient's gurney, Lina and Bartell took the next and Maggie and Taylor the next. I grabbed one end of the final gurney—

And then Corrigan was there at the other end. I wanted to thank him for staying, for supporting my crazy plan but, as soon as I looked into those blue eyes, I struggled to get the words out. He'd lost that cocky hardness for a second and was looking at me with such a mix of lust and longing....

"Let's move!" said Bartell.

We pushed the gurneys out to the ambulance bay and—

I let out a shuddering gasp as the cold hit me. The temperature had plummeted and a bitter wind was howling, lashing our exposed skin. The snow hadn't started yet, but it was close.

We pushed the gurneys into the waiting ambulances and handed the charts to the paramedics. They raced away the second we had the doors shut. A steady stream of cars started to roar out of the underground parking garage: everyone was desperate to get out of town before we got cut off.

All seven of us clustered around Bartell as he started to speak. "We've done all we can," he said. "We're down to six critical patients. I figure I can cope with that. So it comes down to what traumas come in over the next few days." He looked around at us. "If we're lucky, the worst we'll get is a couple of sprained ankles from people slipping on the ice."

I really hoped so. Because it was sinking in that our little group was now all that our town had. Whatever came in, we'd have to deal with it. I wouldn't just be doing consults, I'd be one of the ER docs, right in the middle of the chaos with patients' lives in my hands.

I felt someone looking at me. I turned and the look in Corrigan's eyes sent a deep, hot pulse straight down my body. I was going to have to do this working right alongside him, both of us fighting to resist....

As the last cars tore away, a fresh blast of wind hit us, even colder than before. For the first time in hours, I had time to look up at the sky.

The sheer size of the clouds was terrifying. Gray-white, they were piled deeper than I'd ever seen and they filled the sky from horizon to horizon, spreading rapidly to block out the last scraps of blue. And below them, an impenetrable curtain of white. This wasn't weather like I'd ever seen it. This was on a whole different scale: our little town felt like a child's toy, helpless against what was coming. I watched as the last cars disappeared into the distance. They'd made it out with minutes to spare. The fear rose up inside me, colder even than the wind. *What are we still doing here? What the hell have I done?*

I was suddenly aware of something warm and comforting. I looked down and saw Corrigan's hand holding mine.

The wind rose to a shriek that hurt our ears. The curtain of white raced towards us.

"God help us," muttered Bartell. He hurried us inside and slammed the doors.

And the blizzard hit us.

17

AMY

S NOW, to me, was soft flakes falling slowly from the sky and kids trying to catch them on their tongues. This was nothing like that. Nothing like anything I'd ever experienced.

A howling, shrieking wind had wrapped itself around the hospital, shaking the windows and blasting into every tiny crack to spread its cold. The snow didn't fall, it blew horizontally and swirled until the flakes seemed to come from every direction, plastering the windows and drifting up against the doors. As the blizzard engulfed us, Mount Mercy gradually disappeared from view. First the mountains faded out. Then the street my house was on. Then the lights of Main Street started to vanish one by one: the bakers, the cafe, the bar....

And then, quite suddenly, all I could see was swirling white. *White-out,* Krista had called it. It was as if the rest of the world had disappeared.

I walked over to the doors, transfixed. I wasn't planning to go out. I just wanted to see it up close. But when the automatic doors slid open ahead of me, I kept going, gazing around me in disbelief.

The wind was the first shock. It was so strong it sent me staggering sideways and so bitterly cold it went straight through my scrubs and clawed at my bones. The howl of it was deafening and it rose and fell, always changing, making it difficult to think. I felt my surgical cap lift and then it was gone, carried away into the white.

And the snow... the snow wasn't like I'd known other years, light and full of air. This was thick and heavy, plastering one whole side of my body from ankle to cheek as the wind pelted it against me. Where it hit cloth, it started to melt and soak in, icy water stealing my body heat. Where it hit skin, I went numb. It filled my vision in every direction: I couldn't see more than six feet. It would be terrifyingly easy to get lost.

Already, parked cars and fire hydrants were featureless, soft-edged snow models. The pavement was white, the road markings invisible. I could just make out the glow of headlights in the distance as a few drivers who'd been caught outside crawled towards home. But aside from them, not a thing was moving. Not even me: I'd stumbled to a stop. The deafening howl of the wind in my ears and the endless white everywhere I looked, combined with my head throbbing so hard with cold that I couldn't think... something about it made my brain misfire like an engine that's starved of fuel. I just stood there, dazed.

Until a hand grabbed my shoulder and spun me around. I stumbled and strong hands grabbed my upper arms, steadying me. *"What the hell are you doing out here, you daft feckin' mare?!"*

I looked up into blue eyes that were gleaming with fury and molten with need.

18

DOMINIC

I WAS SO angry with her, I was going to....

What do you call it when you're absolutely livid with someone and all you want to do is kiss them?

She stared up at me, coming out of her daze. "I just..." She blinked and flushed. "I just wanted to see."

"You'll catch your death, you bloody eejit!" I leaned close to make sure I was heard over the wind. And that made it even harder because she was inches from me, looking like some sort of snow queen with all that soft, pale skin and those blue eyes. The stupid cap was gone and her hair had blown loose, plastered damply to her cheek and neck on one side, flying out on the other as the wind caught it. Without thinking, I pushed my fingers through it to comb it back off her ear so she could hear me better. And the feel of her, her skin so cold and her vivid, copper hair dusted with snow, damp against my warm fingers...she was just so fragile, so vulnerable....

I cursed and picked her up. Just scooped one arm under the backs of her legs and the other under her back and hoisted her up against my chest. That woke her up. "What are you—Corrigan!" she squeaked.

I ignored her. Carried her back through the automatic door and right to the center of the ER, out of the draft. And I tried not to think about the way she felt against me, the side of her breast pillowed against my pec. *Dammit, Beckett....*

I set her down and she staggered, huffing with indignation and blowing hair out of her face. People were looking at us and she didn't seem to like being the center of attention. "You didn't have to—"

"It's too cold for messing around," I told her. And I meant it. Even after just a few minutes, she was soaked through from the snow and her skin was bone white. Anyone caught outside in that weather would be dead in a matter of hours. I grabbed her hands and they were like blocks of ice. I pressed them between my palms to warm them.

I scowled at her and she glared at me, still trying to comb her damp hair back off her face. But now that she was out of danger, we were both calming down. *Maybe I overreacted, picking her up.* I didn't regret it, though. She gave one last huff of anger, finally got her hair out of her face and—

And then we were gazing into each other's eyes again. *Damn you, woman. What am I going to do with you?* My whole world seemed to narrow down to the little droplet of melted snow on her soft lower lip.

"Thank you," she muttered.

"Didn't want our only surgeon getting frostbitten fingers," I told her.

"Thank you for staying, too."

I wasn't expecting that one. I tried to shrug and look away, but I couldn't let go of those eyes. How was it that I could fool every other woman I met and not her? She said she was weird, but she asked the questions other people wouldn't, the ones that cut straight through all my bullshit. I finally managed to break her gaze and looked down at my feet. "It was the right thing to do," I said.

I let go of her hands. Then—I couldn't stop myself—I brushed some of the snow out of her hair. And as soon as I touched her again, she gave this tiny little intake of breath and I had to pull my hands back and make fists or I would have just grabbed her and—

"Just be careful, Beckett!" I muttered. And walked away.

19

AMY

A S I STOOD THERE staring at his retreating back, Krista bounded up. *"What was that?* And don't say you were just talking. Or that he 'might be interested.' If he was any more interested, you'd be pregnant."

I shook my head. "I don't know." And it was the truth. Just that morning, he'd pushed me away, but when he'd looked at me just now, when he'd picked me up and carried me in, it was like I was the most important thing in his world. In the bar, I'd been one hundred percent, cast-iron sure that I wasn't going to get involved with a cocky, shallow womanizer. Now the only thing I was sure of was that Dominic Corrigan wasn't what he appeared.

The ER stayed blessedly quiet for most of the morning. We had a guy come in with whiplash after he'd run into another car in the snow and an old lady who'd gotten caught outside and was close to hypothermia. I just hoped it stayed that way. If we had traumas come in, if it became a mad, panicked rush... my insides contracted into a dark, cold ball at the thought. I didn't belong in the ER. I was used to careful planning and precision. Having someone's life in my hands and not having time to think... *what if I screw up? What if I freeze?*

I decided to operate on Rebecca's leg while it was quiet. I sat by her bedside as Lina prepared the anesthetic.

"Will my parents be here when I wake up?" asked Rebecca.

My chest contracted. *The poor kid.* "I'm sorry. The snow might last a while. But they'll be here as soon as they can.

She suddenly grabbed my hand. "But *you* will be, right?"

I blinked down at her and started to say something, but there was suddenly a huge lump in my throat. "Of course," I managed.

"Count backwards from ten for me," said Lina.

I sat there in silence as Rebecca counted, that protective urge welling up in me again. *She's my responsibility.* I was the world's least suitable person for the job. *I have no idea how to be a mom!* But I knew I'd better figure it out fast because, for as long as we were cut off, I was the closest to a mom she had.

"She's under," said Lina.

I swallowed and looked down at the sleeping face with its blonde curls. I don't normally get to know my patients. I meet them for maybe a minute or two before the operation. This was going to be like operating on my own child.

"Amy, you okay?" asked Krista.

I nodded. "Fine," I said, my voice tight. "Let's do this."

Four hours later, I staggered out of the OR. Krista slapped me on the back but I was too mentally exhausted to do more than nod and weakly pat her. *Holy shit.* The operation had gone perfectly but I'd had to work with all those new feelings flooding through me. Rebecca would be fine, but I was an emotional wreck.

I tried to call her parents to give them an update, but the hospital phone had no dial tone. I ventured downstairs to the ER in case it was just our floor, but when I got there, I found Maggie talking to Bartell.

"Every phone's dead," she was telling him. "And it's not just us. I walked down the street and the whole town's the same. The wind must have brought down the phone lines."

I hurried off towards the locker room to get my cell phone. Then had to pull up short when Corrigan stepped out of an exam room, right into my path. We came to a stop with our sneakers touching, my breasts a hair's breadth from brushing his chest. I opened my mouth to apologize, but when I looked up and saw his face, that was forgotten.

He looked exhausted. His scrubs were soaking wet in places and there was still a little snow in his hair. But he looked happy. Not that fake, loud happiness he'd shown at the bar, his party persona. He looked satisfied. *Fulfilled.* For just a moment, that sadness I always saw in his eyes was gone. "What happened to *you?*" I asked.

He sighed and grinned. "A lady pulled up right outside the doors. Went out to see why she wasn't getting out of her car, turned out she was nine months pregnant."

I caught my breath. Obstetrics was shut down! Everything was shut down! "What happened?"

A baby's cry came from the exam room. "Well, she's not pregnant anymore."

Now I knew why he looked so happy. A stupid grin broke across my face. "You delivered it?"

"Taylor helped." He kept looking towards the exam room and his grin matched mine. The baby's cry died away and it sounded as if it was feeding. Corrigan's grin grew even wider.

Emotion welled up inside me, hot and powerful. It was something about the look on his face, the fact he could be so big and strong and still be so...*doting.* And between that and what had happened upstairs with Rebecca, I suddenly felt a wild rush of hormones. *He'd make a great father.*

"You okay, Beckett?"

I realized I was staring. "Yep." And I told him about Rebecca coming through the operation well, and wanting to call her folks.

He reached into his pocket and handed me his cell phone. "Use mine."

I thanked him and got out of there before I did anything else weird. *What's wrong with me?* Ever since I'd met him, I was discovering whole new parts of myself. I'd never wanted kids before because I didn't think I'd make a good mother. But now....

I shook my head and called Rebecca's folks, who were still stuck in a motel waiting for the roads to clear. Her mom broke down when I told her that Rebecca had had another operation, but I managed to reassure them that everything was okay. "We'll monitor her closely, but she should be fine. She may need an operation on her kidneys at some point, but that can wait until we can get her to a specialist unit."

"God bless you, Doctor Beckett," said Rebecca's mom with feeling.

"You're welcome," I managed. I wasn't used to this stuff. I stayed in the OR so I didn't have to meet patients. I was starting to see how much I'd been missing out on.

As I ended the call, I realized something felt different. The howling wind had been so constant, it had almost become background noise, but now it had died away. And there was no movement outside the windows: the snow had stopped. I ran over to the main doors to get a first look at what the blizzard had left.

Drifts were waist-deep along the sidewalks and cars were buried up to the tops of their tires. As I got closer, I triggered the automatic sliding doors and a blast of air rushed in. It was cold like I'd never felt it: it actually sent me stumbling back a few steps in shock. God, the air felt like ice water, it soaked right through your clothes! I wrapped my arms around myself and ventured as far as the doors.

Snow had drifted up against them, almost hip-deep: we'd have to shovel it aside to get patients in and out. I tried poking it with my sneaker and I couldn't believe how thick and dense it was, as much ice as snow. The hills and forests that led up to the mountain were covered, too, the branches of the pine trees laden with blankets of white.

Icicles hung from every roof and windows and windshields were frosted with ice. Some of the strings of fairy lights that lit up Main Street at night were hanging limply down, their wires snapped by the weight of the ice that had formed on them. No wonder the phone lines were down. We were lucky we still had power.

Shivering, I stepped back to let the doors close and went to find Corrigan. When I couldn't find him anywhere in the ER, I pushed open the door of the locker room and—

I was looking at glistening, tanned abs. My gaze slowed to a crawl as it rode each hard ridge: *up* and *down* and *up*...and then it locked onto a drop of water that was sliding down the hard valley of his centerline, following it past his navel, down to his—

"For fuck's sake, Beckett, in or out," said the very naked Corrigan.

Without thinking, I stepped forward and the door swung closed behind me. We were maybe six feet apart. He was still dripping wet and steam from the shower was wrapped like a lover around his body, every inch of tan skin gleaming. All the parts of him I'd dreamed about—*fantasized* about—were right there, perfectly displayed. The chest, so wide and strong, his curving pecs crested by pink nipples the size of silver dollars. The upper arms, even bigger than they'd looked beneath his scrubs, his tattoos shining as if the ink was still wet. I saw what the snake tail was, now: it led up to a staff and wound around it before turning its head back to glare at the viewer. A Caduceus, the symbol of medicine, but styled more like a biker tattoo. And he really did have circular scars that might be from bullets, one on his left pec and two low down on his side, and a long, thin knife scar across his abdomen.

His wide shoulders and tight waist formed a V, an arrow pointing downward, and my eyes obeyed. They found the deep line of his adonis belt and followed it along, past his thickly-muscled thigh, to—

My fantasy had been eerily accurate. Big. Thick *and* long, the head satiny and—

I forced my eyes up to his face. He gave me the wickedest grin I'd ever seen.

I stared at the ceiling. "I just came to give you your phone back."

Out of the corner of my eye, I saw him nodding, utterly relaxed in his nakedness. "Throw me a towel, would you?"

I grabbed a towel off the pile and tossed it over to him, then tried to keep my eyes on his face while he toweled himself off. But my gaze seemed to keep drifting down, following his hands as they rubbed the little jewels of moisture from his chest...his abs...his—

I jerked my eyes away and saw that wolfish grin again. He turned side-on to me as he dried his ass, his hard cheeks dimpled. I couldn't stop thinking about my fantasy, how my fingers had dug into those cheeks, my thumbs right in those dimples....

He lazily pulled on a pair of jockey shorts and then swaggered towards me, a stripper teasing the shy girl at a bachelorette party. I think he was expecting me to blush and hurry away, and that would have been the end of it.

But something happened.

With each step he took, I could see his eyes changing, the heat rising in him. And the look he gave me rooted me to the spot: I *couldn't* run. The mood began to shift. Three steps from me and it had become only partly a game. Two steps. One step. And suddenly, it wasn't a game at all.

It was happening again, just like it had in the cafeteria, in the bar. My breathing had gone fast and tight. I felt like I was falling and my pulse was hammering in my ears. The heat of his near-naked body throbbed through the narrow sliver of air between us and melted me.

His eyes were flicking over my face, eating me up, but his jaw was set, lips pressed together. He was battling with himself and the tension was building with each heartbeat. He almost glared, furious at me for doing this to him. *Me?!* I looked down at myself. And when I looked up....

When I looked up, the anger and the indecision were gone. He slipped a hand around the back of my head. *Oh my God! We can't—* But I didn't pull away.

He leaned down—

Krista burst through the door. "Two criticals coming—" She stumbled to a stop as she saw us. "...in. We need you."

Corrigan and I stared at each other, dumbstruck. *We were about to* —*We nearly*—

Shouts from outside. The rattle of gurneys. We both nodded to each other, dropping our eyes. *Later.* He pulled on a fresh set of scrubs and we ran for the ER.

20

DOMINIC

"WHAT HAVE we got?" I yelled.

Beside me, I saw Beckett's eyes widen in disbelief. In the few minutes we'd been away, the ER had gone from quiet to total chaos. The main doors were open, letting in a freezing current of air. A crowd of guys had just entered with two injured men carried on their shoulders. There were long furrows in the snow outside where they'd forced their way through, the white polka-dotted with red. *This looks bad.*

Taylor got to the first guy as his buddies dumped him onto a gurney. "Head injury," she called, bending over him. "A lot of bleeding. Pupils fixed and dilated"

I raced over. The guy was big, with a bald head and a black beard dusted with snow. We'd have to work fast, he might be bleeding into his brain. "How's the other one?" I called over my shoulder.

The men dumped the second guy onto a gurney. Beckett ran forward to examine him—

"*STOP!*" I didn't wait around to see if she'd heard, just grabbed her shoulders and wrenched her backwards. Her feet slid from under her and she would have gone down if I hadn't kept hold of her. "Look," I said, panting.

The second guy had razor wire tangled around his left leg and a coil of it had spilled off the gurney and was trailing across the floor. She'd almost run right into it.

"Fucking evil stuff," I warned her. "It'll cut you right down to the bone and it likes to spring out at you. We need to cut it off him."

Beckett grabbed a nurse. "Find Maggie! Tell her to bring some wire cutters!"

The nurse ran off. I stepped closer to the patient and saw the blood soaking his pants and dripping to the floor. We couldn't wait: we had to start working on him now, or he'd bleed out.

Taylor and Krista had hooked monitors up to the head injury guy. "This guy's not looking good!"

They didn't need to read out the numbers, I could hear the beeps of his faltering heartbeat. *Shit!* We'd have to work on both of them at once. I made a decision and turned to Beckett. "You're going to have to run one of these."

I saw her freeze. "*What?!*" She looked around her, going white. "I never—"

It hit home, then. *She's never run a trauma.* The closest she'd been to the ER was a six month rotation as an intern. I knew that just being in the middle of all this chaos freaked her out, and I was expecting her to give orders. But we had no choice. I grabbed her arm and pulled her close. "I'll be right here," I told her.

We stared at each other and for a second I was lost in those eyes. *I would have kissed her. If Krista hadn't come in right then, I would have—*

Later. "You can do this," I told her.

She took a panicked breath...and nodded. My heart soared. *Attagirl!* I pushed her towards the head injury guy. I didn't want her anywhere near the razor wire.

I got the gurneys moved around so that both patients were next to each other and I could talk to her as we worked. Beckett shoved her arms into an ER apron and pulled on some gloves. Her hands were shaking.

I cut away the guy's pants and what I saw made me wince. The wire had coiled and tightened around his leg: the more he'd struggled, the more it had dug in, slicing into him like a band saw. It was almost down to the bone in places. Lucky for him, he was out cold. "How's yours looking?" I called.

No response. I glanced across. Beckett was facing away from me, but I could see the tension in her back. Everyone was looking at her expectantly and she'd frozen, unsure where to start. I turned back to my patient and started trying to stem the bleeding while I talked. "What's his pulse ox?"

"Um...85," she said, her voice high and tight.

"Okay. You're going to need to intubate him." It wasn't hard to make my voice soothing. I really felt for her. I remembered how terrifying it had been when I'd run my first trauma and I'd had two years of ER internship by that point. "You ever do that?"

"Once. I mean... I watched a Resident do it." She paused and I imagined her biting her lip. "Four years ago."

"You can do it. Head back, visualize the cords..." I talked her through it, step by step. Credit to her, she didn't miss a beat. Meanwhile, I was trying to put pressure on all the places my guy was bleeding from, but I'd run out of hands. I called Taylor over to help. "*Don't get cut!*" I warned her as I showed her where to press.

"I'm in!" Beckett called triumphantly.

I relaxed a little as I heard a nurse start to pump the intubation bag and fill the man's lungs. "You're doing great!" I called. By now, I had my hands, Taylor's hands and a nurse's hands all pressing on the guy's leg to stop the bleeding. It was working, but it was dangerous as hell. Taylor was actually having to pass her arms through a couple of the razor-sharp coils of wire to reach him. *Where the hell is Maggie with those wire cutters?*

My eyes flicked to the guy's arm: the nurses had rolled up his sleeve to attach a blood pressure monitor and I could see a couple of tattoos: one that was definitely from prison and a weird one that caught my eye. Two crossed rifles beneath a clenched fist. I'd seen that one before.

Fuck.

I looked up at the crowd of men milling around. And this time I spotted them: Colt and his son Seth.

My heart started to pound. "Call Earl, get him over here." I'd thought we were rid of Colt. Now we had his whole gang in our ER. *Razor wire*...at a guess, they'd been breaking into somewhere when these guys got injured.

Just seeing that bastard again made me automatically twist around and check that Beckett was okay: that deep, protective urge again. But it was the wrong thing to do because she looked up and saw my expression, then turned and saw Colt herself. I watched as she went pale. *Shit.* As if she didn't have enough to worry about. Taylor noticed, too, and caught Seth's eye. She looked down at the injured men, then back to him: *what are you mixed up in?* And he just glanced at his dad and gave a tiny shake of his head, apologetic or *can't talk* or both.

Part of me wanted to throw the whole gang out of the hospital. But both guys would die if we didn't treat them. We'd just have to do our jobs and hope Colt didn't turn violent.

At that moment, Beckett's patient crashed.

I heard it first as a collective intake of breath from the nurses and then the steady tone of the heart monitor. "Talk to me, Beckett!"

Her voice was strained. "His heart's stopped! I—get the..." Everyone was talking at once and I lost her voice under the hubbub. So did the nurses: I could hear them muttering in confusion. "You've got to speak up, Beckett!" I called. "People have to hear you!"

I could hear her struggling to make that small voice big. Then it broke free, shaky but clear. "Defibrillator paddles! And 1mg of Epi!"

There was a bustle of activity. I heard Beckett cursing, praying, then the whine of the defibrillator and the thump as it discharged. And then, at last, the steady beep of a healthy rhythm. She'd done it. I craned around and just managed to catch her eye. She was white-faced but she gave me a quick nod of thanks.

Maggie ran up with a pair of wire cutters. *At last!* I had to nod to her where to cut because I didn't have a hand to spare. In a few minutes, we'd have cut this godawful stuff off him and then—

He woke up.

It was the one thing none of us had been expecting. He'd been out cold since he was brought in and it hadn't occurred to us that he'd come round. But as Maggie tried to nudge a loop of wire out of his leg, it scraped a nerve and suddenly he was screaming, half-sitting up. Everything twisted and moved. Maggie's wire cutters snipped. The wire, suddenly free, uncoiled with a metal shriek. We all jumped back from the gurney. But Taylor, whose hands were within the loops of the wire, had to move slower to avoid slashing her wrists. The end of the wire sprang towards her face.

I shoved her aside. And felt it slash into the side of my neck. *Fuck!*

For a few seconds, everyone just stood there, shell-shocked. Then I started giving orders. We gave the patient something for the pain. Then we held him down while Maggie carefully cut the wire away from his leg. Wearing heavy gloves, she finally managed to get the whole bloody coil of it off him and well away from where we were working.

Taylor rushed over to me and started examining my neck. I tried to wave her away, but she shook her head. I glanced down at my scrubs: I was dripping blood. *Oh.* I held still.

"It's deep and messy," she said, her voice tight. "But it missed your jugular."

"How much by?"

"You don't want to know."" She paused and stared up at me. "Thank you," she said at last. She was still breathing a little fast, still imagining how the wire would have slashed across her eyes, her cheeks. "It should have been—"

I put my hands gently on her shoulders. "A scar looks better on a guy," I told her firmly.

Our eyes met and she calmed a little. We nodded to each other. We had each other's backs.

"It's going to need stitches," she told me, taping a pad of gauze over it.

"Him first," I said, nodding towards the guy we were working on.

With the wire out of the way, we managed to stem the bleeding and his pressure slowly recovered. We sutured the wounds and dressed them, then swaddled his leg in bandages. He'd be off his feet for a while, but he should make a full recovery.

I went over to check on Beckett. She'd got the head injury guy breathing on his own, but he was still unconscious. Just as I arrived, she finished giving orders for his medication and the nurses wheeled him off to the intensive care area. I watched Beckett slowly surface from the headlong adrenaline rush she'd been in. She blinked at the ER as if she'd forgotten where she was.

And then she just *ran*. She bolted across the room, dodged around a startled Taylor and disappeared into the locker room.

And I ran right after her.

21

AMY

I RAN OVER to the sinks and stood there gripping the porcelain. I was physically shaking, skin clammy with cold sweat. I ducked low, unsure if I was going to throw up, and sucked in air in shuddering gulps.

When I glanced up at the mirror again, Corrigan was standing behind me.

I shook my head at him in the mirror. "I can't do this." My voice was a pleading rasp.

He moved closer, but I didn't turn around. "What are you talking about? You did *great.*"

"I froze! That guy nearly died!"

"But he didn't. You saved him."

Didn't he get it? I wasn't like him! "I was *terrified!*"

He moved even closer. Now I could feel the presence of him behind me, his heat against my back. "You were scared but you did it anyway. Definition of bravery."

I started shaking my head. Strong hands on my shoulders twisted me around and then he was *there,* not just in the mirror, but real, looming and warm and solid right in front of me, seeing me at my most vulnerable. "I just wanted to stay up there!" I blurted. "Where it's quiet and safe and not...."

"Chaos?" he murmured.

I nodded.

He placed his hand on my damp cheek and I marvelled at how big those palms were. He looked so rooted, so *right,* here, a colossus carved from granite to especially fit the ER, with his strength and his confidence and his big, booming voice. And I was just a dormouse, trying to scurry back upstairs.

I knew he was going to try to convince me. My mind was racing non-stop, a billion reasons and arguments I could throw at him. But he sidestepped it all because he didn't use words. He just gazed steadily down at me and what I saw in his eyes short-circuited my panic.

He believed I *did* belong down here. He believed enough for the both of us.

My chest filled, buoying me up above the fear. And as I calmed, I realized how quiet it was. We were alone in the locker room... *again.* I swallowed. I saw his chest fill as he too remembered the nearly-kiss. It was happening again, that thrumming, breathless whirl that pushed all other thoughts from my head. His eyes fell to my lips. His hand gripped my cheek....

He leaned into me and I tilted my head way back so that I could meet his eyes.

"I can't resist you," he said. Four little shockwaves of silver-edged air that reverberated into my brain and set off a nuclear explosion as their meaning sunk in. Frenzied disbelief and arguments and *what if?* s all swept away by an expanding blast wave of hot emotion. I had to say something, but I couldn't form words. So I just put my hand on top of the hand that gripped my cheek... and pressed it there.

"You're more than anyone here gives you credit for," he said. "You hide away but you shouldn't hide." Each word was low and heavy, big ingots of silver that sunk into my soul. The cocky, teasing tone was gone. His voice came from somewhere down deep.

His hand moved from my cheek, sliding up over my temple, his fingers pushing under my surgical cap and smoothing over my pinned-back hair. I felt the cap tumble to the floor. "You drive me... fucking.... *crazy*," he told me. With each word, his voice grew tighter and my breathing grew faster. For the first time, there wasn't any of my usual *me?!* His voice didn't allow any argument.

His thumb stroked my hair, following its lines, and I felt the tiny tremble in his hand. God, his whole body had gone taut, quaking with the effort of holding back. "There's a sink behind you," he said. "Do you know what I want to do?" His other hand was suddenly on my waist, warm through the thin fabric. "I want to shove these down your legs,"—the edge of his hand nudged the waistband of my scrub pants—"and pick you up, sit you on the edge and just fuck you right here." He leaned in even closer, his lips right at my ear, and his voice became a growl wrapped around a core of molten silver. "I want all of you. I want your tits and your legs and your arse and your sweet, shy—"

He didn't say the last word. He breathed it. In his accent, it was transformed, those four letters turned from something ugly and course into something reverent but just as hotly forbidden. It soaked straight to my core and became a thrashing, urgent heat, an ache between my thighs. I wanted him. I wanted him more than I've ever wanted anything. My breath came in halting, frantic pants. I was delirious for this man.

"But..." His face twisted with the effort of saying it. I felt the muscles in his arms straining. "I...can't....*do that*. You deserve better than a quick fuck, Beckett." My surname wasn't formal, anymore. It was a pet name, a codename more intimate than *Amy* could ever be. "You deserve the fairy tale."

I blinked up at him. He sunk his fingertips into my hair for a second and then started to withdraw that hand and it felt like a knife being drawn from me. I clamped my own hand on top of it, holding it on me. I just couldn't bear to let this go. "Then—Then don't make it a quick—Do...do more! I—" I struggled to put it into words: an invisible ocean current that was barreling me towards him, unstoppable. "I *really like you!"* I said at last, and cursed myself because that didn't even begin to describe it.

But it didn't matter because immediately, I saw it in his eyes: he felt it, too. "We could...be together," I said. Dating. A relationship. Something. I didn't care. I just couldn't go back to being alone. Everything that had seemed so perfect, before he came along, so safe and warm, suddenly seemed so dark and cold.

Both of his hands found my cheeks, now. His thumbs slowly rubbed over my cheekbones as if he was memorizing them, making the most of what would be our very last contact. "No, Beckett. We couldn't. I can't give you that."

I just stared up at him, shell-shocked by what I heard in his voice. He was trapped, wrapped in chains and weighted to the ocean bed. He couldn't surface, however much he wanted to. And he didn't want me to have just the fake him, all arrogance and swagger, the *him* he showed everyone else.

I didn't know what else to do, so I nodded. Felt hot tears weighing my eyes and blinked furiously. "Your neck's going to need stitches," I told him. "Come on. I'll do it."

He gazed at me for a beat, those beautiful eyes full of pain at hurting me. But then he nodded. He understood. If this was it, forever, then I needed to get straight back to working with him, to prove to myself I could. He led the way out of the locker room and I grabbed my surgical cap and followed, silently wiping my eyes on my sleeve.

In Exam One, I sat him on the table and busied myself setting up a light just right, and getting the suture kit ready, and generally anything that meant I didn't have to think about what we'd just lost. I was about to pull the curtain closed when Corrigan put his hand on my arm. "Hey!" he called to someone in the hallway. When the man spun around, startled, I saw it was Seth. Colt's son. He'd been talking to Taylor and the expression on both their faces, the way their cheeks colored, eased my pain a little. They were just so sweet together. *At least someone's happy.*

Corrigan jerked his head. Both of them obediently trotted over to us. *How does he do that? Everyone just obeys him.* When they were inside the exam room, Corrigan motioned for me to close the curtain. That made it cramped, but private.

"About time you told us what happened," said Corrigan, pinning Seth with a look.

"It was just an accident!" Seth was an even worse liar than me. "We were hiking. Some farmer had put razor wire across a trail and we didn't see it until it was too late."

"You regularly go hiking in waist-deep snow?" Corrigan shook his head. "How'd the other guy crack his head?"

"He was trying to help. Slipped and hit his head on a log."

This time *I* shook my head. "Not a skull fracture like that. He must have fallen from a height, onto concrete or rock."

"Why are you lying to us?" asked Taylor. There was real hurt in her voice and I saw Seth instantly weaken. *He really likes her.* "We can help them better if you tell us what really happened."

Seth huffed and scowled, looking everywhere except her eyes. But Taylor crossed her arms and pouted and every time he looked at her, I saw his resistance crumble a little more. I silently sutured Corrigan's wound, waiting....

"Okay," Seth said at last. "Okay, look—"

The curtain was ripped aside. I looked up from my suturing... right into Colt's coldly gleaming eyes. I froze. Prey-still, a mouse who sees the shadow of a hawk. I didn't dare breathe.

I was only half-done with Corrigan's neck wound. He turned his head very slowly, the thread still connecting us. "Private discussion," he told Colt.

His glare would have made any other man back away, but Colt took a step into the room, pulling the curtain closed behind him. *Shit.* Now we were hidden from the hallway. No one would see what he did.

"You don't talk to my people without me," Colt told us. *My people.* Like a military unit... or a cult. "We'll be leaving, now. All of us."

It took a few seconds for his words to register. Taylor found her voice first. "You don't mean the injured guys?" she asked in disbelief.

Then, off his silence. "You're insane! They can't leave, they need care!"

I saw Colt go tense, the tendons in his neck standing out like ropes. He was close enough that I could smell him, stale tobacco and whiskey and a tang that could have been boot polish or gun oil. I wasn't sure if it was the word *insane* or just Taylor daring to resist him, but he was getting wound up.

Seth saw it too, and took a half step forward. "She's right, dad," he said.

His gentle tone was right, but it was the worst thing he could have said. I saw Colt's eyes flick to Taylor and he drew in a long, shuddering breath. He could see Seth liked her and it enraged him. I saw his hand slide down to the knife on his belt and my insides went cold. This guy was seriously unhinged and we were all alone with him.

Corrigan slid off the table and blocked Colt's path. Everyone drew in their breath. He was bigger than Colt but Colt was savage in a way I can't explain, a snapping, vicious jackal who could take down a lion.

And then I saw something that really terrified me. For just a second, as the adrenaline slammed through his system, there was a wild look in Corrigan's eyes. A *come on, then!* look.

In that second, he didn't fear death. He welcomed it.

"Your man with the leg wounds, you can take," I blurted. My heart was pounding so hard it hurt. I couldn't believe I was daring to speak. "But the other guy, with the head injury, he still hasn't regained consciousness. He needs constant monitoring." And then I added, "He might not wake up."

Because I'd realized what this all boiled down to. Colt didn't want us talking to his men. He was willing to risk their lives to prevent it.

Colt stared at Corrigan for long seconds, neither of them backing down. It was so tense I wanted to scream. I saw Colt's fingers stroke the handle of his knife once, twice—

And then he nodded, jerked his head for Seth to follow, and stormed out of the room. Seth gave Taylor one last, mournful look...and then hurried after his father. And they were gone.

All three of us let out a long sigh of relief. I started suturing again: I had to focus on something to calm me down. But I could feel Corrigan staring at me and at last I had to look up into his eyes.

There was scalding anger, first, but it didn't sting: I could feel it wrapping around me, a protective fire. He didn't want me putting myself at risk.

Then his gaze softened. He glanced around at Taylor, at me, at himself. And he sighed and nodded. *Thanks.* And beneath the gratitude, that *pull,* that deep longing.

We tore our eyes away and I carried on suturing. But we couldn't fight this. Not forever.

I finally finished, cut the thread and the three of us walked back out into the ER. Colt was preparing to leave. Two of his men were carrying the guy with the leg wounds, who was panting and growling with pain. Earl and Lloyd pulled up in their police SUV just as they were loading him into a pickup.

Corrigan waved them over and we huddled in a quiet corner, out of earshot of the patients. "It's all done now," he told Earl. "But we had another run-in with that guy."

Earl cursed and looked over his shoulder at Colt. "Sorry I wasn't here."

I patted Earl's arm. "You can't be here all the time. You've got a whole town to protect."

"I'm gonna stop by more," he said. "I insist."

Out of the corner of my eye, I caught Lloyd rolling his eyes, but he was smirking, too. The affection between the pupil and his mentor was easy to see. The two had been partnered together for over a year now and I got the impression that Earl was almost like a father to the young guy. But it felt like there was something I was missing. Why was Earl so keen to spend even more time here, when he already came around so often? He kept casting furtive glances towards the back of the ER, but when I followed his gaze, there was nothing obvious he was looking at. Just the critical care beds, the fire exit, Maggie balanced halfway up a ladder fixing a light—

"I think something's going on," said Corrigan. "That Colt guy is unstable. Dangerous. He's got guys following him around, but they're not just a bunch of thugs: I saw a tattoo on the leg guy, two crossed rifles with a clenched fist. Colt had the same one, mixed in with all that other ink. They're an organized gang...or something else. And Colt's son, Seth, he's in it, too."

"But he doesn't want to be," said Taylor.

"And they're bringing in extra people," said Corrigan. "People who *aren't* part of the gang. Like that old guy yesterday, he was an ex-con from Florida."

"Like Colt's putting together a crew," said Lloyd quietly. "For a job."

We all went silent for a moment as that sank in. "*Here?*" I said at last. "What is there to steal in Mount Mercy?" Our bank is tiny, a one-room place with a couple of staff.

"Today, one comes in with razor wire wrapped round him and one's fallen from a height. Like they were trying to get over a wall, someplace really secure." Corrigan looked at Earl. "You know anywhere around here that looks like that?"

Earl thought about it. "The mining company, maybe? They have pretty high walls. I'll do a drive by and check." He frowned. "That tattoo: two crossed rifles? Clenched fist?"

Corrigan nodded.

Earl narrowed his eyes. "I swear, I've heard of that somewhere. Let me check it out. C'mon, Lloyd." And he pulled his peaked cap onto his head and headed off towards his cruiser, Lloyd hurrying behind him. Cold wind blew in as the automatic doors slid open and I wrapped my arms around myself. The doors shut, but the chill remained.

Colt and his men had invaded our sleepy little town. They were planning something awful. And with the town cut off by the snow, no one from outside could come to protect us.

We were on our own.

22

COLT

I T WAS COLD, as I slammed Seth up against the dumpster. Cold enough that the breath that exploded out of his lungs was a white cloud and my spittle damn near froze on my lips.

But I've never minded the cold. Cold strengthens a man, just like sieving out the ice crystals to strengthen liquor. It was a hell of a lot colder in that prison yard in Denver, with nothing to do to keep warm but trudge back and forth...and plan.

"What did you tell that blonde bitch?" I snarled. He was struggling, but I held him easily, didn't matter that he was thirty years younger. He'd gotten soft, without me around. I pressed my thumb hard into his windpipe.

"*Nothing!*" he wheezed. "*Swear!*"

I pressed harder, cutting off his air completely. I knew I should kill him, family or not. I'd seen the way he looked at her, even though he knew she was one of *them*, part of that government machine.

I could feel the life going out of him, second by second. His skin was turning blue, his eyes pleading. But he didn't try to kick me or grab for me. He was still more scared of me than he was of death and that was something.

I waited until I saw the little veins in the whites of his eyes begin to throb and burst and then I dropped him. He crumpled into the snow and just lay there, heaving in air. The rest of my men hung back near the mouth of the alley, making sure no one came in. I'd sent Max back to camp in a pickup on account of his leg, but the rest of us would walk the five miles. Better for fitness, better for discipline. No one was dumb enough to argue.

"We have to call it off," croaked Seth. "The roads are blocked. How do we get out of town, afterwards?"

"The snow's a blessing," I told him. "No cops can get through. No one will even know what happened here for days, maybe weeks. I called Isaac, over in Denver. He's going to fly us out in a chopper."

"What about Max? He can't run, with that leg. Can't even walk. We're a man down."

"Isaac can use a gun. He can take Max's place. But you gotta protect him, when it all goes down. He's our only way out of here."

"What about Harry? What if he wakes up and talks?"

"He won't. He's loyal." I knew that was bullshit. Everybody talks, sooner or later. That's why I hadn't wanted to leave him in the hospital. But it had been smarter to leave, let that big Irish bastard and the red-headed bitch he was sweet on think they'd won. "Get back to camp," I told Seth. "Make sure Reynolds has done his job, then wait for me. I got shit to take care of."

I stalked back to the hospital. In a big city hospital, there would have been all sorts of security but a little place like this had one guard, tops, and he'd been sent home with all the other staff when the blizzard hit. I just strolled right in and headed straight for the back of the ER, where they were keeping all the critical cases. I spotted Harry straightaway. His head was all wrapped up in bandages, but he was breathing. I headed towards him, but hung back at the last minute. A few beds further down was a little blonde-haired kid and that red-haired surgeon, Beckett, was sitting on the edge of her bed. She'd recognize me if I got too close.

"I don't get it," said Beckett. "Show me again?"

They were playing some kids' game where they touched their spread fingers together in sequence. "It's the number of letters in the name of your favorite color, then the number of letters in the name of your favorite band, then the number of letters in the first name of your one true love," said the kid authoritatively.

Beckett blushed. They started up the game again and, while they were distracted, I quickly walked over to Harry's bed and pulled a curtain across to hide me. I shook him, but he didn't stir.

Beckett's voice from outside, "One, two, three, four, *five.*"

I found the switches for the monitors and flipped them off.

Outside, Beckett started to count to fourteen. I stood there staring at Harry. *Dammit!* He was a good soldier. A believer. But I couldn't take the chance, not with fifty million on the table.

I pulled the pillow from under Harry's head and pressed it over his face. He didn't struggle.

"One, two, three, four, five, six, *seven,*" said Beckett. "Pinky finger. What does that make me?"

"Strong of heart," said the kid.

Harry's chest stopped moving.

And I put the pillow back under his head and slipped quietly away.

23

AMY

AFTER THE SUDDEN RUSH of the double trauma, the ER went quiet as the grave. I couldn't get used to the sudden swings: I'm used to having surgeries neatly scheduled all day. *How does Corrigan do this?*

I couldn't sit idle so I did the lumbar puncture one of the critical patients had been waiting on. It took a few hours and the whole way through, Krista was looking at me across the table with a gleam in her eyes. I knew what she was dying to ask. When the operation was over, she told Lina and Adele that we'd clean up the OR and, before the door had even closed behind them, she pounced. *"What happened in the locker room?"*

I pulled my mask off. "It all just suddenly got... out of control. If you hadn't come in... I think he was going to kiss me."

"You *think?* I saw the way you were looking at each other. If I hadn't come in, you would have been naked up against the lockers! But *since* then? Have you talked to him?"

I stripped off my gloves and threw them in the trash. I loved Krista but I didn't want to get into this, especially now, at the end of a long day. I was worn out and I hadn't eaten since that morning. "We talked. But it's not going to happen."

Krista looked disappointed, but then nodded sagely. "He just wants to fuck, you want more."

"No! We both want more. But he....." I wasn't sure how much I should say. I felt as if he'd taken me into his confidence, somehow, being so open with me. "...can't."

"Men like that never can. Don't worry, we'll find you someone else."

But I don't want someone else. "He's not 'like that,'" I blurted.

She frowned at me, confused.

"He's not shallow! There's more to him!"

"It is *Corrigan* we're talking about, here? Big hands, big ego, big—"

"Yes! But—" Something was happening that didn't happen very often: I was getting mad. Maybe because I knew what it felt like to be underestimated, even if it was in a very different way? My whole life, everyone—me included—had been telling me I was too introverted for this job, too shy for that man. "You don't know him like I do!" I snapped.

Krista blinked at me. Then her eyes went big. "*Shit!*"

"What?" I asked, thrown.

"You like him!"

The shock made my anger fall away. I tried to brazen it out, but I'd gone bright red. "Everyone likes him!" I said, looking at the floor.

"Everyone thinks he's hot, everyone wants to fuck him, you *like him, like* him." She actually looked scared. "Amy, he's not that kind of guy."

That needled me. I felt the anger starting to build back up again. "Why does everyone think they know what kind of guy he is, when no one even properly talks to him? He's hurting. He just needs—"

Krista cut me off with a horrified squeal, clapping a hand over her mouth.

"What?"

"You said the fatal words. *He just needs.* You want to fix him!"

I opened and closed my mouth a few times, unable to find words. "I know how it sounds...."

"It sounds like you're trying to fix a bad boy."

"He's not a bad boy, he's just—"

"*Misunderstood?* Oh, Amy, bless you, you're so naive!"

"Stop patronizing me! He's just acting! It's an act!"

"Oh, and there's a sweet guy underneath?"

"Yes! He cares about kids and babies and—"

"You want a *baby* with him now?!"

I lost it. "You know what? I'm sick of being the shy friend you're always trying to help! I can run my own life!"

And I stormed out of the OR, leaving her open-mouthed.

I made it down to the end of the hallway before I faltered and stopped. *What am I doing?!* I was never like this, all emotional and out of control. Not until Corrigan came along.

I turned around and slowly walked back. When I walked back into the OR, Krista was silently cleaning up. I picked up a broom and helped. Neither of us said a word for a few minutes.

"I'm sorry," I said at last.

"No, *I'm* sorry," Krista said immediately. She lifted her head to look at me and her eyes were moist. "I can be too pushy. I just didn't want to see you get your heart broken."

"I'm just strung out from being down in the ER. And I'm all messed up about Corrigan. I *do* like him."

She ran to me and pulled me into a deep, warm hug, and it was the best feeling in the world. "You're not my shy friend," she said into my shoulder. "You're just my friend."

I nodded, my own eyes getting hot. "Krista?"

"Mm-hmm?"

"You're my best friend. Don't go anywhere. 'Kay?"

"'Kay."

When we eventually broke the hug, we finished cleaning up. And when we'd done that, Krista went off to find somewhere to get some sleep, while it was still quiet. I stood at the window looking out at the town. I barely recognized Mount Mercy with the buildings half-buried in snow.

The fight had woken me up to something. I'd assumed it was over, between Corrigan and me, because he'd said so. I'm a dormouse. I always do what I'm told.

Except... it wasn't *right*. I knew he was in pain and I was the only one who could see it: even Krista couldn't. Maybe I was the only one who'd *ever* seen it. Soon, he'd break the rules and he'd be bounced on to some other hospital, or he'd lose his license completely, and this chance would be gone forever. And this thing we had together... it was *real*. Just thinking about him made something inside me rise and float like a balloon. I *needed* him. And maybe... he needed me.

The idea of me doing what no other woman had been able to seemed laughable. Maybe Krista was right, maybe I was naive, and maybe I *was* trying to fix him. But.... I felt something inside me harden into stone.

I wasn't quitting.

This dormouse was going to fight for her man.

When I ventured into the ER, it was still eerily quiet. Taylor was treating an old lady with a broken wrist, but no one else was around. They were probably grabbing a nap while they could: until the roads reopened and more staff could get in, we'd all have to work continuously and sleep when we could. Maybe I should do the same. The sun hadn't quite set, but I was exhausted. If I got my head down, I could probably—

Someone grabbed my arm and pulled me through the curtain into Exam Two.

I yelped and slammed into a big, warm body. I jumped back and looked up, but I'd already recognized that vanilla and sandalwood scent.

"*Shh,*" said Corrigan before I could speak.

I stood there open-mouthed. I was furious at the way he'd grabbed me but the glowing aftershock of the contact was still throbbing through me: the way his pecs had pressed into the upper slopes of my breasts, the way one of his thighs had pressed right between mine...."*What?*" I hissed.

He moved me further away from the curtain and spoke quietly. At first, I thought it was just because people were trying to sleep. His Irish accent was even more magical when he spoke softly, like silver silk caressing my ears. "That head injury case you worked on?" he began.

I nodded that I remembered.

"He didn't make it."

My eyes snapped wide, my mind full of all the things I might have done wrong.

He raised a placating hand. "Nothing you did. As far as I can tell, he just stopped breathing." He pressed his lips together for a moment. "His monitors were switched off."

I blinked. I'd never heard of that happening. "It *was* crazy," I whispered cautiously. "Everyone was running around... people are strung out. Maybe a nurse made a mistake?"

He crossed his arms. "You know the nurses here better than me. You think one of them could have messed up like that?"

I thought about it. "No." My stomach knotted. Now I knew why he was speaking so quietly, why he'd pulled me in here, out of sight. "You think someone killed him?"

"I think Colt killed him. Or sent someone to kill him. He really didn't want us talking to that guy."

I imagined Colt creeping through the ER, right next to us, but unseen, and wanted to throw up with fear. *I was right there. Jesus,* Rebecca *was right there!* "What do we do?"

"I don't know. We need an autopsy and an investigation and an APB for Colt. That's all state police stuff and they can't get here."

We heard the electronic hum of the main doors sliding open. "That's probably Earl and Lloyd," whispered Corrigan. "I called them. Can you grab them?"

I slipped out of Exam Two and looked across the room towards the doors. It *was* Earl. The setting sun was behind him and I'd have recognized that big, cuddly silhouette anywhere. And behind him was the lean outline of Lloyd, awkwardly shifting from foot to foot. I started forward to say hi.

Just at that moment, Maggie emerged from the basement, lugging a huge bag of tools and muttering something about *cheap pipes that weren't worth a damn.* She nodded towards the doorway. "Earl."

Earl came to attention and whipped off his peaked cap. "Ma'am," he said, breathless. His eyes tracked her as she walked away. His gaze only broke off when it crossed my own disbelieving stare.

"*Maggie?*" I mouthed silently at him.

He flushed crimson and looked at his feet, wedging his cap back on his head.

That's why he was always dragging Lloyd to the hospital? I hurried over and pulled him forward. "Earl, you have to tell her how you feel!"

He shrugged and mumbled. He was pushing sixty, but suddenly he was a teenager, more nervous and awkward than Lloyd. "Ah, I don't—She might not—"

"She *would!*" Both of them had been single for at least a decade. Both of them were lonely. "Earl, you have to say something!"

He shook his head. Behind him, Lloyd caught my eye and shrugged helplessly: *welcome to my world.* He must have figured it out months ago and he'd had no luck convincing his mentor, either.

I brought them to Exam Two. "Beckett agrees with me," Corrigan told Earl. "It wasn't an accident. That guy was murdered, most likely by Colt."

Earl looked queasy. The worst thing he normally had to deal with was a couple of drunks or a fender bender. "I got worse news. I found something on Colt. He pulled a printout of a newspaper clipping from his uniform pocket and unfolded it. "Told you I recognized the name."

It was a front page story from a Denver newspaper. The man in the picture was much younger and looked less bitter, but he was definitely the same man. "Colt Blackwood," I murmured. "Sentenced for... oh my God."

Colt had led an ultra-right militia called the Colorado Guardians of Freedom, or CGF. It had grown over the years from a small band of extremists into a statewide movement suspected of multiple counts of arson, murder and extortion. Colt himself had become quite rich and owned a sprawling ranch...until the FBI raided it, confiscated everything, and sent him to federal prison. "Why did I never hear about any of this?" I asked.

"Look at the date," said Earl.

I focused on the tiny numbers at the top of the page. Colt had been sentenced twenty years ago.

"That's why I couldn't place him, at first," said Earl. "He just got released a few months ago."

Corrigan spoke up. "The men he has with him, they're—"

"Members of his militia, yeah," said Earl. "That tattoo, with the crossed rifles and the fist? That's their symbol."

"So he's reforming his militia. But what's he doing *here*?" I asked.

Earl let out a long sigh. "Been trying to figure that out myself. Drove by the mining company. Some of the razor wire was missing from the top of a wall. The place was all shut down on account of the snow, but I called the boss and had him come in and yep, they've had a break in. They're making a list of what's missing now." He shook his head. "But what would they want with mining equipment?"

Corrigan thought for a moment. When he spoke again, he had a sick look on his face. "Earl, do they keep explosives there?"

Earl drew in his breath...and nodded.

Oh Jesus. So an ultra-right militia was in our town and they were stealing explosives? "We have to get some help," I croaked.

Earl nodded. "I'll call the FBI. I don't care if the roads are blocked, this is too big. They can send a damn helicopter if they have to." He pulled out his phone, then frowned at the screen. "*Dammit!* Check yours."

Corrigan pulled his out. I ran to the locker room and got mine. None of us had a signal. "The wind must have taken out the cell tower," said Earl. "It's right at the top of the hill, pretty exposed."

We were completely cut off. Not only couldn't we call for help, we couldn't send a warning. *Oh God...* Colt could do anything here, and no one would even know.

We heard the main doors to the ER slide open and a blast of frozen air lifted the curtains. All three of us raced out just in time to see a man stagger in. He was barely through the doors when he fell forward—he would have hit the floor if Corrigan hadn't grabbed him under the arms.

The guy was in his twenties with short, sandy hair and a light build: he could have been any college kid from the city. But he was in a bad way. His jeans were soaked through and clinging to him, his jacket—a light thing, no more substantial than a dishtowel—was plastered with snow and frost caked his hair and eyelashes. And he was trying to say something, but he was too weak and frozen to get the words out. "*So,*" he said, looking right at me. "*So.*"

"He's ice cold," said Corrigan. "Heated blankets, warm saline, *now!*"

The ER came alive as we lifted the man up onto a bed. I winced as I saw his fingers. They looked as if they were about to burst, skin stretched tight over swollen redness. I'd never seen frostbite before. Corrigan saw me looking and gave me a little shake of his head when the patient wasn't looking: he was probably going to lose at least some of his fingers.

"*So,*" said the man again. His eyes were pleading, desperate to tell us something but his lips, his jaw, his vocal cords were all too cold to work properly. While the others swaddled him in blankets and got an IV going, I tried to understand. He was getting more frantic, not less, even though we were helping him, so it wasn't himself he was worried about. I looked down at his clothes. His jeans were soaked right up to the waist, like he'd waded here through deep drifts. And he was so cold, he must have been walking for hours. Someone was *out there,* in the snow, way out of town.

"*Sophie,*" he managed at last.

24

DOMINIC

"No," said Bartell. *"Absolutely not!"*

I pointed through the ER's glass doors to the world outside. "It's, what, ten degrees out there? The sun's going to be down in an hour and then it's going to get even colder. She's already been out there for hours, she can't have long left."

"You're a doctor," Bartell told me. "Not a paramedic!"

"We don't have any fucking paramedics!" I snapped. "We're *it!*"

As Sophie's boyfriend had warmed up, he'd managed to tell us how their car had slewed off the road, up in the hills outside town. How she was trapped in the wreckage and, with the cell service down, he'd been forced to hike for hours through the snow to get help.

Bartell ran a hand through his hair, gave an exhausted sigh, and nodded. "The roads will be blocked," he warned.

"Yeah," I muttered, pulling on my thick orange parka. "I'll have to drive as far as I can and then walk the rest of the way." I started throwing medical gear into a paramedic bag.

A field surgery kit landed in the bag. I spun around and found Beckett standing there, jaw set in determination.

"No," I told her. "No way."

"You think you're going to find her on your own?" she asked. "I know the roads around here. Besides, she might need surgery."

I glared and took a step towards her. I know how to use my size to intimidate.

But she just stood her ground, determined. She didn't *want* to go out there: I could see the fear in her eyes. Being out in the wilds, in this weather... that was as far from her safe, snug OR as it was possible to get. But she was going to go anyway because—

Because she didn't want me to go alone.

"Let's get going," I grunted.

And we ran.

25

AMY

THE PARKING GARAGE was almost empty. I ran towards my car while trying to do up the zipper on the huge paramedic's parka I'd found in a closet. Skidding to a stop, I blipped the lock and—

"You can't be serious," said Corrigan behind me. "You live in the mountains of Colorado and *that's* your car?"

I blinked, hotly embarrassed and angry at the same time. "What? What's wrong with it?" My car is a little electric thing, just big enough for two (as long as your shoulders aren't too wide). It's small, quiet, and efficient: the planet doesn't even know it's there.

"It's very you," said Corrigan. Then he grabbed my arm and pulled me over to *his* car, a big red pickup with a light bar on top and huge chunky tires. You didn't *get* in, you *climbed* in. The engine came to life with an angry, chest-thumping roar and we tore out of the parking garage already pushing forty.

Some of the roads near the hospital had now been plowed but as we reached the edge of town, the pavement disappeared beneath a hard, packed-down crust of snow as slippery as ice.

As we turned into a bend, the hiss of the tires on the snow suddenly disappeared and the world went utterly silent. Corrigan cursed and turned the wheel... but nothing happened. Instead of turning, we slid towards the edge of the road, the headlights catching a wall as it loomed up to meet us. I grabbed a grab handle and closed my eyes—

The tire noise returned as they finally found grip. We swung around, fishtailed, and then straightened out. Corrigan let out a sigh of relief and slowed the pace...but only a little. We couldn't go slowly or we'd never reach Sophie in time.

We skidded another three times on our way to the hills. I spent the journey grimly clinging to my grab handle, wondering what the hell I was doing. Even paramedics wouldn't be out in snow like this: this was a job for specially-trained rescue teams, not ER doctors. Certainly not a surgeon.

But when Corrigan had been planning to go on his own, all I could think about was that moment when he'd faced off against Colt. Part of him had wanted a fight. Had longed for it, even. And I put that together with all the dangerous places he kept going and....

There was no way I was letting him go into danger on his own. However much this scared me, losing him scared me more.

The snow deepened and thickened as we climbed up into the hills, coming up over the top of the wheels. Eventually, on a narrow track that cut into the forest, the wheels began to spin. Corrigan pulled over. We'd have to go the rest of the way on foot.

26

DOMINIC

B ACK AT THE HOSPITAL, we'd worked out a plan. We'd reach Sophie and get her out while Krista got hold of a local man with a snowplow and got him to clear the road along the bottom of the hills, all the way back to the hospital. We'd have to carry Sophie down to the road and meet them, and they'd then take her back to the ER. It was a mile from where we were now to the crash, then maybe another mile to the road.

That hadn't sounded so bad, back in the warm. But as soon as I opened my door and the cold flooded in, everything was different. I'd never felt cold like it: the temperature was so low, it was actually painful just moving your exposed hand or face through it. And when I stepped down, the snow was up above my knees. It was worse for Beckett: it was high up her thighs. We were both wearing thick parkas but they did nothing to protect our lower halves. Moving through the snow was like wading through an ice bath. Both of us shuddered. *Jesus!*

I grabbed the bag and we started to move, working our way uphill through the trees. The sun was sinking rapidly, now, throwing out one last blast of orange fire that was carved by the tree trunks into golden wedges atop the snow. Despite the fierce cold, it was beautiful.

I saw Beckett gazing around her in wonder. I got the feeling she'd never been out in the wilds in the snow, despite living here. In fact, I got the feeling she'd never been out in the wilds *at all*. She'd missed out on all this, huddled in her OR.

But at least she'd been safe there. That protective urge came back, stronger than ever. If we got into trouble there was no cell service and no one to come for us. The lack of cars on the road and the way the snow deadened all sound made it seem even lonelier. All we could hear was the crunch of our shoes: it was like we were the only two people in the world.

I was fighting with myself. I didn't want her here. But there was no one I'd rather be alone with.

It got tougher and tougher as we climbed higher. Our scrub pants were soaked through and the cold crept into our muscles, then our bones. Every breath of air was painful: it was so far below freezing, the air felt like a million sharp-edged ice crystals, burning our lungs. A mile in this would seem like ten. "Talk to me," I said. I'd been on plenty of long hikes in Africa and one thing I'd learned was that talking makes them go faster.

Beckett glanced across at me, as horrified as if I'd asked her to strip naked.

"Anything," I pressed. "Tell me about growing up."

And slowly, grudgingly, as we panted and shivered and forced our way through the drifts, she told me. She told me about how her dad had won awards for his painstaking work, spending weeks teasing out the secrets of some minute insect's anatomy. How he was even more shy and awkward than she was. She never used the word *Asperger's, but* all the signs were there. When I heard about her mom dying, it suddenly all made sense. A shy kid, raised by a dad who was probably a high-functioning autistic. No wonder she'd gotten used to hiding, no wonder she needed order and quiet.

And now she was having to deal with the ER, in a crisis, with some far-right maniac on the loose. She was braver than even I'd given her credit for. A big swell of hot emotion rose up inside me, so fast and strong it took me by surprise. She needed protecting, dammit! From the world, but from herself, too. She needed to be gently tempted out into the daylight, to be shown the world she was missing. She needed—

Me?

My jaw set. Memories of Chrissy grabbed hold of me and tugged me down, down into the blackness. I couldn't give her that. I couldn't give anyone that.

We reached the top of the rise. The trees thinned out and the ground mercifully leveled off. And there it was in front of us, a car crumpled from impacts with trees but still recognizable, a dark shape visible in the driver's seat.

Beckett was a second faster than me to react. She ran forward, staggering in the deep snow. The last rays of sun sparkled on the surface, blinding bright. Hiding the—

I gave an animal cry of fear and lurched forward. Grabbed for her and missed. Snagged the hood of her parka and *hauled,* pulling her right off her feet. I tumbled backwards and we both went down on our asses with her on top of me. At first, she couldn't see what I'd saved her from. Then the sun's glare faded a little and she went pale.

Less than six feet in front of her, the ground fell away. We'd emerged from the forest on a cliff that plunged a hundred feet straight down. And the car was balanced right on the edge.

27

AMY

W E SHUFFLED slowly towards the cliff edge, Corrigan's hand grasping mine. As we got closer, we dropped to our hands and knees. The snow had drifted up into a bank that hung out over the edge in places and if we didn't feel our way, we might fall through into nothingness.

The car was resting with its front wheels over the edge. As we drew level with the driver's door, my shadow fell across the woman inside and she moaned and turned towards me—

And the car slid.

We hadn't realized, but the ground beneath the snow sloped down a little towards the edge. Between the weight of the engine dragging it forward and the slick, icy ground, any tiny motion would send the car sliding right off the cliff.

"Jesus!" Corrigan threw open the door, lunged inside, grabbed Sophie's shoulder, and tried to pull her out. But she jerked to a sudden stop and screamed in pain. Her leg was caught.

Corrigan looked at me helplessly. The car slid soundlessly past us, inch after inch....

And stopped. The front doors were now level with the edge. I let out a breath I didn't realize I'd been holding.

"We've got to secure the car," said Corrigan, his face pale. "I'll try to find something. Stay with her."

I nodded, as shaken as him. "Try not to move," I told Sophie, but she didn't respond: she was only semi-conscious. She had long, chestnut hair and it had fallen forward over her face. Very carefully, I reached in and brushed it back so that I could see her. She couldn't have been more than 18 or 19 and she was pretty, with delicate features that matched her slender, elegant figure. But the cold had turned her skin, bone white and her breathing was shaky: maybe hypothermia, maybe something worse.

I tentatively reached in again and held her wrist, feeling for her pulse. She was shockingly cold: she couldn't last much longer.

"Beckett!" I turned and saw Corrigan watching me, horrified. "Get your hand out of there!"

"I'm just checking her pulse. I can pull it back." But I knew what he was afraid of because I was thinking the same thing. If she grabbed me in panic and held on as the car went over... or if the door closed on my arm.... I tried not to look at the town spread out below, the houses like toys.

Corrigan was cursing himself. "Why didn't I bring a fucking rope?"

I shook my head. I hadn't thought of it either. We were doctors, not rescue workers. Then I finally found her pulse: weak and getting weaker. "I think she's bleeding from somewhere," I told Corrigan. "We have to stop it or we'll lose her."

He was looking around frantically for something to use. "As soon as we make sure the car's safe!"

Sophie gave a low groan. I could feel the life draining out of her. Corrigan was right, it was way too dangerous. But....

I'd never understood why ER doctors took the chances they did. By the time patients reached me, those choices had already been made, for better or worse. I never knew how easy I had it. Because now, kneeling right next to this woman, watching her die....

What would he *do?*

I grabbed the surgical kit, ran around to the other side of the car, and quietly opened the door. By the time Corrigan looked round, I was sliding into the passenger seat, lowering my ass into it as if it was upholstered with eggshells. "Beckett, *no!*" he yelled.

I touched down, holding my breath... the car didn't move.

I tried to do everything in slow motion, to make every movement smooth and steady, even though I was a bag of nerves. I pressed my back as hard into the seat as I could, trying to get my weight as far back as possible. Shining a flashlight down into the foot well, I saw I'd been right: Sophie was bleeding steadily from her calf. I could see where her ankle was pinned by metal that had bent inward.

Corrigan arrived, frantic and out of breath. "Get out of there!" The Irish in his voice was stronger, when he was stressed.

He put out his hand to grab me, but I shook my head: even that, I had to do gingerly. "I can do this," I told him. "If I don't, she's dead."

We stared at each other. I saw his hand twitch. He wanted so badly to pull me out... but at last he nodded.

Getting an IV needle into her vein took five tries. My hands were numb and stiff with cold, the tips deathly white, and I could see each panicked breath I took as a dense little cloud. I finally got it in and hung a bag of blood from a coat hook: that was a start, but it wouldn't do any good unless I could stop the bleeding.

Very, very carefully, I rolled forward and down until I was lying across Sophie's lap, my head, and shoulders in the footwell. I tried not to think about the fact that there was nothing underneath me but a hundred foot drop. Holding the flashlight between my teeth, I tried to imagine I was back in the nice, safe OR, with Bach on the speakers and Krista cracking jokes and Lina keeping an eye on the anesthetic and Adele passing me sponges and—

It all seemed really, really far away.

But I could see the bleeder, I could *see* it, it was *right there,* and if I could just rotate the leg *a little*—

As I clamped the bleeder, Sophie cried out and arched in pain under me. My stomach dropped through the floor. "Sophie! Please don't move!"

She groaned and thrashed.

And the car started to slide.

I tried to back out, but there was no quick way to do it: I had to twist myself back up into my seat. As my eyes came above the dashboard, I saw the nose of the car tilt down, more of the town lurching into view. I lunged towards the door, but it was too late to climb out: the door was already over the edge.

28

DOMINIC

WHEN RACHEL was about a year old, Chrissy bought this fancy backpack. It was a complicated web of straps that looped around me and around the baby and basically let her ride on my back. I thought it was stupid, but Rachel loved it: as soon as I had her in it, she was chortling and clapping, happy at suddenly being six feet off the ground.

And then... there was this noise. A hissing, nylon slithering. I felt the straps go loose across my chest. Either the thing was defective or I hadn't done it up right, but she was falling. And I did what you'd do, on instinct, which is to turn around, but of course that didn't help because she went with me. And I could hear her laughter turn into a wail and feel the straps coming loose but no matter which one I grabbed, it didn't seem to help, and I knew she was falling but I couldn't stop it—

Rachel wound up dangling from one leg and escaped with nothing more than a bump and some tears. But that feeling of something happening and being completely unable to stop it... that's exactly what it felt like when I saw the car sliding off the cliff. All I wanted to do was run to it and grab the bumper, but I had just enough sense left in my head to know that would do no good. My eyes searched the same ground I'd been searching for the last five minutes and suddenly, out of desperation or pure dumb luck, I saw what I needed: a rock the size of a watermelon. I grabbed it and sprinted.

The lack of noise as the car slid was eerie, just a creak and crunch of snow beneath the body. Moving slowly but picking up speed.

I've never run so fast in my life. If I slipped, even once, I'd be too late.

The car tilted down, scraped... and I dived to the ground and shoved the rock in front of the rear wheel like a footballer player scoring a touchdown. The car jerked, rocked..., and stopped.

The driver's door was hanging open over space. Beckett was clinging to the seat, terrified, looking down at the drop: there was no way she could climb out on her own. I leaned right out, straining, and managed to grab her hand. I wasn't waiting around for any of that *count to three* bullshit, I just pulled her out of there and turned, flinging her round in an arc to land on the soft snow behind me.

I nearly lost her. I stalked over to her. "*You fucking stupid—What were you thinking?*" I roared.

She just stared up at me, still sprawled on her back in the snow.

I nearly lost her. "*You—*" My throat closed up. I couldn't speak.

She stared up at me, white-faced and mute.

I nearly lost her. It pounded through me with every heartbeat. I grabbed her by the wrist and hauled her to her feet. I was shaking with fear and anger and—

I felt it rise inside me, soaring and swelling, taking my breath.

I didn't just *like* her, or care for her, or any of those weak little words. They didn't cover it, not anymore.

I felt myself *lift*...and then those chains from my past pulled tight and wrenched me back down. I was the worst bastard in the world, for feeling that way. *What about Chrissy? And Rachel?*

I froze, torn between past and future. All I could do was stare down into her eyes. God, she was so painfully, heartbreakingly beautiful. Neither of us had noticed, with all the panic, but it had started to snow again and tiny flakes were dusting her cheeks and gleaming in her copper hair. She was looking up at me with big, frightened eyes.

All I wanted to do was kiss her. But I didn't deserve her. I knew what I deserved.

"I clamped the bleeder," said Beckett in a small voice.

"You clamped the bleeder," I repeated. I closed my eyes for a second and felt the world sway around me. I felt sick when I thought of how close I'd come to losing her. "Of course you did," I leaned down and touched my forehead to hers. "Damn you, Beckett," I whispered.

Does she know? Can she not know?

I turned away and marched back towards the car.

29

AMY

T O TAKE A LOOK at Sophie's trapped leg, Corrigan had to stretch out with his legs on the cliff, his arms and head in the car and his midsection suspended over space. I knelt on his legs to help pin him in place and tried not to look at the town a hundred feet below. Even with the danger, I couldn't stop thinking about what just happened. He'd looked at me as if he—*Oh God!* It kept replaying in my head and every time, I went heady. But there was still something holding him back, something he couldn't break free of, and I had no idea what it was.

He squirmed backwards onto the cliff and then motioned me over to the trees, out of earshot of Sophie. The sun was down, now, and the light was draining from the forest rapidly, leaving impenetrable shadows that made it easy to trip. The snow was getting heavier, the flakes slow and silent, and the size of dimes.

"We can't free that ankle," said Corrigan. "The car's all twisted and bent. If we were on a freeway and we could get to the fender, maybe we could pry it apart. But it's hanging over space."

I wanted to scream. All we needed was a tow truck to pull the car back onto the cliff, or a jaws-of-life from a fire truck, or a cutting torch. The blizzard had set us back a hundred years. "Then what do we do? She's freezing, she can't wait."

"I know." He looked at the car, then back to me, and there was pity in his eyes. "You're going to have to take the leg."

I just blinked at him. It was so far outside what I'd even consider, I just didn't understand. Only when I saw how sad he looked did I get it. "*What?! No!* I can't—" I looked at the car and lowered my voice. "I'm not *amputating her leg!*"

"Beckett, if you don't she's going to die. We have to get her out and get her warm *now*. There's a saw in the medical kit. I'll get it. You...." He nodded awkwardly towards the car.

You tell her. I felt like the cliff had fallen out from under my feet. This was worse than going back a hundred years, this was medieval! But however much I shook my head, he was right. I'd felt how cold she was. She *would* die if we didn't get her out.

I walked back to Sophie, heart hammering, and knelt down right on the cliff edge. Even then, with the front of the car hanging out over the edge, I was still too far away to touch her. I had to raise my voice just to talk to her. "H—Hey." I began. "How are you doing?"

It was getting dark fast and I could barely see her in the shadows inside the car. "Better," she said. The blood transfusion must have lifted her pulse and woken her up a little. "Cold."

"I know. Listen, Sophie...." My throat was clamping down, trying to snatch each word away. "We need to get you out. There's a snow plow coming, we can get you to the hospital, but—" *Oh God, how do I do this? I'm the world's worst person at talking to people, especially about something like this. Why is he making me do this? He'd be so much better at it.*

But it was my responsibility. If he'd offered, I wouldn't have let him and I think he knew that.

I took a deep breath and closed my eyes. "Sophie, to get you out, I'm going to have to remove your left leg below the knee."

She gave a strangled gasp and then said *No* just as I started to speak again. *No* as I told her we could knock her out with pain meds so that it wouldn't hurt, *No* as I told her it was the only way. *No. No, no, no!*

"*I'm a dancer!*" she sobbed as I finally stopped speaking. "I have a place this fall at Fenbrook Academy! You can't take my leg. This is my *life!*"

Tears had filled my eyes and were tracing hot lines down my frozen cheeks. "I—"

"*Please!*" she begged. "*Please don't!*"

I stood up and went over to Corrigan. "She's a dancer," I told him. "A ballet dancer."

I didn't think he'd understand. I knew he was jaded, knew he'd made the call on a hundred cases like this in the ER, not to mention Africa and other warzones.

But I saw him mouth a curse as he looked towards the car. It was fully dark, now. He weighed the bone saw in his hand and I stared at its vicious teeth as they gleamed in the moonlight.

"I never asked you for anything before," I said. "But I'm asking you for this. Find another way."

Corrigan drew in a deep breath. Another. Then he tossed the saw back into the medical bag. "I'll have to try to pry the metal apart from the outside, to free her leg," he said. There was a strange finality in his voice, a kind of relief, as if all roads had been leading to this.

"How? We can't get to the front of the car."

He looked towards the cliff edge. "I'll have to climb down, underneath it."

30

DOMINIC

THERE WASN'T a good place to climb down on the driver's side of the car. I'd have to climb down on the passenger side and climb all the way across underneath. With no rope.

As I lowered myself over the edge, I was almost glad it was so dark. I had to feel for footholds but at least I couldn't see how far away the ground was. The wind was a clue, though, whipping across the ground below me and gusting vertically up the cliff face to tug at my coat. I realized my feet were numb. I couldn't really tell if I was putting them on firm rock or packed snow that would crumble when I put my weight on it. But it was too late now.

I climbed sideways, underneath the car. It acted like a roof above me, blocking the falling snow, but also blocking the moonlight. I couldn't see a damn thing. I had to take it slow, feeling my way, and that left too much time for thinking. When I'd realized my full feelings for Beckett, everything from my past had risen up to claim me. The *guilt.*

Chrissy.

Rachel.

Rachel was why I was down there. She'd wanted to be a ballet dancer, too. But there was another reason.

I looked down at the blackness beneath me. Would it be such a bad way to go? A freezing rush of air, the ground invisible as it came up to meet you—

Suicide is a mortal sin. But if I slipped or my grip gave out or the car fell on top of me....

People think you're a hero for doing dangerous things. They don't realize you might have your own, selfish reasons.

I reached the driver's side of the car and held on to the cliff one-handed while I took out my flashlight. It would have been a hell of a lot easier to hang onto the car, but if I did that I'd pull the damn thing over the edge. I got the flashlight switched on and pointed it up at—

It slipped through my numb fingers and fell, the beam twisting and slashing through the night like a lightsaber, revealing the drop below me. I watched it, heart hammering. It was a long time before it dropped out of sight.

I took out a pry bar and, by feel alone, worked it into the dented mass of metal and started trying to loosen it. There was nothing to brace against so I had to use raw muscle, straining and grunting. I started to wonder how the hell I was going to climb back across with no strength left in my arms.

That doesn't matter, a dark little voice in my head told me. *Just get Sophie out. Make sure Beckett is safe. The rest doesn't matter.*

I gritted my teeth and heaved on the pry bar, the metal creaking, and groaning.

"That's it!" yelled Beckett from the darkness. She was in the back of the car, ready to pull Sophie into the rear seat and then out through the rear door. "I can feel her leg coming loose!"

I heaved again, using both hands. The bar slipped and suddenly I was balancing on just my feet, toppling backwards into space. I had to grab *something.* My hand found one of the wheels. I jerked to a stop, but the car started to slide. *Fuck! Fuck, fuck, fuck!*

"It's moving!" screamed Beckett. "I can't stop it!"

I got the pry bar in again and tried to force the metal apart, but Sophie's leg was still trapped. In desperation, I started pounding my fist on the crumpled metal, bending it inwards and upwards. I managed to get my hand up inside the footwell and bent aside the metal that had caught on her shoe—

"She's free!" I heard grunting and then a limp body being dragged out of the car. "She's out!"

I let out a breath. The car was still sliding forward. Slowly, but it didn't have far to go before gravity would take over and carry it the rest of the way. I pulled my hand back—

Fuck. My coat was caught on something inside the footwell. I couldn't pull my arm out. And I didn't have a free hand to unfasten my coat and shrug it off.

Beckett's head appeared over the edge of the cliff. "She's out! Climb up!"

God, she was so beautiful. But I'd got what I'd wanted. What I deserved.

"I can't," I told her. "I'm caught."

The car slid slowly forward... taking me with it.

31

AMY

I FUMBLED for my flashlight and shone it so that I could see him without blinding him. He looked up at me with a strange sort of calm. "It's alright, Beckett." The car slid inexorably forward. "It's okay."

I knelt there staring down into those blue eyes. He'd always been going to go out like this, risking his life to save a patient. His path had been mapped out long before I'd ever met him. He was like some comet on a collision course with a planet, blazing across the galaxy with just enough drinking and jokes and sex to ease his pain until impact. He should have sped straight past me: I'd only been drawn into his orbit by chance. And it was ridiculous to think someone as tiny and insignificant as me could alter his trajectory.

"Get Sophie down the hill," he told me.

I stared, tears coursing down my cheeks and melting the snowflakes that had settled there.

And I decided.

"*No!*" I snapped viciously. I wasn't going to let this wonderful, big-hearted man go. I didn't care how hopeless it was, or how dangerous it was. I grabbed Sophie by the shoulders and dragged her through the snow to the back of the car. "You *press down!*" I snapped, pointing at the trunk. "You *press that thing down,* no matter what!"

She nodded and put her weight on the back of the car. It kept sliding, but it slowed a little.

I put my flashlight between my teeth and took out a scalpel. Then I climbed back into the car through the rear door.

Corrigan saw what I was doing and came to life. "*NO!*" he roared. "*No! Get out of there!*"

By now I was wriggling between the front seats. *I am not letting him die.*

"*BECKETT!*"

I shoved my head and shoulders into the footwell. The movement made the car tip forward, sliding faster. "*I can't hold it!*" yelled Sophie from behind me.

"*BECKETT, GET OUT OF THERE!*" Corrigan's voice was raw and fractured.

My hands were shaking. The light from the flashlight was jerking and twitching as I panted, lighting up dirt and torn carpet and candy wrappers, twisted metal and—

There! Poking in through the mangled steel, a hand. I grabbed it and squeezed it.

The car lurched and tipped.

I saw the loop of orange fabric that was snagged. Slashed it free with my scalpel. The hand withdrew and was gone.

I twisted and climbed. As my shoulders pushed between the rear seats, it registered that I was *climbing,* clawing my way up a forty-five degree slope: the car had tipped right up and was going over. I kicked and twisted and scrambled, focusing on the open rear door and the moonlit forest that was moving horribly fast past it—

I fell out onto the snow, one arm and one leg hanging over the cliff. I rolled to safety as the car's bumper slid almost silently past my head and the whole thing disappeared into the blackness. I looked around. Sophie was lying gasping in the snow. There were tire tracks where the car used to be. Nothing else.

A few heartbeats of total silence and then an almighty crash from below: shattering glass and tortured, screaming metal.

"*Corrigan!*" I clawed my way on my forearms to the edge, hoping, praying....

And looked down into his upturned face. For a few seconds, we just stared at each other. Then he got one hand up onto the cliff edge and I pulled and he heaved and he clambered up. As soon as he was there, he just grabbed me and rolled me into a full-body hug. He was on top of me and the whole of me was pressed against the whole of him, my face buried in the crook of his neck, his arms locked so tight around my back that it felt like he'd never let me go. I felt his words as hot rushes of air against the back of my neck. "That's not what you *do,* Beckett! That's not what you do, you *eejit!* You're meant to be safe! Why did you do that?!"

I pulled back from him enough to look into his eyes. "Why do you want to die?" I searched his face for answers. "You're *good* and a great doctor and I really like you!"

He stared at me and went silent. His eyes were imploring me not to do this, not to tempt him. I knew I was tearing him in two, but what was this blackness I was dragging him away from? What had hold of him so tightly that he was ready to let it drag him down to his death?

A noise shattered the silence. Distant and muffled by the snow, but recognizable: a car horn. The snow plow was here.

Corrigan got to his feet, his eyes never leaving mine. He reached down, grabbed my hand and hauled me up, but he didn't let go of my hand. His strong fingers squeezed mine, over and over, and I could feel the tension all the way up his arm. He was a hair's breadth from jerking me forward and kissing me. "Come on," he said at last. "We have to get her down the hill."

I nodded. But this wasn't over and we both knew it. We couldn't continue like this: the tension between us had ratcheted too high. Either he'd manage to break free of what was holding him back...or I'd lose him forever.

32

AMY

STRAPPED to the side of the medical bag was a folding backboard and we used it as a stretcher to carry Sophie. She'd passed out again, from the cold or the effort of helping save Corrigan, and her skin was frighteningly pale. Corrigan was right: we had to get her down the hill to the snow plow, *now*.

But carrying the stretcher through thigh-deep drifts was a frozen, heart-stopping hell. The snow was getting heavier and it blew into our faces, half-blinding us and numbing our skin. My scrubs were long-since soaked through and the snow felt as if it was pressing against my bare legs, turning my thighs and calves into lumps of concrete. I soon had no feeling in my feet and that made it impossible to get a sure footing. With the path twisting its way downhill, that led to some terrifying moments because, when one of us slipped, we didn't have a hand free to stop ourselves. By halfway, my shoulders were on fire, my legs were screaming and my abdomen was burning from trying to stabilize me.

Corrigan was almost a silhouette in front of me: I could just see some of his black hair, shining in the moonlight, and the edges of his broad shoulders where the falling snow whipped past them. I could see the tension in him: he knew I was watching him. Every hundred yards or so, he'd look back to check I was okay and the need, the longing in his eyes was breathtaking. A battle was going on inside him and all I could do was keep shuffling forward and wait and hope and pray.

Finally, the snow started to turn amber as the glow from the snowplow's lights trickled through the trees. I'd started to shiver and couldn't stop, and my fingers were gripping the backboard so hard, afraid of dropping it, that I wasn't sure I'd be able to let go.

We emerged from the forest and there it was: a big yellow double cab pick up with a snow plow mounted on the front and emergency lights on the roof. Krista was riding shotgun and she and the driver jumped out when they saw us. Krista ran over, gently pried my fingers from the backboard and took my end. I wanted to hug her. I've never been so glad to see her in my life.

Between the four of us, we got the backboard into the bed of the pickup truck: it would be cold, but it wouldn't take them long to get back to the hospital now that the roads were clear. Krista knelt down in the back of the pickup to keep an eye on Sophie. "I got this," she said, waving me towards the cab. "You're frozen, you take the cab."

I eased my freezing body into the pickup. The warmth hit me like I'd stepped into a sauna. And the dryness, the simple pleasure of *not* having snow hitting my cheeks and forehead, for the first time in what felt like hours....

And then a second wave of warmth hit me, this time through my thighs and ass and I groaned. *Heated. Seats.* I seriously considered stripping my soaked pants off right there and then and the hell with modesty.

And then I looked up and saw that Corrigan, instead of getting into the rear of the cab, was about to close the door.

"I've got to go back for my car," he said. "We might need it."

I stared, open-mouthed. I knew exactly what this was: he couldn't take being close to me, feeling like we felt. But that meant he was going to walk off into the darkness: two miles through the snow, alone.

He slammed the door and stepped back. The driver started to

turn the pickup around. Corrigan backed away and then turned and headed back up the hill.

The driver got the pickup pointing towards town and the hospital. *Home.* All I had to do was sit tight and I'd be safe and warm. We began to accelerate. Outside, Corrigan's orange parka had almost disappeared into the night....

"*Stop!*" I threw open my door. "Wait! Sorry! Stop!" The driver pulled up and I was out before we'd even stopped moving, stumbling in the snow, the cold even more of a shock after the few moments of warmth.

Krista shouted my name but I shook my head. "I'm going with him!"

And I raced after him into the night.

33

DOMINIC

CLIMBING UP THE HILL was even harder than going down it. I had to lean forward for balance, fighting for grip. The wind was getting up, whipping sounds away from me, and the parka's hood blocked my ears but I thought I heard someone shouting and then—

Beckett arrived beside me in an explosion of snow and panting. My eyes bugged out. *But I left her—*

I spun around to see the snowplow's lights fading into the distance. *Shit!* She couldn't be out here with me! The temperature was dropping fast, it was dangerous. I'd have to call them back....

Then I remembered: no cell service. I cursed under my breath and glared at her.

She lifted her chin, resolute. "I wasn't leaving you out here on your own."

Damn you, Beckett! But it was myself I was mad at. If I'd just gone back in the snow plow with her and stuck it out, instead of running back into the darkness..... But I was ready to snap. Every time I looked at her, the pull towards her was almost more than I could take. What had happened on the cliff top had made everything jump into high-def, pin-sharp clarity. I was in love with this woman. I couldn't deny it, but I couldn't give in. I couldn't do that to Chrissy and Rachel.

"Come on," I muttered. "We've got to hurry."

The snow wasn't just falling anymore, it was blowing horizontally and falling more thickly. By the time we'd made it back to the cliff top, our tracks had been completely covered. I turned a slow circle, trying to figure out which way my car was. I could feel Beckett looking up at me and I knew she wanted to talk. But I picked a direction and set off instead.

The snow came thicker and thicker, the drifts shifting and changing until I couldn't recognize anything. The temperature had plummeted and I'd started to shake, but I was more worried about Beckett: she'd gone pale and was stumbling as if sleepy, and I knew that meant she was dangerously cold. It felt like we'd been walking too long. Shouldn't we have reached the car, by now?

Then my shin whacked into something hard. At first, I thought it was a fallen tree, but it was too smooth, too regular. I ran my hand over it. Metal.

As I saw the shape of it, stretching off to the left and right, realization slowly dawned. This must be the fallen cell phone tower. But Earl had said that was right up at the top of the hill. We'd overshot the car by half a mile. *Dammit!*

Beckett crouched down at the base of the tower, where it had broken. "Look," she said, raising her voice over the wind.

I looked... and felt a slow, cold sickness rise in my gut. The metal was blackened and scorched. Explosives. It hadn't blown down. Someone had deliberately cut the town off from the outside world.

I took Beckett's hand and helped her up. But as she got to her feet, she wavered and almost fell. *Fuck!* She'd stopped shaking and that was a really bad sign. "Come on, Beckett!" I snapped, trying to sound angry to hide how worried I was. I hooked an arm under her shoulders and supported her, letting her lean against me as we stumbled along. *Fuck! Fuck! You idiot, Corrigan!* Why hadn't I got in the snowplow with her? I'd failed to protect her, just like I'd failed to protect Chrissy. *If something happens to her....*

It felt like an hour before I glimpsed my pickup through the snow. By now, Beckett was just a dead weight, slumped against me. I wrestled her onto the back seat, jumped into the front and started the engine. I had to get her back to the hospital *now*—

The engine wouldn't turn over.

I tried it again, but it was utterly dead. Either the cold had killed the starter motor or the gasoline had thickened in the tank. I thumped the steering wheel. *Fuck!*

I scrambled into the back seat and turned on the light. *Oh God:* it was worse than I'd thought. She was semi-conscious, barely stirring when I said her name, and her skin was deathly pale. I needed to warm her up, but it was barely any warmer inside than outside: I could see my breath and every surface I touched was freezing. I fired up the heater, but, without the engine running, it was a measly breeze of tepid air.

I lay down with her and wrapped my arms around her, pulling her on top of me. But there were too many layers: the insulation that had kept the cold out also kept my body heat in.

I stripped off my coat and then hers. Pulled her close again. Now I could feel how cold her body was and it scared me. She just soaked up my warmth with no movement, no sign of life. And her scrubs were making it worse, the pants were soaked through with melted snow. I dragged them down her legs and off, pulling her sneakers off, too, trying to ignore the glimpses of long, graceful thighs. When I took her feet in my hands, they were like blocks of ice. "Jesus, Beckett, come on," I muttered. I could hear the fear in my voice, now. *I'd* done this. My weakness. I should have been strong enough to just get into the snow plow and resist her.

I started rubbing the circulation back into her with long, hard strokes, trying to get the blood moving in her calves and thighs. Then up her sides, through her scrub top, my palms rubbing the thin material over her waist, her arms, her shoulders. Over and over, working frantically at her, until at last I started to feel the tiniest hint of warmth creeping back into her. At first, it was only in her torso, her body still jealously guarding its heat, keeping it away from her extremities. But as I kept rubbing, as the car gradually warmed from my body heat, her color started to creep back. Her neck turned from white to pink, then her hips and her thighs. I wrapped her up in both coats, using them as blankets while I kept working on her legs. She stirred, then her eyes fluttered open.

"Are you okay?" I asked in a rush. I tried to keep my voice level, but it was useless: I was terrified.

She blinked. Frowned. Experimentally shifted her legs against the coats. "Where are my pants?" she asked.

I wasn't ready for the wave of relief that hit me. It sliced through me, washing everything else away, then lifting me up and making me heady and stupid. "Oh, Jesus, Beckett," I croaked. Her face was still so pale. I cupped her cheeks in my palms, feeling my warmth soaking into her—

And then, suddenly, I was kissing her.

34

AMY

I ALWAYS THOUGHT I knew how he'd kiss me. You looked at Dominic Corrigan and you knew how a man like that kissed: with *those* lips and *that* attitude, he'd kiss you and he'd own you. It would be brutal and hot, open-mouthed and panting, a kiss that melted your whole body.

But the first kiss wasn't like that at all. It took me right back to my teenage days. Not to a kiss I'd ever actually had, but to the kiss I'd always dreamed of. That lift-you-up, heart-fluttering kiss that literally takes your breath away because it's so sudden and impulsive, that kiss that makes you stagger, makes you reel, makes you swoon. He didn't kiss me to own me, or dominate me, or show me how hard he wanted to fuck me. He kissed me because he couldn't *not* kiss me.

He kissed me because he loved me.

Hard lips crushing down on mine, a mingled gasp of wonder, shock and need from both of us. Then twisting and moving, every tiny touch of his lips against mine sending a surge of energy through me, my heart racing, my face going hot under his palms.

"Wow," I croaked as he pulled back to look at me.

"Yeah," he said. Emotion made the Irish thick in his voice. "Well, it was a long time coming."

The kiss had taken us both by surprise but it had broken the dam. He stared down at me. I stared up at him—

We fell on each other, him lunging down and me surging up from the seat to meet halfway, chests pressed together and arms tangled around each other. This time, the kiss was urgent and deep, drinking each other in. I was gasping, inhaling the raw spirit of Dominic Corrigan and he was panting down the essence of me. My hands were in his hair, fingers sliding through the thick black locks, luxuriating in them. Then they fell to his shoulders, palms circling on the heavy muscles: God, he was like a wall against me, so big, so solid: I wanted to cling to him, hang off him.

We twisted around each other like eels, unable to keep still. His hands went wild on my back, crushing me to him, exploring the shape of me through my scrub top. Then they found my rump through my snow-soaked panties and squeezed hard. I yelped and wriggled, a bolt of heat twisting through me, and he growled and started stroking my thighs and hips. I let out a strangled groan and kissed him even harder, unable to let go of his lips for more than a second.

The kiss was changing again, turning wild and sexual, turning *Corrigan*. He sought me out and demanded that I open, and I did... but I did more. I couldn't be passive, not with this man. I couldn't just *be kissed*. His kiss was like a drug that set me free: my hands grabbed at his shoulders, his back, his ass as my tongue met his.

The heat thrummed through me, pounding in my ears, blocking out all thought. I felt him grab the clip that held my hair up and pull it free, none too gently, and I didn't care. He kissed down my throat and his stubble burned my cheek and I didn't care about that, either. We were beyond politeness. We needed each other.

His fingers dug into the cheeks of my ass and his thumbs pressed into the creases at the tops of my thighs. I was captured, held fast for his kiss. His thumbs circled in those sensitive spots and I started to gasp and thrash, my panting lips stroking his.

Then he pushed my scrub top up to bunch under my arms. I had my eyes closed but I could feel the sudden warmth of his chest through only one flimsy layer of cloth. Then the seat either side of my head squished as he pushed himself up on his forearms and I knew he was looking at me. Our breathing filled the car: my tight, quick pants; his much bigger, deeper breaths as his eyes roamed over me. He suddenly scooped his hands under me, unclipped my black bra and pushed it up out of the way. I lay there, my skin warming under his gaze, my nipples tightening into aching peaks.

He fell on me, those big hands wrapping around my waist to pin me there as his mouth opened wide to engulf one breast. I clutched at his arms, his muscles rock hard under my fingers, as his tongue circled and lashed, pleasure twisting and spiraling outwards to fill me. Maybe scared of crushing me, he suddenly pulled me on top of him, lying back on the seat with me straddling him. He pulled my upper body down to meet his mouth, his hands stroking and squeezing my breasts as his tongue licked at them.

My thighs were clamped around his torso and I was practically grinding myself against the hard ridges of his abs. My breath came in shuddering pants. This man made me completely lose control. I groped for the bottom of his scrub top and pushed it up, letting my fingers rollercoaster over the peaks and valleys of his six pack. The more I touched him, the more I needed to touch him. My fingers pushed the material higher, higher, revealing his deep center line and the hard slabs of his chest. I ran my thumb over one nipple experimentally and he growled, his whole body stiffening beneath me. He wrapped his hand around the back of my head and tugged me down for a kiss.

My breasts, slick and shining from his mouth, pillowed and dragged along his chest as I sank down and flattened myself against him. He was too tall to lie completely flat along the seat so his knees were raised and I wound up with my ass in the air and pressed back against them. I felt him lift himself off the seat a little and heard the rasp of fabric as he pushed down his pants. And then his cock sprang free and slapped against my inner thigh, hot and hard and ready. I drew back from his kiss a little, our lips a few millimeters apart, and felt him hook his thumbs into my panties and shove them down my thighs. My eyes flew open and I drew back a little more. He was staring up at me and then his hand was on my thigh, sliding upward....

My eyes widened. He cupped me, stroked me. I could feel how slickly wet I was....

"I've been dreaming about doing this," he murmured. The combination of the lust in his voice and the silver of his accent seared into my mind and just melted me. "Been thinking about it ever since you put your hands on my hands, that day in the ER. I wanted to know what you—"

Two fingers parted me and slid deep. I shuddered and gasped and he grinned, watching the pleasure in my eyes. His thumb found my clit and started to circle. "...what you sound like when you come," he finished.

I stared down into those blue eyes, unable to speak. God, he was an expert, his fingers just the right combination of thick and strong, deft and quick. I started to rock atop him and he began to smooth his other hand over my bare ass cheek, enjoying the way it tensed as I moved. Waves of pleasure were rippling out from my groin, making me buck my hips and squeeze around him, my hair lashing his face. His fingers moved faster, fucking me, thumb circling and circling. My fingers dug hard into his biceps, my forehead lowering to press against his....

I came, arching my back and clenching and spasming around his fingers. I was planning to be silent, tried to bite my lip, but he was too good. It got loose, a rising cry that turned into a staccato burst of high little yells as the lust in his eyes overpowered my shyness. I didn't need to hide anymore. Not with him.

I swayed atop him, dazed. He was pulling his wallet out of the pocket of his scrub pants, taking something out. His knuckles brushed my inner thigh as he rolled a condom on and then the head of his cock was nudging at my folds and—

He drove up into me, spreading me—God, *stretching* me deliciously. My world narrowed down to the glorious feeling of that hot hardness stroking into me and the press of his body between my knees. He put his hands on my shoulders and pushed me back until I was kneeling astride him, head lowered to clear the ceiling. He filled his hands with my breasts, squeezing them in time with our slow movements, smoothing my hair across them in a silken curtain and using it to caress my nipples. We were working together, him thrusting up as I pushed down and back and God, it was amazing. I'd always been passive, before, I'd never been with anyone I could unleash and be myself with. It went on for long minutes, every slow, silken thrust ratcheting the pleasure higher. My toes started to dance and curl against the seat, my fingers crushing his shoulders. Already, I was getting close again. And the look in his eyes only drove me closer. With every stroke into me, his eyes narrowed and his body hardened under my hands. He needed more, needed to fuck me faster, harder. But he couldn't, not like this....

He suddenly pushed me off him, hooking my leg over him and sliding out from under me. Before I knew what was happening, he'd pushed me along the seat so that I was on hands and knees, my face close to the fogged-up window. I felt his knees push between mine, spreading my thighs, and gulped again as I realized what he was going to do. He pressed down on my naked back, making me arch my back and present myself to him. And then both of us cried out as he plunged inside me again.

He could go deeper, like this, and he slid inside me all the way to the hilt, until I felt the heat of his body against mine. He started to move and he was iron and silk inside me, filling me, every sweet backwards drag and quick, hard thrust making the pleasure spiral higher inside me. I pressed my cheek against the cold glass, the blizzard just a hazy blur outside. He began to slam me, his fingers curling around the crease of my hips to pull me back onto him.

His voice was ragged, the Irish raw and savage, nuggets of silver in freshly-broken rock. "*Christ,* Amy, you're amazing." He grabbed my rump, his fingers rough with need. "Always knew you would be."

I was incapable of speech. With every thrust, the pleasure compressed, tightening and tightening towards the point of bursting. His thrusts were so strong, now, that I was being shifted along the seat and had to brace my hands against the door. My climax was like a living thing inside me, now, hurling itself back and forth, demanding release.

His thrusts got faster, faster, building to a peak. As he slammed into me, he slowly pulled me back against him until I was kneeling, my back pressed against his chest. He filled his hands with my breasts, pinching the nipples lightly, and the pleasure compressed and brightened: *God, yes!*

And then he pushed me forward, burying himself in me while pushing me up against the window. My breasts, still damp and super-sensitive, pressed against the cold glass, the chill shock of it against my hot flesh indescribable. I knew there was no one outside to see but the feeling of being so wantonly, filthily *on show,* coupled with the press of his hard body against me, the endless, silken stretch of him inside me—

I screamed my orgasm out into the snow, shuddering around him again and again. He put one hand under my chin and twisted my head around for his kiss, our lips meeting just as he growled and shot inside me.

35

AMY

W E LAY with him spooning me from behind, both of us naked. The rear seat was warm from our coupling and, with both coats layered over us as blankets, it was cozy. Him being so big, I was close to the edge of the seat, but he had both arms wrapped around me and it didn't feel precarious at all. I felt warm in a way that went beyond simple temperature, protected in a way that went beyond being out of the snow. All my blankets and comforters and the log fire at my apartment, all of my burrowing...these arms were what I'd been searching for all along.

There was just enough moonlight to see by. I could see blurry movement through the fogged-up windows and hear the wind: the blizzard was still howling outside. But in here, all was safe and cozy.

I was wondering whether I needed to start calling him *Dominic,* now. *Dom?* I liked it, but I couldn't get used to it after so much *Corrigan.* "Are you going to start calling me Amy now?" I thought aloud.

He hugged me even tighter to his chest. "No," he said, and nipped my earlobe with his teeth. "I like *Beckett* too much."

I sort of writhed against him. The way he said it, *Beckett* was like my sexy, sultry, alter-ego. I felt his cock harden against my ass. The man was insatiable.

I closed my eyes, comfortable and secure. He was a superb cuddler. It was the final proof that the cocky, womanizing Corrigan was a fake. *This* was his natural state, to be with someone. This must be what he was like when he was married, before he changed. Which reminded me of something I needed to broach, if we were together. "Do you see them often?"

He sounded genuinely confused. "Who?"

"Your ex." I paused. "You're divorced, right?"

He went completely still behind me. Had I got it wrong? I was so sure, all the signs had been there. I twisted around in his arms so that I could look at him....

When I saw the expression on his face, my stomach fell a thousand feet. *Oh. Shit.* My words echoed in my head: colorful baubles I'd tossed happily into the air, only to feel them explode like hand grenades. I knew I had no social skills, but how could I have gotten it so utterly, horrifically wrong? I searched his face, flailing for an escape hatch, a way to take it back—

Two words, drawn from somewhere unimaginably deep, hauled up to the surface in a process that was all fractured, razor-sharp edges and bitter, toxic pain. He didn't say them, he cleared them from his mouth as quickly as possible. "Chrissy." Then, even harder: "*Rachel.*" He swallowed. "They died two years ago. Rachel would be eight, now. Rebecca's age."

My mouth opened and closed silently. I could feel the tears in my eyes: the pain radiating off him was so immense it soaked through me, stealing my words. I'd done enough damage, I wasn't going to ask *how.* But he must have seen the question on my face.

"They were murdered," he said.

Dealing with death is part of my job. But no matter how hard it is, that sort of death can be broken down with logic. It's lifestyle and disease and age, surgical complications, even mistakes. *Murder?!* That was something that happened in books and movies. Losing someone

I could conceive of. Having them *taken from you?* Not just his wife, but his daughter, too?

I threw my arms around him and clutched him as tight as I could. The emotion was a hot swell of pressure inside me. I couldn't form it into words so I kept my jaw clamped shut and it leaked out as tears. *How could they,* kept going through my head. *How could anyone do that to this man?*

He rubbed my back, gently trying to soothe me. But that was the wrong way around, *I* needed to be soothing *him!* I clung to him as if I could draw the poison from him if I only pressed myself close enough. *I'm here,* I kept thinking. *I'm here now.* I didn't care that it was ridiculous, that he was the strong one who'd traveled the world and took everything in his stride and I was the one who usually hid away in the OR. I needed to help my man.

When I finally pushed back and looked up into his face, I shook my head in disbelief. "How do you cope?" I asked.

He stared right back at me. "I don't."

That didn't make any sense to me because obviously he *was* coping, he'd filled the years since with women and travel. I just hugged him close again and, wrapped together, we eventually dozed.

I woke about an hour later. It was still dark, but something was different: I couldn't figure out what, at first. Then I got it: the wind wasn't howling. When I looked outside, the snow had stopped.

I realized he was awake, too. "We should try the engine again," he said. I nodded dumbly as he pulled on his scrubs. I was still shell-shocked by what he'd told me, but I was taking my cues from him: we'd talk about it when and if he wanted to. Part of me was glad of the change of subject. I needed some time just to process.

He climbed into the front and tried the engine. It grumbled twice, then caught. He threw a grin at me over his shoulder. "I think we thawed it out."

I blushed, remembering, and struggled into my own scrubs. Climbing into the passenger seat beside him, my mind was racing. Even without what he'd told me about his family, this would be an awkward moment. *What now?* Were we... *together?* What if that had just been a one-night stand for him after all? What if—

He grabbed me under the arms and pulled me into his lap. Before I knew what was happening, his lips were coming down on mine. I opened under him and it became a deep, slow kiss, full of reassurance and love. When he broke it, he looked down into my eyes. "Okay?" he asked.

"*Mm-hmm,*" I nodded breathlessly.

He pushed a lock of hair back from my face. His eyes were solemn... and determined. Acknowledging that making this work would be hard. Telling me he was damn well going to try.

We set off down the hill, crunching through thick snow. It took us a full hour to make it back to the hospital, but, when we did, Taylor and Krista met us at the door.

"Sophie's going to be fine," Krista told us, her eyes on Corrigan. "No other traumas came in. It's been quiet. I even grabbed a nap."

I let out a long sigh of relief and hugged her. "Thank you for holding the fort."

Krista and Taylor high-fived, good friends already. "Meh," said Krista. "This doctorin' ain't so hard."

I'd always thought of the ER as cold and drafty but after the long walk through the snow, going inside was like climbing into a warm bath. Maggie was balanced precariously at the very top of a stepladder, reaching up into the ceiling space to fix a light, and Earl was watching her from across the room, twisting his hat in his hands. I gave him a look: *tell her!* He shook his head.

Taylor took Corrigan off to check on the critical patients. Krista pulled me aside the second they were out of earshot. "You two were out there a suspiciously long time."

I started to tell her she was wrong... and then remembered that I couldn't, for once, and turned scarlet. Krista's jaw dropped. We joke about my non-existent sex life so often, something actually happening hadn't occurred to her. "*You didn't!*"

I looked at the floor. But for once, as well as blushing, I had this big, stupid grin on my face.

"*Oh my God! Tell me everything!*"

"Me too," came Maggie's voice from above.

I shook my head, remembering. Later. Maybe. If we did tequila shots.

At that second, it went black.

Not dark: *black.* Not only did every light in the hospital go out, every light in the street outside did, too. And with the moon behind a cloud, that left us in pitch, suffocating blackness. A shrill, discordant chorus of alarms sounded from the critical area: all the ventilators warning that they were now running on battery power.

"It's okay!" Maggie's voice. But she didn't *sound* okay, she sounded panicked. Then I remembered she was perched ten feet in the air. "The wind must have brought down the power lines. The emergency generator will kick in in a couple of—*shit!*"

In the darkness, I had to fill in what was happening from the sounds. A rush of air as she fell. A creak as she grabbed hold of a pipe and dangled. A clang as her foot searched for the stepladder and kicked it instead. It toppled and crashed to the floor, missing me by inches. Heavy, running footsteps—

A scream as she fell. I winced, but there was nothing I could do: I knew the ladder was right in front of me, waiting to trip me. She was falling eight feet onto a hard floor, she'd crack her head right open—

There was a soft *whump.*

The lights flickered on. The ventilator alarms died away.

Earl was standing underneath the hole in the ceiling with Maggie in his arms. She was looking up at him in shock and he was looking down at her in a very particular way.

"Earl?" she said in disbelief.

"*Ma'am,*" he said.

I grabbed Krista by the elbow and towed her away. I may be socially inept, but even I know when two people need a moment alone. Behind us, I heard Earl mumbling something, her calling him a big lunk... and then silence. I sneaked a peek. They were kissing. *Yes!*

"I'm going to go check on Rebecca," I told Krista, and walked off towards the critical area, grinning.

Rebecca was dozing, but she woke up as I approached. I whispered *hi,* keeping my voice low because the other patients were sleeping.

"You look different," whispered Rebecca curiously.

My hair was down. I hadn't thought to put it up again after Corrigan had pulled it free while we were... I coughed. But I wasn't sure that was it. I felt giddy and light. I looked over my shoulder, seeing Corrigan at the far end of the row of beds, before I realized what I'd done.

Rebecca drew in her breath. *"You're in love!"* she whispered, awestruck. "With Doctor Corrigan!"

I spent about three seconds trying to form a denial before I gave in and nodded. My grown-up head was saying things like *you can't use the L-word. Not yet.* The whole rest of me was *squeezing* and singing, yes *I can.* "How did you know?" I whispered.

"My mom got the same look after she met my step-dad," she said proudly. Then, at the mention of her parents, her face crumpled.

I leaned close and grabbed her hands. "Hey, *hey,* don't worry," I told her. Talking to her was getting easier each time... and leaving her was getting harder. "As soon as the snow clears, they'll be here, okay?" She reluctantly nodded. "Now try to get some sleep."

As she snuggled down, I remembered to check her chart. Everything was fine except—

Oh God.

"Everything okay?" asked Rebecca.

I managed to control my face. "Yes, sweetie," I whispered. "Go to sleep, everything's fine."

It was the first time I'd lied to her.

36

DOMINIC

I SPENT about twenty minutes hunting for Beckett before I thought to go upstairs and check the surgeon's break room. I strode in and sighed in relief as I spotted her standing in the shadows. Then I glanced around and whistled. Everything was sparkling clean, there were plump armchairs, a bean-to-cup coffee machine and a jar of amaretto biscuits. The ER break room was a frat house by comparison. "Wow," I said. "So this is how the other half lives."

She drew in her breath and I heard the rapid tremble. I rushed forward, grabbed her hand and pulled her into the light: yep, her eyes were full of tears. "What?" I demanded. "What's going on?"

"Rebecca's kidneys are failing," she croaked. "They're blocked. Damage from the crush injuries. I knew it was a danger, but I didn't think it would happen this fast."

My chest closed up. "What do we do?"

"There's nothing we can do until tomorrow. I've given her Sorbitol, we need to wait for that to bring her potassium levels down first...."

She trailed off. I took hold of her shoulders. She suddenly looked so fragile. "What is it?"

"The only way to save her kidneys is with a pyeloplasty. I've never done one before, it's a job for a specialist renal surgeon. And with an adult I could do it keyhole, but Rebecca's too small, I'd have to open her up. She's already weak. She could die on the table."

"And if you *don't* do it?"

"She'll live... but her kidneys will fail and once they're gone, she's on dialysis for the rest of her life." Fresh tears welled up. "She's a minor, she can't make the decision. Her parents are meant to, but I can't reach them!"

Oh shit.

Her voice fractured. *"How the hell am I meant to decide?* Do I risk killing her, to give her a shot at a normal life?"

I closed my eyes and pulled her to my chest, wrapping my arms around her and cradling her head against me. Her silent tears made warm blotches on the front of my scrubs. "You think I should do it?" she asked after a few moments.

That *was* my instinct. If it had been an adult then sure, roll the dice and to hell with the rules. But this was a kid. I thought of Rebecca hooked up to a dialysis machine once a week for the rest of her life, hoping she got lucky on the transplant list. But then I thought of her parents showing up and Beckett having to tell them their daughter was gone because of a decision she'd made. There *were* no easy answers. "I don't know," I said at last. I stroked her hair. "I know you're an amazing surgeon. If anyone can pull it off, you can. And I know you care about her. You're the closest thing that kid has to a mother, right now. You've got to go with your gut, do what you think's right. I've got your back either way."

Krista opened the door. When she saw us hugging, her face lit up. Her mouth opened for one of her smartass comments...and then she saw the expressions on our faces and bit it back. "You two should head home," she said gently. "It's still quiet."

Beckett shook her head. "We can't just leave you here."

"Yes you can!" said Krista firmly. "You have to! Both of you are exhausted. Taylor and I can handle the graveyard shift, but we need you two fresh for tomorrow."

She had a point. It could be days until the snow cleared and we had to sleep at some point. And now that she'd said it, I realized how utterly spent I was. A full day on my feet, followed by trekking up that hill in the snow, rescuing Sophie, carrying the stretcher, struggling back up the hill. We'd only dozed in my pickup and only for an hour or so. I was ready to drop. I looked at Beckett: she looked exhausted too.

Krista could see we were weakening. "If there's an emergency, we'll send someone to come get you."

"My apartment's just down the street," I said without thinking. Then I realized how it sounded. Beckett blushed and, for once, I think I did, too.

"*Go!*" said Krista, grinning.

We went.

37

AMY

T HE FIRST THING I noticed was that I was warm. *Really* warm, cozy in a way I'd never experienced before.

Firstly, I was sprawled face-down on a big, heated mattress that was the perfect blend of hard and soft. I sent my hands out on sleepy reconnaissance missions, feeling around until I'd confirmed that the mattress had shoulders and abs and was, in fact, Corrigan.

Secondly, I was under the best comforter I'd ever felt. It was soft enough to mold to our bodies and hug us but dense and thickly satisfying, its weight pressing me firmly into my pillow of Irish pec. *I never, ever want to move.* The only part of me that was cold was my nose, because that was above the comforter so that I could breathe. So I ducked my head and snuggled in tighter.

"*Christ, woman!* Your nose is like a feckin' icicle!" Corrigan captured my head between his palms, kissed my forehead and then pressed one warm palm against the tip of my nose to thaw it.

"I really like your bed," I said seriously.

He fingered the comforter appreciatively. "Well, you don't want to mess around when it comes to duvets."

I hadn't considered that he might have the same need for coziness that I had. I'd thought of him sleeping on the floor with a sandpaper blanket. Every day, I was learning new things about him. "*Duvet?* That's what you call this?" He nodded. "Teach me something else," I said.

His face lit up and his voice dropped into a silver-edged growl. "I've got a few things I could teach you."

We were both naked, I realized. And his cock was stiffening rapidly against my thigh. "*Words!*" I yelped. "Teach me words!"

He pointed through the open door to the bathroom. "That's a tap," he said, pointing to the faucet. "We're in my flat. You're a lass." He rolled us over so that he was on top. "And if we fought, we'd be having a *row*." It rhymed with *cow*.

"Now you're just making them up," I told him. My voice had gone high and tight. He'd landed between my legs and he was *very* naked. We looked at each other and I bit my lip. "What, um...what *did* you want to teach me?" I asked, shocked at my boldness.

He gave a truly wicked chuckle and ducked his head under the duvet. A split-second later, I cried out and arched my back, clutching at the pillows.

~

We didn't want to leave Krista and Taylor alone at the hospital too long, plus there was no power so no way to cook breakfast and we were both starving. But before we headed out, we had to brave a freezing cold shower.

I endured it for about twenty seconds and then leapt out, naked and shivering, trying to rub some warmth into myself with a towel. It occurred to me that I didn't have anything to wear except yesterday's scrubs. There were fresh ones at work but I could do with something to throw on until then, maybe a t-shirt. While Corrigan showered, I had a look in his closet but there were just a few shirts: he'd only partly unpacked. I pulled open a dresser drawer—

Staring up at me was a toy rabbit. A gray one, with pink ears, clearly much loved: I could see where a little hand had crushed its paw tight and where its feet were faded from having been dragged along the ground, Someone had taken this thing *everywhere* with them.

Rachel.

I heard Corrigan jump out of the shower in a cloud of curses. I quickly shut the drawer, grabbed a shirt from the closet and pulled it on, my heart hammering. I forced a smile onto my face as he walked in but I knew we needed to talk.

He took my hand and we headed out onto Main Street to try to find something to eat. When the daylight hit my face, it reminded me: *today's the day.* I had to make the call on whether to operate on Rebecca. I wasn't any closer to a decision, but I couldn't put off making it much longer.

Last night's snow was already being shoveled off the sidewalks and, amazingly, most of the stores had opened for business, using candles for lighting and wood burners for heat. The bank seemed to be closed, but that made sense: without power, their computers would be useless.

The cafe was rammed. Everyone in town was searching for breakfast and the cafe was the one place in town that had a grill fired by propane tanks. "All I can offer you is a table outside," said Martha, the elderly owner.

It was cold but crisp and we had our thick coats. "We'll take it," I said quickly and we sat down before someone else grabbed it, then got our orders in: eggs, bacon and coffee.

A family with two small children took the only other table and my mind snapped back to Rachel's rabbit. *How do you cope?* I'd asked him in the pickup. *I don't.* The answer hadn't made sense to me, then, but it did now. That fierce Irish stubbornness I loved so much...it had kept him going but only because he'd refused to accept death's authority. He hadn't moved on. He'd spent the time since their deaths treading water, filling his life with the constant adrenaline rush of the ER. And when that wasn't enough: bars and women and danger, *Doctors without Borders* and trips to warzones. *Oh, Corrigan!* I just wanted to hug him. *He hasn't let them go.*

My mind followed that to its logical conclusion and I didn't like it.

If he hasn't let them go...God, he must feel like he's having to choose, them or me. No wonder he'd seemed so torn, these last few days. The guilt surged up inside me. *What the hell do I do?*

I didn't have any answers. I wished my mom was still alive: if I'd ever needed some motherly advice, it was now. But I was going to have to figure it out myself, one day at a time.

One thing couldn't wait, though. Something I'd seen on the cliff top that I was seeing now through fresh eyes. Something I had to talk to him about. I drew in a big breath of freezing air—

"Um," I said. *Brilliant, Amy.*

He frowned at me and waited.

I grabbed his hands to give me strength. "When your hand got caught," I said, "and the car was going to carry you over the cliff, you said *it's okay.* You looked like...you were ready to go."

He looked away. "It was just for a second."

Every dormouse instinct in me begged me to let it go. Confronting people isn't in my nature. But he needed to hear this.

I shook my head. "It's not just that one time. When you faced off with Colt at the hospital, part of you wanted the fight. And the Congo. And Libya. All those warzones." I took a deep breath. "I—I think part of you wants to die because you feel guilty about...them. And I don't want anything to happen to you."

Corrigan stared at me, stunned at what I'd just blurted out.

I looked down at the table, heart thumping. "Sorry," I mumbled. "I probably should have been more subtle. I sort of skipped social skills 101."

He just kept staring at me. Each time I dared to glance up, his expression had changed. He went from shock to fury and then to sadness and finally defeat. I couldn't take that. *I've made things worse!* I kept my eyes fixed on the table.

Until a warm finger hooked me under the chin and lifted my head so that I was looking into his eyes. Eyes that had changed again to show deep affection...and hope.

"You're not the one who's fucked up, Beckett," he said. He went silent for a moment. I could see him struggling, bracing himself to get the word out. I don't know if he realized he was squeezing my hands, but I hoped it helped. "*Yeah,*" he said eventually. He looked almost surprised that he'd managed to say it. "Yeah," he said again. "I did want—I did want to die. Sometimes."

I had to fight past a huge lump in my throat to speak. "*Did?*"

He looked deep in my eyes for a long time before he finally nodded. He wanted to be sure and I think he wanted me to *know* he was sure. "*Did.*"

And he pulled me by the hands towards him and leaned forward and drew me into a slow, tender kiss. I could feel the cold wind lashing my cheeks and playing with my hair but it didn't matter: a warm glow was pulsing through me, right down to my toes. And I understood something: he was my missing puzzle piece, the perfect balance for me, just as my mom had been to my dad.

When we broke the kiss, Martha was standing there next to us, plates in hand. She said nothing as she set them down, but she had a huge grin on her face.

We ate quickly, before the freezing air cooled the food too much, and it was fantastic: crispy strips of bacon that melted in your mouth, mounds of piping-hot, buttery scrambled eggs and huge mugs of steaming coffee. There's something about a hot breakfast when you're really, really cold. I watched Corrigan as I sipped my coffee, feeling the first stirrings of hope.

An alarm started to blare, a long continuous bell that I'd never heard before. As I looked up, the doors to the bank burst open. Wasn't the bank *closed?*

It took me a second to register that the men pouring out of the bank all had guns. "Oh Jesus," I whispered.

A police SUV had been cruising down the street. It screeched to a stop and Earl and his young partner Lloyd jumped out, guns drawn.

"*Get down!*" yelled Corrigan, even as he grabbed me around the waist and bore me to the ground.

And then the world became deafening gunfire and breaking glass as the shooting started.

38

DOMINIC

G UNFIGHTS always look so exciting in the movies. That's because they don't show the collateral damage. When you're a bystander, it's very, very different.

There were at least ten gunmen, some carrying bags in one hand and handguns in the other, some toting assault rifles. As they poured out of the bank and tried to cross the street, they came up against Earl and his young partner, Lloyd, firing from behind their SUV. So they fanned out instead, spreading the fight all the way down Main Street right when it was full of people going to work. My ears rang with the staccato chatter of gunfire. And then, between the shots, the screaming started.

I'd been under fire before, in the Congo, even taken a few bullets myself. I knew we had to get behind something, but we were caught out in the open: there was nothing. All we could do was to get down low and pray. A gunman ran past us and one of the cops fired at him and missed. I heard the bullets pass overhead and the plate glass window of the cafe came crashing down in a million glittering shards. The people inside began to run and scream, but there was nowhere *to* run: the place was too crowded for them to move.

I already had Beckett down on the freezing sidewalk and I was trying to cover every inch of her body with mine. My heart was slamming in my chest. *What if she gets hit? What if I lose her?* I knew the most dangerous thing in the world is someone firing a gun indiscriminately and right now, both sides were in a wild panic, spraying bullets at anything that moved. Earl and Lloyd were just small-town cops and probably hadn't ever been under fire before: they were operating on instinct, scared out of their minds. And the gunmen just plain didn't care.

A second cop car pulled up behind Earl's and the gunfire increased. *Should we run?* That meant standing up and that made us bigger targets. Even as I thought it, a woman fleeing across the street screamed and fell to the ground. I didn't even see the stray shot that hit her. I stared at her twitching body, trying to figure out how to get to her...and then she went still, a life just snuffed out. I pressed Beckett even tighter against the sidewalk, my heart pounding.

And then, in the midst of all the chaos, I glimpsed a face. One of the men firing an assault rifle was Colt.

I started to recognize other faces. The old guy who'd come in with palpitations. Some of the men who'd carried the two injured guys to the ER. This was Colt's gang, or militia, or whatever the hell they were. *They're bank robbers?* That's what they'd been planning?

I looked down and saw Beckett staring at Colt, too. "*Here?*" she mouthed over the gunfire. I knew what she meant. A tiny local bank like the one on Main Street wouldn't have enough cash to be worth robbing. And why weren't they wearing masks? Didn't they care that everyone could identify them?

Then I saw Seth, Colt's son. He was sheltering behind a parked car and next to him was a man in a tan jacket. Seth had a hand on the man's arm, as if telling him to wait. Almost as if he was the man's bodyguard.

Beckett gave a horrified moan beneath me. I followed her gaze and—

Oh God, no.

Taylor was standing about thirty feet away. She was still holding a takeout cup of coffee and she was rooted to the spot, face pale and eyes huge. She must have wandered into this just as it started and now she was frozen.

And two of the gunmen were running right towards her, gunfire chewing up the storefronts behind them as the police tried to hit them. I could see it all coming in sickening slow motion. Even if I could leave Beckett, there was no way I could get to her in time—

Seth sprang to his feet and started running, shoving other people out of his way. I saw Colt yell at him, furious, but he kept going, charging towards Taylor. He slammed into her like a linebacker, carrying her to the ground behind a car just as bullets raked the wall where she'd been standing. Seth lay there panting and frantic, his arms wrapped around Taylor's waist to hold her there. He glanced our way and for a second, our eyes met. I glanced down at Beckett. I understood.

Colt yelled orders to his men and they started to flood across the street towards an alley. He called for his son, but Seth shook his head, still protecting Taylor.

The man in the tan jacket made a run for it. Earl yelled at him to stop. Colt raised his gun and fired and my stomach knotted as I saw Earl fall. Lloyd dropped to his knees next to his mentor, his mouth wide in shock. Then he jumped to his feet and fired wildly at Colt, screaming in rage. Most of his shots slammed into a parked car near the guy in a tan jacket—

The whole street shook as the car's gas tank exploded. The few windows that had survived, shattered. My head throbbed and my lungs ached as the pressure wave hit us. Beckett screamed beneath me.

The shooting stopped.

For a few moments I just lay there, stunned. All I could hear was a ringing in my ears and my vision was blurry. When I got my senses back, I quickly rolled off Beckett and flipped her face-up, my heart racing. "Beckett?" What if she'd caught a piece of shrapnel from the explosion? "*Beckett?*"

She opened her eyes. I patted her down, looking for injuries, but she was fine, just dazed. I pulled her to her feet and then wrapped her up in a hug, lifting her right off the ground. She nestled her head into my shoulder. I closed my eyes, panting in relief. *If anything had happened to her....*

"Oh my God," whispered Beckett. She was looking over my shoulder.

I slowly opened my eyes and looked around.

Main Street lay in ruins. Every window was shattered, bullet holes riddled the signs and the car that had exploded was on fire, sending thick black smoke twisting down the street in choking clouds. Four of the gunmen were down and the cops were scrambling to get cuffs on them. The rest were disappearing into an alley. As I watched, Colt grabbed hold of Seth and dragged him roughly away from Taylor, then ran with him into the alley. Seth looked forlornly back at Taylor as they were torn apart and she stared back at him, tearful and accusing. *How could you do this?*

The injured lay everywhere: cops, civilians, gunmen. The family who'd been sitting next to us outside the cafe must have tried to make a run for it, because the father was bleeding from his chest, the mother from her arm. People inside the cafe were screaming, begging for help, one woman stretched out on the counter as a man tried to stop her bleeding.

Earl lay on the ground, the front of his uniform soaked in blood. Lloyd was kneeling next to him, tears running down his cheeks. The gunman in the tan jacket was rolling on the ground next to the burning car in agony, his hands over his eyes.

And more. So many more. My training kicked in. We needed to declare a major incident, call local hospitals, have them send extra ambulances and doctors—

Then I remembered and my throat closed up. We didn't have any of that backup. We didn't even have our normal roster of staff.

I looked around and met Beckett's eyes. Then Taylor's.

All we had was the three of us.

I took a deep breath and we ran into the chaos.

39

AMY

T HIS CAN'T *be real*. The town I knew so well was barely recognizable. With every step, my sneakers crunched broken glass and kicked tinkling shell casings. Everywhere I looked, another person lay bleeding, the snow stained red around them. And the ones out here were only the beginning. The store fronts were gaping black maws lined with jagged teeth. I couldn't see who was screaming inside and part of me didn't want to.

We stopped next to Taylor, who looked as shell-shocked as me. "I just...." Her face was as pale as the snow. "I just came out to get coffee—"

Corrigan pulled her into a hug. Even as he patted her back, he was looking around at the injured, deciding priorities. *How is he unaffected?* I was freaking out.

Then I got a look at his expression. He wasn't unaffected. He was just used to this sort of horror.

He gave Taylor ten seconds, then gently pushed her back. "I'll be in there," he told us, pointing to the cafe. It looked like hell in there: all I could see was the silhouettes of bodies crammed together, people panicking and screaming and struggling to get out.

It made sense: the cafe needed someone who was big enough to push through the crowd, who wouldn't get trampled. But I didn't want to be left out here. The ER was bad enough, but this was something else entirely. Twenty or more people were yelling for help. Some of them would die before I could help them. Some of them would die before I could even *reach* them. I was shaking. I couldn't stop shaking.

Corrigan took hold of my shoulders. "Amy. You'll be okay."

I shook my head, gazing around me in disbelief. People I knew, dying. Stores I visited every day, destroyed. "I—" I choked helplessly. My head went light.

"*Beckett,*" he snapped.

I came back to him.

He looked deep into my eyes. "You can do this," he told me. There was absolutely no doubt in his voice. "You're just scared. It's okay to be scared. But you can do this."

My heart was still hammering so hard it was painful but his words unfroze me. I drew in a shuddering breath and clung onto those words like a life preserver. Then I nodded.

And he was gone, sprinting off towards the cafe.

I turned around. Everywhere I looked, someone was screaming for help. *Who do I help first? Who do I leave to die?* I felt the panic rising again.

It's okay to be scared. You can do this.

Taylor was frozen, too. She stared at me, her eyes huge. I had to get her moving and I couldn't even get myself moving.

"Earl," I told her, pointing to the fallen cop. "Help Earl."

"*I'm just a student!*" she whispered, tears in her eyes.

I grabbed her hands and squeezed. "Not today."

Then I ran to the man who'd been sitting with his family, eating breakfast next to us. He was on his back, hands clutched to a wound on his chest. His wife was sprawled next to him, bleeding from her arm, trying to comfort her kids. When I checked over my shoulder, Taylor was still standing there...but then she nodded to me and ran to Earl.

I fell to my knees beside the man. Blood was pumping between his fingers. It was so bitterly cold, I could see steam rising from the wound. "It's okay," I said out loud. "I'm a doctor."

The woman touched my arm in thanks. She'd thought I'd been reassuring *them.*

I tore away the man's shirt and reached for—

I blinked. *What the hell am I going to use?* I didn't even have a first aid kit with me!

I pressed on the wound while I thought. The bleeding barely slowed.

"Is he going to be okay?" sobbed the wife. The children were crying too. I was a hair's breadth from joining them.

What would Corrigan do?

I looked around and found one of the walking wounded, a bald man with a gash on his cheek. "*You!* I need your help!" He came over. "Run to the hardware store and get me all the dishtowels they have. And a knife, I need a small, sharp knife." He hurried off. I found another person, a woman in her sixties. "And you: I need you to go into the stationary store and get me bulldog clips. The smallest ones you can find." She ran.

While we were waiting, I told the man's wife to show me her arm. "You'll be okay," I told her. "The bullet went straight through. Keep pressure on it." Any other time, she would have been rushed to hospital. Only in this hell could a bullet wound be minor.

The supplies began to arrive and I started frantically treating people, using dishtowels as bandages and bulldog clips to clamp arteries. The father looked like he'd make it. The store owner I treated next was touch-and-go: he'd been shot in the leg and had lost a lot of blood. Then a teenage girl who'd been hit in the neck by flying glass. She was shaking with cold and shock and I realized I was still wearing my thick winter coat, so I pulled it off and wrapped it around her. One man had been thrown against a truck by the force of the car exploding and was lying on the ground with a possible cervical spine fracture. I didn't have a neck brace to put on him so I mounded snow up all around his neck and packed it in tight to immobilize him.

I wish Corrigan was here. I felt stupid thinking it because I knew he was going through hell himself, trying to save lives in that dim, cramped cafe, patching wounds in freakin' candlelight. And I felt guilty because who cared if I was upset and panicking, when people were fighting for their lives all around me? But I *did* want him. It didn't matter that I was a surgeon, I was still human and part of me just wanted to cling to him and cry my eyes out.

But they needed me. So I kept going. *Why aren't the ambulances here yet,* I wondered.

Then it hit me. *Oh Jesus: nobody's called it in!* We'd come to rely on people using their cell phones: after any shooting, a whole flood of people would dial 911 within minutes. But the phone lines were down. The hospital had no idea anything had happened.

I grabbed a teenage boy who'd escaped uninjured. "Run to the hospital," I told him. "Ask for Doctor Bartell and tell him we have twenty or more wounded with at least ten criticals. Tell him to send everybody. *Everybody.* You got that?" He nodded and I pushed him away. "*Go!*"

For maybe fifteen minutes, I ran around treating everyone I could, holding the hands of the ones I couldn't. Corrigan still hadn't emerged from the darkness of the cafe. I wanted to check on Earl but Taylor was kneeling over him and there were too many others who needed me. *Is he alive? Dead?*

Vehicles started to arrive, skidding and slipping on the hard-packed snow. We'd used all our ambulances to evacuate patients when the blizzard arrived so Bartell, expert organizer that he was, had begged, borrowed or stolen anything he could: pickups, vans, SUVs, all driven by nurses. Krista led the way in a postal truck.

We got the most urgent patients loaded and I was turning from the truck when Corrigan suddenly appeared in front of me. He looked as if he'd been through a war. Like me, he'd given away his coat and his shirt had been torn to rags: I realized he must have been tearing strips off to use as bandages. His jeans were stained with blood and his eyes had the same haunted look that mine probably did. "Are you—" I began.

He grabbed me, lifted me right off my feet and folded me into his arms. He didn't say anything for a moment, just crushed me to him. I could feel the pain throbbing out of him. We knew we had to go but this couldn't wait. I didn't know what he'd seen in that cafe, maybe I never would. I just knew he needed me to make it okay again, just as I needed him. He buried his lips in my hair and laid a trail of kisses down my scalp, kissing me to make sure I was still real. His chest pressed into me, heaving with emotion. "Sorry," he muttered. "Just...."

I nodded frantically. "I'm the same."

He pushed back from me and cupped my cheek, his hand wonderfully warm against my skin. There was shock in his eyes, even though this sort of hell wasn't new to him. Since he lost his wife he'd been in all sorts of disaster zones and war-torn cities. What was new to him, I realized, was having someone to come back to. A big, hot swell of sympathy hit me. *He's had to go through this so many times on his own....*

He bent down and kissed me, slowly tasting me and then drawing me in. The pleasure and happiness rolled down my body in a slow wave, making all the horror drop back. I put my hand on his arm and I could feel his body relaxing, too.

We allowed ourselves that one, slow kiss and then jumped into the front of the truck with Krista. We'd done what we could here. Now we had to get the injured back to the hospital. My stomach twisted as I saw the convoy of vehicles behind us in the wing mirror. *How are we going to cope with this many patients?* Corrigan was sitting next to me and I squeezed his hand in fear. He nodded: he was thinking the same thing.

The ER was about to be utterly overloaded.

40

AMY

I'VE ALWAYS BEEN SCARED of the ER. But I've always been a little in awe of it and the people who work there, too. It's loud and it's chaotic and things move too fast, but those things are also strengths: I always felt like the ER was crazy enough, fast-moving enough, to cope with anything.

But it couldn't cope with *this*.

When the fourth critical case was wheeled in, you could feel the panic in the air. By the time we'd reached the seventh, the place was in uproar and there were still three more outside. We would have been swamped even *with* our full staff.

What made it worse was the mix of patients. Some of them were gunmen, handcuffed to gurneys. Some were cops, still with loaded guns. Both had seen their friends killed by the other side. Then there were civilians who'd all been shot or injured by one side or the other. Some were crying, some were threatening, everyone was yelling. It was my own personal hell, a crowded, deafening pressure cooker that could explode at any time.

Corrigan caught my gaze from across the room and nodded at me. *You can do this.*

I took a deep breath and kept going.

Within a half hour, though, Taylor, Corrigan and I were all stretched to breaking point. We were trying to take the most urgent cases first, but we had to keep swapping as more patients crashed and threatened to bleed out. We were panting, desperate, trying to hold it all in our heads at once: *this* guy needs to be intubated *now,* this one needs a chest tube, this one's vitals are failing. Even Corrigan started to lose his cool. There were just *too many*—

"The hell with this," said Bartell suddenly. He'd been standing in the center of the room, keeping an eye on things, but now he marched into his office. Through the open door, I saw him wrench off his tie and toss it aside, then pull something out of the bottom drawer of his filing cabinet. When he marched back in, he was shaking out a crumpled, decade-old white coat. We all stood there open-mouthed as he pulled it on.

"I *was* a doctor, you know." He indicated his suit. "Before all this bullshit. Now: what have we got?"

And he pulled on some gloves and started saving lives with the rest of us.

My next patient was Earl. He'd taken two bullets to the chest, one missing his heart by about a millimeter and one nicking a lung. Taylor had done her best to stabilize him in the street, but he'd lost a lot of blood. Maggie was right beside him, her eyes red from crying. There wasn't really room for visitors, but from the look in her eyes, *no one* was going to make her move. Lying handcuffed to a gurney next to Earl was one of the gunmen. He'd only been shot in the leg, but he'd lost more blood and his pressure was dangerously low. "Get another bag of O-neg into both of them," I told Krista.

Lloyd suddenly got in my face. He'd taken some shrapnel in the arm and was walking around the ER hooked up to a drip, jacked up on adrenaline, shock and guilt. "Why are you treating *him?*" he snapped at me, pointing to the gunman.

Corrigan stepped protectively in front of me, hands up to placate him. "We're treating everybody!"

"This is bullshit!" yelled Lloyd.

Krista appeared from behind me and I sighed in relief. I turned to take the bags of blood—

She was only holding one.

I took it but frowned at her. "Thanks, but we need two."

She was white-faced. "That's the last one."

What? I shook my head. "No it isn't. It can't be, we always keep at least ten bags on hand."

Bartell overheard that. He turned from his patient, saw the bag I was holding and looked ill. The whole ER quietened down as he pressed a hand to his forehead and wiped it down his clammy face.

"It's my fault," he said. "We were due a delivery. The truck was on its way from Denver when the blizzard warning came. I completely forgot."

"That's *it?*" I asked in a small voice. "That's our last bag?"

He silently nodded. As administrator, organizing things was his job. He looked not just humiliated but crushed at having overlooked something as basic as blood.

To my amazement, Corrigan stepped up and put a hand on his shoulder. "It's not your fault, mate. None of us are at our best."

Bartell gave him a stern look, unsure if he was being sarcastic, but Corrigan's expression was completely sincere. Bartell nodded and sighed, accepting the olive branch.

"Okay," said Corrigan. "This is what we're going to do. Maggie?" She looked up, still red-eyed. "I need you to go into town and get everybody who's not injured and get them here, now, donating blood." She started to argue but he cut her off, nodding at Earl. "Maggie, this is the best thing you can do for him, okay? I need you to do it because I trust you to get it done."

Maggie blinked uncertainly, then nodded. She planted a kiss on Earl's cheek and marched out into the street.

When I looked round, Corrigan was looking at me. No: *everyone* was looking at me. Corrigan's eyes were full of pity. I didn't understand at first. Then I realized I was still holding the last bag of blood. It would be close to an hour at the earliest before we could get the first donated blood. Both Earl and the gunman needed a transfusion *now*.

Oh crap. What do I do?

Corrigan stepped forward but I put my hand up to stop him. However tempting it was to huddle behind him, Earl was my patient. It was my responsibility. I took a deep breath. "We're giving this bag to him," I told everyone. And nodded at the gunman.

Lloyd muscled forward. *"ARE YOU KIDDING ME?"* He was shaking with anger. He pointed to his mentor and looked around the room for support. "It's *Earl!*"

There was a low rumble of agreement from the rest of the ER. Staff, townsfolk... everyone loved Earl.

Every cell in my body screamed at me to back down. A week before, I would have done. But I stood my ground and looked Lloyd in the eye. "Earl can have the very first bag of donated O-neg we get," I told him. "But this guy needs the blood more."

Lloyd stared at me. I stared right back. I could feel Corrigan's eyes on me, willing me on.

Lloyd dropped his eyes and stalked off, cursing. I let out a long breath and handed the bag of blood to Krista to hook up. "I'm sorry," I told Earl.

He weakly shook his head. "I trust you, doc."

Those four words sent me close to tears. *What if I'm wrong?* What if I just saved some scumbag and killed Earl? Unable to speak, I patted his shoulder.

To my surprise, he gripped my wrist and pulled me close. Corrigan frowned and came over as well.

"I gotta tell you something," said Earl. "In case...."

"You're going to be *just fine!*" I told him sternly, not liking where that thought was going.

"Just in case," he croaked. "Mining company tallied up what Colt and his men stole. Some drills, some jackhammers... and you were right: explosives."

"Did they use them at the bank, to open the vault?" asked Corrigan.

Earl shook his head and pointed to a man in a suit, across the ER. "I talked to the bank manager, when they were bringing us in. They didn't blow the vault door, they drilled it. And they stole *eight crates* of explosives. Enough to put a hole in the world."

All the talking exhausted him. His eyes closed and he passed out, leaving Corrigan and me staring at each other in fear.

The next few hours were a blur. I was way, way, *way* out of my element, right at the center of the chaos. Every few seconds, another patient stopped breathing and needed to be intubated, or they crashed and needed resuscitation. When I *was* doing surgery, it wasn't anything like I was used to. There wasn't time to be careful or neat, or to plan or double-check. I was cutting, clamping and suturing as fast as my fingers would move. Every patient was thirty seconds from death: if I made *one* mistake... it felt like being in a falling elevator, waiting for the impact.

There wasn't time for Corrigan and I to speak but I could feel his eyes on me as we worked. Rooting for me, believing in me, willing me on.

Eventually, the blood started to arrive and that bought us some breathing space. Earl got the first bag and his color started to improve. Maggie ran in to check on him, then ran back to the waiting area to keep the blood drive running. From what I could see, she was doing everything short of physically dragging people out of their homes and squeezing the blood out of them.

Second by agonizing second, we started to claw our way back from the brink. The number of patients crashing slowly fell. First we could think, then we could breathe and, finally, I stepped back from one patient and looked around and there wasn't another one waiting.

My exhausted brain couldn't wrap itself around that concept. There must be *something* I needed to do. I hurried off to see who needed help but, as soon as I took a step, I staggered on legs that had become limp noodles. Strong hands caught me under the arms and a solid, warm chest pressed against my back. Lips brushed my ear, Corrigan's voice a low, silvered rumble I felt as much as heard. "Stop."

I was so wired on adrenaline, I tried to shake him off. But he wrapped his arms around my waist. "*Stop,*" he said again.

I stopped. I let my body flop against him and it was the best thing I'd ever felt: a big, warm, vertical mattress. As soon as I stopped, the tiredness soaked in. My arms hung limp and heavy from my shoulders and my fingers were throbbing and aching from clutching a scalpel. I felt used up and wrung out: I'd never been in such a state of tension for so long. I looked up at the clock. *That must be wrong. It was eight in the morning when the shooting started.* Now it was after three. *Seven hours?!*

"We did it," he told me. "We saved them all. You did *great,* Beckett." He looked at someone behind me. "You too, Taylor."

I turned and saw an exhausted Taylor nod in thanks. Then I closed my eyes and the world became a big, warm, dark bath I could sink into. Corrigan's chest was the most comfortable thing in the world. It occurred to me that I was in the middle of the ER and I wasn't freaking out. It was still busy, still loud, still chaotic, but compared to the last seven hours it felt like a freakin' Japanese meditation garden.

Corrigan gently turned me to face him. Warm fingers tilted my chin up—

I realized at the last second what he was going to do and my eyes flew open. For a second, all my shyness came back. This wasn't like the cafe, this was the hospital, the middle of the freakin' ER, surrounded by people I knew. I wanted to bolt, but his arms were like iron around my waist.

And then his lips met mine. I sort of squeaked, shrinking under him... and then I just melted and opened. There was a deafening hush as everyone stopped working to stare. I swear even a patient who'd been coughing non-stop went silent. Corrigan's hand slid onto my cheek, his fingertips sliding into my hair. My surgical cap tumbled off my head and fell to the floor. There was an undercurrent of raw, sexual need: there always was, with Corrigan. But the kiss just throbbed with love. It poured into me, lifting me up right when I was at my lowest. I went giddy and light: my hands grabbed his shoulders and I clung on as if I was on a roller coaster.

I gulped and panted. Opened my eyes and saw Krista staring at me, open-mouthed. Then she grinned, but she gave Corrigan *the look*. You know the one I mean, the *that's my best friend so you'd better watch it* look. I had a feeling that pretty soon they'd have *the conversation*. I got butterflies. No one had ever had call to have *the conversation* about me before.

When I looked back to Corrigan, he was staring down into my eyes with such helpless, possessive *want,* I swallowed and crushed my thighs together. Those eyes that had once been like a frozen sky had thawed completely, but it meant I could see the pain inside him fighting with the love. The more he felt for me, the more he felt he was cheating on Chrissy and Rachel. *How do I get him to let go?* And then a stab of guilt. *Is it wrong to want that?* I just wanted him to be happy, to be free!

Krista came over: but not for *the conversation*. At least, not yet. "I just checked Rebecca's levels," she said. "The Sorbitol worked. You could do the pyeloplasty... if you want to."

I closed my eyes for a second and felt the room tilt around me. I still had no idea which was the right option: operate and risk Rebecca's life, or play it safe but sentence her to a lifetime on dialysis. What if there was another emergency, while I was operating? What if I messed up? Krista, like Corrigan, was playing it carefully neutral. I understood why but it was maddening. *Someone tell me what to do!* I've never felt so alone.

And then I felt a soft hand take mine. And another, bigger hand take my other hand. I wasn't alone. I opened my eyes and looked at the two of them. They couldn't tell me what to do, but they were there for me.

I drew in a deep breath. I didn't know what I was going to say until I said it.

"Prep her for surgery," I told Krista. "Get Lina and Adele. Let's do this."

41

COLT

O UR CAMP was just that, a half-dozen tents pitched in a clearing, deep in the forest, along with some pickups and the van. We'd put a snow plow on one of the pickups so we could keep the backroads we used clear but we couldn't do anything about the bitter cold. At night, the water would freeze in your canteen if you didn't keep it in your sleeping bag with you. Sleeping on the ground, pissing in a latrine pit...we were living like savages. It hurt. It hurt *bad*. Time was, I'd have been lounging in a fat armchair by the fire with my feet up, a whiskey in my hand and an adoring wife by my side. The land I owned stretched so far, the boundary was out of sight.

They took all that away from me. But I was taking it back.

I bent down next to one of the bags from the bank and opened the zipper. As the light from the snow hit the contents, my face was bathed in a glorious yellow glow. *Fifty. Million.*

I'd rebuild. The CGF would be stronger than ever.

But only if I kept us pure. No dead weight. If someone screwed up, they were done. Mostly, they'd already been punished for their mistakes. Harry had already paid with his life. Max, who'd gotten all that razor wire around his leg, was likely crippled for life but, if he lived, I figured I could find a place for him as quartermaster or something. But there was one more source of weakness.

The other guys were sitting around the fire, desperately trying to keep warm, but I found Seth at the edge of the camp, pale and antsy and gazing down towards the town.

I fingered the knife on my belt and started walking towards him. He was too smart to run. I'd chased him down enough times, when he was a boy, pinned him to a tree and taken my belt to him. But he started to back away, keeping six feet between us.

"You had one job," I told him. "Didn't ask much. Just one thing."

"I never asked to be part of this!"

I frowned at that. 'Course he hadn't had to ask. I'd let him have that honor, something any real man would covet, because he was my blood. "I told you to keep Isaac safe. Nobody else mattered." My voice was loud enough for the other men to hear but I didn't care. They all knew they might have to be sacrificed for the cause. "But instead, you were cozied up to that blonde with the big tits."

"Don't talk about her like that!" It was the first time I'd heard some fire in his voice.

"Is it because she's a doctor? She remind you of that bullshit where you thought *you* were going to be one, and go work for the government? Where you forget where you came from?"

"No! I just—"

I drew the knife and it cut off his words as surely as if I'd sliced them out of the air.

"Isaac," I told him, gliding the blade across my finger to test it, "was the *one person* we needed."

Seth swallowed. "Please—"

"Without our *pilot*," I grated, circling around him, "we can't use the chopper. Without the *chopper*, we have no way out."

He turned to follow me as I circled him. "Sir—"

"I need you to know how disappointed I am." My voice was tight. "My entire plan could fail, because of you. The CGF could *end*, because of you."

"*Dad*—"

I ran at him. I'd been slowly creeping forward as I circled, too gradually for him to notice. He tried to get out of the way, but, too late, he realized I'd tricked him into standing with his back against a tree. There was no place to run. Three quick steps and my knife went *up* and *in*—

Seth cried out in shock and fear.

"Damn you, boy," I muttered. I was pressed right up against him, chest to chest. "Damn you to hell." There were tears in my eyes, at the weakness.

Not his weakness. Mine.

I stepped back. I'd stabbed the knife between his body and his arm, burying the tip of the blade in the frozen wood. It was his eyes. He has his mother's eyes.

I tugged the knife free, turned and walked away. "I got to go fix what you messed up," I said.

His voice was shaky. "The hospital? You're going there? *No!*"

I kept walking. He cursed and ran to catch up.

42

DOMINIC

IT DOESN'T MATTER which hospital you're in or even which country you're in: worried people look the same. Mothers and fathers. Sisters and brothers. Sons and daughters—that's always tough. They cry and they pray and they drink too much coffee as they wait for news. But most of all, they pace. I must have watched a thousand people pace.

I'd never been the one doing the pacing, before.

The surgery had started four hours ago and I was as worried about Beckett as I was about Rebecca. If it went wrong, if the kid didn't make it, Beckett was never going to forgive herself. I could tell, just from watching them together, how much she liked Rebecca. She'd make a great mom. There was a part of me that was already imagining some idyllic existence with me and her and, someday, kids. But then the memory would slam into me. That night. The dark house. *So much blood.*

How could you? How could I feel this way about someone who wasn't *them?* And it was getting harder. I felt like a swimmer clawing for the surface, the memory dragging me down by the ankles and the future just out of reach, bright and glorious above the surface. The more I fell for Beckett, the harder my past dragged me away from her. I either had to break free and be with her or let her go and sink down into the darkness forever. Right now, though, I just wanted her to be okay.

She emerged from the OR. "How is she?" I demanded. She was still in gloves and mask so I grabbed her wrists instead of her hands. "How did it go? Is she okay? Are you okay? Talk to me!"

She was saying something, but it was muffled.

"What?" I asked, heart pounding.

"Let me take my mask off!"

Oh. I let go of her wrists, chastened. *Too much coffee.*

She pulled down her mask. "It went well."

I knew by now how much of a perfectionist she was. If Beckett said it went well, the surgery must have been a work of art. I picked her up and hugged her.

"I've got her on a ventilator for now," said Beckett into my shoulder. "But she should be able to come off it in a couple of days."

I gently pushed her back so that I could look at her. Both of us were drunk with relief. The ER was under control, Rebecca was okay... *we made it.* I leaned down and kissed her. Soft and sweet at first, exploring her lips as I breathed in her scent, my hands sliding down her back to her rump. Then it turned hot and dirty as I squeezed her there, our mouths open and frantic, panting—

We broke as Krista, Adele and Lina emerged from the OR, pushing the sleeping Rebecca and her portable ventilator on a gurney. They were heading down to the ER but there wasn't space in the elevator for us, too, so we let them go ahead. Krista winked at Beckett as the doors closed.

I realized it was dark outside. The operation had taken the whole afternoon and it was past seven. "Come on," I told Beckett. "We need to get you something to eat. You haven't stopped since breakfast. And I want to check on Taylor, too." The poor kid was just a student, but she'd seen more in one day than most doctors see in a lifetime.

I couldn't be bothered to wait for the elevator to come back up so we took the stairs, holding hands the whole way down. Both of us were exhausted. Maybe, if it stayed quiet, we could grab a few hours' sleep in a spare room. And before we slept....

I was still thinking about sex when we emerged into the ER. The silence should have been a warning, but it was only when I heard a rifle being cocked that I pulled up short. As my eyes adjusted to the gloom of the hallway, I saw Colt in the shadows and Seth beside him. Both had guns trained on us.

"We're here for our man," said Colt, his voice a low rasp.

I pushed Beckett behind me, but I knew it wouldn't do much good. Colt was carrying an assault rifle and I'd seen its power that morning. The bullets would go right through me and hit her.

I glanced around. We were in a quiet hallway near the back of the ER, thankfully away from the patients. Colt and Seth must have slipped in through an unlocked door at the rear. There were three staff nearby, all standing with their hands raised, silent and terrified. My heart nearly stopped when I saw that one of them was Taylor. We'd strolled right into a hostage situation.

"You can take your guy," I told Colt. The fear made the Irish come out strong in my voice: my stomach was churning, thinking what one of those high-powered bullets could do to Beckett, or Taylor, or one of the patients. "Just put the gun down and I'll take you right to him."

Colt walked towards me. He didn't swagger, didn't try to prove he was a big man. There was no wasted movement at all: everything about this man was pared down to the bone. He didn't stop until the muzzle of his gun was an inch from my cheek. "How about you take me right to him,' he countered, "and then maybe I'll put my gun down."

I smelled gun oil and burnt powder. I've had guns pointed at me a few times, by gang members in LA and militia in Africa. But those guys—little more than kids, usually—were always fired up on adrenaline. Most of the time they were as scared as you were. Colt was different. There was no fear at all in his eyes: twenty years in jail had burned it all away and now he had nothing more to lose. His anger was still there, but time had hardened and sharpened it into a vicious weapon. No fear, plenty of anger. This guy actually would shoot. *We have to get him out of here.*

And then, to my horror, Taylor gave a choking sob of disbelief. An intake of breath as she prepared to speak— *No, Taylor! Don't!*

"How can you be a part of this?" she asked Seth.

Colt swung smoothly around to point the gun right at her face. Behind me, Beckett caught her breath in fear and grabbed my shoulders. Taylor went stock-still.

"You got some advice on how my son should live his life?" Colt asked Taylor.

I thought about trying to grab the gun but Colt could easily pull the trigger before I got it off him. Seth was standing in the perfect position, behind his dad. But he wasn't going to rebel against him: too scared or too loyal, or both. "Sir!" he said desperately.

Colt ignored him. He pushed the muzzle of the gun against Taylor's lips. "You think you're going to tempt him away from me?"

Taylor didn't move. Tears were filling her eyes. Seth's breathing changed, becoming quick and labored. He had his gun pointed at me, but the barrel started to tremble as his anger built. *Taylor.* The one thing that could override his fear of his father. But if it turned into a gunfight between them, we could all die.

Colt pried Taylor's lips apart with the muzzle. She had her teeth firmly locked together, but he didn't try to open them. He just slid the muzzle along them and the hallway was so silent, we could all hear it, *chink chink chink.* Beckett's fingers dug into my shoulders and I heard one of the hostages offer up a prayer.

"Dad!" snapped Seth.

Colt twisted his head around, surprised. He frowned, then looked at his son with a strange mixture of pride and disgust. His gun was still pressed against Taylor's mouth and his finger caressed the trigger once, twice....

He jerked the gun out from between her lips and pointed it at me. "Take me to him," he ordered.

We moved as a group, Colt's gun against the back of my head. This was getting worse and worse: we were entering the main part of the ER, now, crammed with staff and patients. I've treated shooting victims enough times to know that the worst place in the world for a gun to be fired is somewhere like this: a place with no solid walls, just curtains and partitions. The bullets would just keep going, taking lives until they finally hit something that stopped them.

Luckily, it was evening. The lights in the rear part of the ER were turned down low and most of the patients were dozing, so we crept through pretty much unnoticed. The patients who woke stared at the guns in fear, but I put a finger to my lips. I knew there were still cops hanging around the hospital and I didn't want anyone to raise the alarm and fetch one or this would turn into a firefight.

We had three of Colt's men in the ER, all of them handcuffed to gurneys. But Colt pushed me straight past the two with bullet wounds and only stopped when we reached the man in the tan jacket I'd seen Seth protecting. He had bandages wrapped around the upper part of his head. "What's the matter with him?" demanded Colt.

The man snapped to attention and tried to blindly find the source of the voice. "Colt?"

"He was right next to the car when it exploded," I said. "A few burns to the face, some burns to the corneas."

"You saying he's blind?" The muzzle of Colt's gun rubbed impatiently at the base of my scalp.

"No. The burns are only light. The bandages can come off in another day."

"Get him out of those handcuffs. I'm taking him with me."

I nodded. I just wanted Colt out of the ER.

But at that second, a yell broke the quiet. "*Freeze!*" All of us whipped around. *Shit!* It was Lloyd. He was standing there, gun drawn. Tired and strung out and worried about Earl and staring straight at the guy who shot him.

"*No!*" I yelled. I put my hands up, pleading. "*Wait!* We can do this peacefully. They're leaving!" My heart was hammering against my ribs. *Beckett. Taylor.* Two nurses and me. All of us were between Lloyd and Colt, right in the firing line. And all around us were patients and other staff. *Shit. Shit, shit, shit.*

"Put your gun down!" yelled Lloyd. He was silhouetted by the moonlight coming in through the windows and I could see his finger tensed on the trigger.

Colt's gun stayed rock-steady against the back of my head. Out of the corner of my eye, I could see Seth slowly raising his gun to protect his father. "No!" I yelled. "We can't have any shooting in h—"

I think Lloyd fired first, when he saw Seth raise his gun. Then Colt's gun was jerked away from my head and he was firing, too. Time slowed down. It seemed to take an eternity for me to reach Beckett and tackle her to the floor, covering her body with mine. Colt was standing right over us, the spent shell casings falling like rain, the detonation of each shot slamming painfully into our eardrums.

Seth had his gun raised, ready to support his dad, but when he saw Taylor still standing, he grabbed her around the waist and pulled her to the floor.

Another cop heard the shots and ran to join Lloyd. More bullets slashed through the air above us, some so close I could feel the wind as they passed. I crushed Beckett to the tiles as hard as I could, that soft copper hair against my lips, the scent of her and feel of her filling my senses.

And that's when I knew. The thought of her being snatched away from me scared me more than anything I'd ever known. *I had to be with her.*

In my mind, I hugged Chrissy and Rachel as hard as I could...and then I finally let them slip away.

For a second, I thought we'd be ripped apart. That's what I'd been scared of, this whole time, that if I let them go, they'd be *gone*, whipped away from me and lost in the blackness. But they just floated there, close enough for my fingertips to brush theirs. They weren't going anywhere. But now I could rise up, grab hold of Beckett —I drew in a long, shuddering breath—and be *free.*

It felt amazing. Tears were welling up behind my closed lids. I pressed myself to Beckett as tight as possible. *Why did I wait so long?* Colt's assault rifle roared again, bullets slashing mercilessly through the air above us. *What if I never get to tell her?*

A scream, from behind Lloyd. I opened my eyes and saw one of the nurses stagger and fall as a bullet clipped her leg. I looked beyond her and realized with a sickening lurch that the cops were standing in front of the exam area, where the rooms only have curtains for fronts. And Colt had backed up against the patient area. "*Stop!*" I yelled. But my voice was lost under the gunfire.

Colt grunted as one of the cops hit him in the leg. He fell to one knee, slapped a new magazine into his gun—

"*No!*" I yelled.

Colt sprayed the whole area around the cops with bullets. The cops ran for cover and I saw the curtains twitch and flap as bullets slashed straight through the exam rooms. Then the cops returned fire and I heard shots go right past Colt and into the patient bed area. *Oh Jesus.* It was Main Street all over again but ten times worse: this was our home, this was where we lived. Everyone in the firing line was either someone I worked with or a patient who was already critical. God, *Rebecca* was in one of those beds!

Colt stopped to change magazine again, snarling at Seth to cover him. But Seth was still shielding Taylor with his body. The cops pushed forward and Colt finally had to break and run, heading for the stairwell. One cop gave chase. Lloyd tore Seth away from Taylor, slammed him to the floor and handcuffed him. Taylor half-sat up and stared at him, her eyes brimming with tears. Seth didn't resist, just stared at the floor.

I scrambled to my feet and checked Beckett, but neither of us were hurt. I clutched her to my chest in relief. "Somebody turn the lights on!" I yelled.

The cop chasing Colt yelled to Lloyd, "He's heading for the basement! I'm going after him!" Lloyd raced to join him and they disappeared down the stairs.

The lights flickered on, painfully bright after the darkness. After the deafening gunfire, it seemed weirdly quiet. Then, as my ears recovered, I started to hear the sobbing, the whimpers of pain. God, there were bullet holes everywhere. "Who got shot?" I yelled, looking frantically around. "*Who got shot?!*"

43

COLT

EACH STAGGERING STEP down the concrete stairs sent a bolt of white-hot pain up my thigh. Blood was pumping steadily through my pants: moving was making it worse.

But the cops were right on my ass. And I wasn't going to get caught, not when I was this close. I owed it to my wife. The CGF was our family's legacy.

Our family. I still couldn't believe the fire I'd seen in Seth's eyes when I'd threatened to shoot his little blonde doctor. He'd finally stood up to me: I was almost proud. It meant the blonde was dangerous, of course. I should have killed her there and then. But I'd been weak. I couldn't do it to him. I knew what it was like to lose someone you were crazy about. Deborah made me feel the exact same way, from the day we met right up until the end.

Deborah. Thanks to the government, she'd died alone while I rotted in a cage, unable to hold her.

They'd pay.

I gritted my teeth and struggled on down the stairs. The basement throbbed with the sound of a generator. There were drums of spare fuel and, at the far end, a gate that led through to the basement parking garage and freedom.

Footsteps pounded down the steps behind me. The cops. They'd cut me down before I was halfway across the parking garage.

I unscrewed the cap on one of the drums of fuel and heaved it over. Fuel glugged and spread over the concrete floor, sloshing up around the remaining drums. I fired two shots at the ground just as the cops arrived. On the second one, I saw a spark and then the spilled fuel erupted into flames. The cops dodged back, cursing, their way blocked. And I ran.

I'd failed to get our pilot back. Now I needed to get him *and* Seth. But I had a plan.

That red-headed surgeon...she was going to help me fix everything.

44

AMY

T HE FIRST PERSON I checked was Rebecca. She was okay, thank God. But as we raced around checking each room, we found more and more injured. A man who'd been brought in earlier in the day, injured by flying glass, had been hit in the stomach by a stray round that cut straight through Exam One and Exam Three before hitting him in Exam Five. We were lucky the other exam rooms had been empty.

One of the bar staff from Krüger's Tavern, who'd only come to the ER to donate blood and then had volunteered to stay and comfort the injured, had been hit in the arm. The bullet had gone straight through and she'd be okay but she was white-faced and shaking. *What did I do wrong,* her eyes asked me. *I was only trying to help.*

Of the staff, one nurse had been shot in the leg and another was unconscious after a bullet had grazed her temple: if she'd been standing even an inch to her left, she'd be dead. It was terrifying: all this from one gun battle that had lasted less than a minute. Lina and Adele had been in the ER but they were both okay. "Find Krista," I begged Lina. "We need her."

Lloyd returned from the basement. *Colt must have gotten away,* I realized in despair. He looked around wide-eyed at the disaster he'd helped wreak. "I was just—Oh God, I was just trying to—" He looked at me. "I'm sorry."

I nodded. "It's okay. Just help us." And I put him to work fetching supplies.

Corrigan and I worked frantically to save the guy who'd been hit in the stomach. I could feel him looking at me and, whenever I glanced up, the look in his eyes took my breath away. Something had changed. He was bursting, desperate to tell me something and my chest kept switching between light and fluttery and cold and dark as I thought about what it might be. When we finally finished and stabilized the guy, he suddenly grabbed my wrist. Opened his mouth to speak—

"*How could you?*" yelled Taylor behind me.

I squeezed Corrigan's hand. *Later.* Then I spun around to look. Taylor had been working on the nurse who'd been shot in the leg, desperately trying to save as much of the muscle as she could, and now she'd finally lost it and was railing at Seth, who was sitting handcuffed on the floor. "These are my *friends!*"

Seth stared at the floor. From the utter misery on his face, he was as horrified by the devastation as she was, and being torn apart by guilt from his part in all this.

"Look at me!" she snapped, tears in her eyes.

Corrigan patted her on the back and then walked over to Seth and hoisted him to his feet by the collar, then slammed him against the wall. Seth kept his eyes on the floor. "Time you told us what the *fuck* is going on." His voice was low and dangerously cold. "We've got a whole ER full of injuries because of your dad. There are people lying dead tonight because of your dad. The only reason I'm not pounding your head against the wall right now is because you saved her—"—he jerked his thumb at Taylor—"—*twice.*"

Seth finally lifted his head and looked at Taylor. I've never known anyone look so utterly trapped. "Why do you follow him?" I blurted.

Seth kept his eyes on Taylor but he answered my question. "Because he's my dad," he said hopelessly.

I thought back to what Earl had told us about Colt's life. His wife had died while he was in jail. So not only had Seth grown up without a dad from...what, the age of seven? He'd also had to go through losing his mom, all on his own. For twenty years, all he'd heard from his dad's far-right buddies was how his dad was this legendary figure, practically a folk hero. When his dad finally got out of jail and asked for his loyalty, of course Seth had grabbed at that last chance to be a family. I thought about how much I loved my dad. Wouldn't I have done the same?

"Just tell us what's going on," I said more gently. "What were you stealing?"

I wasn't expecting him to give me a straight answer. But Taylor's tear-filled eyes did what no amount of threats from Corrigan could have. Seth finally weakened. "Gold," he said.

"*What?*" It was ridiculous. Gold? In our tiny bank?

Seth let out a long sigh. "Back in the Eighties, the government wanted to make sure they still had cash reserves after a Soviet nuclear attack. So they hid stashes of gold bullion in remote locations around the country. Fifty million per location. No one is meant to know where they are. Not even the bank managers. They tell the bank it's part of some Federal program to reinforce their vault, get them to close for a weekend, dig up the vault floor and bury the gold underneath."

"How did your dad know the gold was there?" asked Corrigan.

"One of the construction workers who hid the gold was sent to jail," said Seth. "Became friends with my dad. And eventually, he talked."

Suddenly, it all made sense. That's why they'd broken into the mining company: drills to get into the vault, jackhammers to dig up the floor. But: "What are the explosives for?"

Seth looked at me, his face blank. "What explosives?"

I exchanged looks with Corrigan. Whatever they were for, Colt hadn't shared that part with his son.

"And him?" asked Corrigan, pointing at the guy in the tan jacket. "Why is he so important?"

"He's a helicopter pilot," said Seth. "He was meant to fly us out of here."

It was a near-perfect crime. With the phone lines down and the cell tower destroyed, Colt and his men would be long gone before the state police even heard about the robbery. And with fifty million dollars, Colt could build a far-right militia that went far beyond Colorado. The thought of that man in control of an army made me want to throw up.

Corrigan drew me close. "It'll be okay," he said. He lowered his voice so that Seth couldn't hear him. "Colt and his men didn't even wear masks. We know who they are! Even if they do escape, the FBI will hunt them down. Colt is going back to jail."

I nodded again but...something didn't feel right. Colt was smart. Why had he and his men been so careless, these last few days, when they could have easily hidden their faces?

Corrigan pulled me into a hug. "We got lucky," he said firmly. "Everyone's going to be okay. For four gunshot wounds, that's pretty amazing." He looked at Taylor, worried. "How are you holding up?"

Taylor took a deep breath. The poor girl was too emotionally worn out to speak, but she bravely gave him a thumbs-up.

Corrigan took my hands in his and pulled me close. "I need to talk to you," he told me. I'd never heard his voice so solemn. But there was a thread of tension there, too: God, yes, he really *needed* to talk to me. I nodded and looked around for somewhere private. "Let's go—"

"Can someone get me some more gauze?" asked Adele, turning from a patient. "Got my hands full."

"I'll get it," I said. I made an apologetic face at Corrigan. He nodded, but kept hold of my hands and only reluctantly let them go when our arms were at full extension.

Normally it would be a nurse's job to run back and forth with supplies, but we were way beyond titles and stations now: everyone was helping out. I was a long, long way from my cozy burrow of the OR...but for the first time, I felt as if I was part of a team.

I pushed open the door to the supply room and stopped dead in my tracks. There were two bullet holes in the wall. Krista was lying on the floor, two bullet wounds in her chest and a lake of blood on the floor around her.

I fell to my knees beside her. *"HELP! SOMEBODY HELP ME!"*

45

AMY

"GET THE crash cart!" I yelled. I was kneeling astride Krista on a gurney, desperately pumping her chest as Corrigan pushed us full speed down the hallway. I was yelling orders at nurses as we passed them. "All the blood you have! She's B negative!" I knew her blood group because we'd both donated blood at the same session, the first week I'd arrived in Mount Mercy. And then she'd taken me to Krüger's and I'd got wasted on two tequila shots because the blood loss made me even more of a lightweight than normal and she'd helped me home and—

Krista!

We crashed through the door into the ER and Corrigan started to slow down but I shook my head. "No, her heart's damaged! I need her upstairs in the OR, now!"

"We have to get her breathing first—"

I lost it. "Goddamn it, Dominic, don't argue with me!" Tears were running down my face. "She has *one chance* and that's to get her on bypass *right now* while I fix her heart!"

He looked me in the eye...and nodded. "Okay. You're the surgeon." And he pushed us towards the elevator.

"Lina! Adele! I need you too!" I yelled. They ran into the elevator with us, loaded with blood bags and pulling the crash cart.

The elevator doors started to close. I kept the chest compressions going, my hands slick with my best friend's blood.

The elevator doors stopped, still a foot open. Bartell stood there, his arm blocking the door. "*What are you doing?*" I screamed, almost hysterical. "We have to get her upstairs!"

"There's a fire." He was pale-faced and sweating.

"*What?!*"

"It started with the generator fuel in the basement: Colt started it to cover his escape. We thought we could put it out with extinguishers but it's spreading. Firefighters are on their way but we have to evacuate the hospital."

I shook my head. He opened his mouth to argue. "I don't operate on her *right now,* she dies!" I snapped tearfully. "Get everyone else out. We're going upstairs." I glanced around at the others but they all nodded: they were with me.

Bartell sighed, nodded and withdrew his arm.

Upstairs, we rushed Krista into the OR and scrambled to get her onto a heart bypass machine and a ventilator. "Gown up," I told Corrigan. "I need you to assist."

"I never—" he began.

"I'll tell you what to do."

And we went to work. But when I opened her up, I felt sick. She was a mess. The first bullet had clipped her heart, but at least it had passed straight through. The second one had hit a rib, spraying bone fragments into her organs, and then tumbled through her body, tearing into a lung and slicing an artery. I saw injuries every day, but this was brutal. "I don't know if I can fix this," I said, my voice going tight and quavery. "There's too much damage. It's—" Tears filled my eyes. I couldn't focus. I could barely think. This was my *friend!* She should be standing next to me, assisting, not lying on the table all—all—

"Hey," said Corrigan from behind his surgical mask.

I looked up at him.

You can't touch, when you're in surgery. Your gloved hands have to remain sterile. So he couldn't wrap me up in his arms or put his lips next to my ear. He couldn't smooth his hand down my back to calm me or put his finger under my chin to keep me looking at him. He could only look me in the eye. But it felt as if he was doing all those things.

"She has you," he said. "And you're the best."

And I believed it because he believed it. I blinked back the tears, swallowed... and *focused.*

And slowly, agonizingly, the wreckage of Krista's body began to make sense. I started to see places where, if I was careful and delicate enough, I could maybe begin to piece things back together. I took a deep breath... and began.

Corrigan stood right next to me, holding clamps and suctioning away blood when I asked him to. His hands were huge next to mine. Not clumsy, just *big,* and with so much strength: he was like a giant trying to pick up a Fabergé egg. And he couldn't get out of the ER mindset of frantic patch-it-and-pray. That works when you're trying to open airways and restart hearts, but it's disastrous when you're repairing delicate organs. "Slow," I said gently. "Slow and easy."

"But—" he nodded at the clock. We could only keep Krista on bypass for so long.

"You have to not let it faze you," I told him. "Don't take your time. But take as much time as it needs."

He nodded and tried. I loved that he tried. I knew how hard it was, to be totally out of your comfort zone.

Twenty minutes in, I thought I smelled something, but pushed the thought away. A few minutes later, I heard Lina sniff. She looked up at me, worried.

"Okay," I said carefully. "That's smoke." As soon as I acknowledged it, I felt my heart start to race.

"How are we doing?" asked Corrigan, his voice calm but strained.

"Halfway there."

We kept working. After another five minutes, I started to notice my hands were sweating under my gloves. Corrigan's forehead was glistening. The room was warming up.

The door suddenly crashed open and a cloud of smoke rolled in. A firefighter emerged from it. "Out!" he ordered, holding the door and pointing to the hallway.

I looked at the smoke and fought down the rising panic. *The hospital is on fire.* My safe little sanctuary was being destroyed. I shook my head. "We're not leaving."

He frowned at me, then stepped inside, letting the door swing shut. "Don't argue with me, we got gas lines and oxygen cylinders and all sorts of shit on this floor. The whole place could go up."

I kept working. "Your job is to save lives?" He nodded. "Well, so's mine. And she's going to die if I don't keep going."

The firefighter glared at me, then looked down at Krista's face. He had gray eyes and thick, black hair and was quite good looking, if you liked the rough look.

"You go and do what you need to do," I told him. "But I'm not leaving her."

He looked at me, looked at Krista again...and then nodded and left. More smoke and scalding hot air rolled in before the door swung closed, gathering in clouds near the ceiling. I coughed. "I can manage on my own," I told the others. "You should go."

Lina shook her head, silent and stoic as always. Adele's eyes were huge and scared, but she shook her head, too. I looked at Corrigan.

He frowned at me disbelievingly. Then he slowly shook his head. "You really don't get it at all, do you, Beckett?" he asked. And those blue eyes fixed me with such a look of deep, aching love that my chest went tight.

I pressed on. The room was getting hotter, now. Adele stuffed some sheets under the bottom of the door, but the smoke got thicker and thicker: it was becoming difficult to breathe. Outside, we could hear heavy boots and the hiss of hoses, shouted orders and—wait, was that... was the fire close enough that I could hear its roar, or was it just my imagination?

If I'd been the person I was a week ago, there's no way I could have kept working. But all that time in the ER had taught me to shut things out. I worked on, Corrigan dabbing away the sweat as it coursed down my forehead. And finally, just as the smoke became unbearable, I tied off my final suture and we were done. Now the moment of truth: would Krista's heart beat on its own? "Internal paddles," I said, my voice high and tight. Then, "Clear!"

Krista's heart contracted as the current coursed through it. Relaxed... and then grudgingly began to beat on its own. "Attagirl," I breathed, my eyes suddenly full of tears.

The firefighter burst through the door again. His face was grimy with soot and his uniform reeked of smoke. "Thought you'd want to know," he said, "fire's out." He nodded at Krista. "You save her?"

I nodded weakly.

He held up his fist. I blinked at it for a moment, and then mimed fist-bumping him, stopping short so I stayed sterile. *I've never done that before.* It felt good.

I closed Krista up and Lina and Adele took her downstairs to the critical care beds. Apparently, the ER had escaped the fire: the mostly-empty parking garage beneath it had acted as a fire break and the flames had spread outward and upwards instead. The surgical floor had actually come off worst. I stared open-mouthed at the blackened walls right outside the OR. The surgeon's lounge had been destroyed, the fancy coffee machine a melted wreck. "Looks like you'll be joining the rest of us downstairs for a while," said Corrigan.

I slumped against his shoulder. I was utterly exhausted, plus I was a little shell-shocked at seeing my burrow laid to waste. "We should go see if they need our help," I mumbled.

But he shook his head, took me by the hand and marched off along the hallway, towing me behind him. "Bartell is down there organizing everyone. He'll come get us if he needs us."

I had to almost run to keep up. I'd never seen him like this before. He was a man on a mission. "But—"

"No buts." He pulled me into one of the other operating theaters.

The air was fresher and cooler, here, because the door had stayed closed. With the lights off, the only light came from the moon, shining in through the window. He hauled me towards the center of the room and I looked around, confused. "What are we doing in—"

He spun me around and pushed me back until my ass hit the operating table, then put his hands on my shoulders to fix me in place. I opened my mouth to speak again—

"*Beckett!*" He used *that* voice.

I gulped. I could see the emotion in his eyes and it made my stomach flip-flop. God, his whole body had gone tense: his hands were like iron on my shoulders. I remembered how he'd tried to tell me something, just after the shooting. It seemed like a lifetime ago. He'd been desperate to get me alone ever since and now he *had* to tell me....

I shut the hell up and listened.

He rubbed his hand down his face, his stubble rasping. "When I met you, I thought, 'she's hiding. Hiding away up here.'" He laid one hand on my cheek and smoothed it back, knocking off my surgical cap and sliding his fingers into my hair. "'I need to bring her out into the light.'" He shook his head. "I didn't realize *I* was hiding, too. That's what Africa and Libya and working in bad neighborhoods was all about. I was burying myself in it so I didn't have to think or feel. You were the first person to make me want more again. *You* stopped *me* hiding."

My mouth had gone dry and I was taking panicky little breaths. I nodded.

"The more I fell for you—and I *have* fallen for you—"

I bit my lip.

"—The more I thought about Chrissy and Rachel. Felt like I shouldn't be with you." He was struggling to get the words out, now. "Like I was being torn between you and them."

Oh God, no....

His voice slowed right down. "I can't be with you both," he managed.

This is where he does it. This is where he tells me it's over. I couldn't look at him as he said it so I pushed him back, tried to wriggle out from between him and the table.

He frowned and pushed me back into place. "*No!* Listen!"

I listened, my face and eyes going hot.

"I let them go," he said quietly.

I felt my eyes widen. I never meant to hurt him. Had I hurt him?

He understood and shook his head. "I let them go," he said again. And he sounded... peaceful. For the first time, the pain in his eyes was gone.

I drew in a little breath of hope. And then both his hands were buried in my hair and his lips came down on mine.

46

AMY

HIS LIPS PARTED MINE, his thumbs stroking across my cheekbones and tilting my head back to meet him. The kiss was slow and deliberate, loaded with meaning. With every tiny caress of his lips against mine, he let me know: I was his.

His tongue teased over my lips and then plunged deep to own me. I'd never known anyone to be so absolutely certain of anything, so completely *sure* that this was the future they wanted. Corrigan was stubborn as hell and this whole time, that had been holding us apart as he refused to let his family go. But now that he'd made up his mind, that same stubborn, unstoppable intent was all focused on *me*. And it was glorious. My heart lifted and I just melted inside, the hot emotion sluicing down and then rising up as pure joy.

A slow rhythm began that wound all the way down our tightly-pressed bodies, chests grinding and hips circling. I felt the swish of my hair falling free as he removed the clip. He buried both hands in it behind my head and then gently combed his fingers down its length. He kissed across my cheek and into my hair and finally just dug his nose between the soft strands and inhaled. "*Amy,*" he said with his next breath, my name a blast of heat against the top of my head.

When he spoke again, his voice had an ache in it, a neat wound painfully tight. My name, said *that* way, in *that* accent, slid straight down my spine, a shining silver pebble that landed weighty and urgent in my groin. "*God, Amy....*"

I pressed in close to him, suddenly breathless, and explored his chest. I slid my palms over the hard curves of his pecs, feeling his heartbeat through the thin scrubs. His hands were moving, too, tracing down my back to cup and squeeze my ass. My heart was dancing: *he's here. It's real. We're together.* And along with that light, heady excitement, there was another kind, dark and heated, vibrating down my body in dense waves, making me crush my thighs together and press myself even harder against him. The feel of him, the scent of him, had a physical effect on me: I could actually feel my eyes go big and start to dart around and hear my breath going trembly. That part of me I kept locked down deep, that I only let out when I was alone in bed, safely secret under the covers? Dominic Corrigan brought it bursting right up to the surface.

I was obsessed. I wanted to lose myself in this man, to throw myself right into the very center of some green, ancient land that smelled of wet rock and crisp air and disappear into him forever. My hands wouldn't stop moving: I wanted to grab as much of him as possible, wanted to fill my senses with him. My fingers slid over his sides, thumbs riding the hard ridges of his abs—

That did it. That unleashed him. He gave a kind of growl, grabbed my waist and lifted me right off my feet. He molded me to him, those big hands tight on my ass, as his lips found mine in breathless, frantic hunger. I wrapped my legs around him, my breasts pillowing against his chest. He marched us across the room like that. Each step made me lift and bounce, stroking my clit against the hardness of his six-pack. One of my outstretched feet caught an equipment trolley and I felt it tip, then heard the crash as hardware scattered across the floor.

A second later, he reached the counter he'd been heading for and swept it clear so that he could perch me on the edge. Kidney bowls clattered to the floor but I didn't care. With his hands freed, Corrigan rammed my scrub top up to my neck, flipped up the cups of my bra and began to roll and squeeze my breasts, his thumbs stroking over my nipples. My yell of shock and pleasure drowned out the metal ringing as the bowls rolled across the tiles.

"Christ, you're beautiful," he muttered. He barely broke the kiss to speak, as if he couldn't bear to stop kissing me. He kept his lips so close, I could feel every hot breath and the *b*s and *f*s made little feather-light kisses that drove me absolutely crazy. He squeezed my breasts in a slow, insistent rhythm. "Right from the first time I saw you," he told me, "I wanted to kiss you. Wanted to fuck you. And I won't ever, ever stop."

The words were pure molten silver, burning into my brain and making me groan and lock my ankles around his calves, pulling him harder against me. All the barriers between us were finally gone and I wanted him like I've never wanted anything or anyone, a soul-deep ache that I had to satisfy *now*. I grabbed the hem of his scrub top and pulled it up his chest and off. The few seconds where his arms were trapped and we couldn't touch each other felt like an eternity. When he hurled it aside and grabbed me again, both of us sighed out loud in relief.

He devoured me with frantic, open-mouthed kisses that started on my hungry lips and worked down my neck and between my breasts. My hands went wild on his shoulders, his pecs and his back, delighting in the feel of him: solid, heavy muscle beneath smooth skin. He was panting, I was panting. The more I touched him, the more he touched me and the more out of control we both got.

He grabbed the hem of my scrub pants in one fist, bunching it up, and *pulled*. The pants dragged down around my hips, then whipped down around my ankles and off as I lifted my ass. It was only when I felt the cold counter under me that I realized my panties were gone, too.

He kissed down the length of me, from throat all the way to groin. As he crouched, I felt his hot breath in the soft hairs there, felt his rising excitement as quickening rushes of air against my damp folds.

And then he stopped. Just for a second. As he stood up, his whole body was rigid with tension, his breathing ragged. He was *just barely* holding himself back: I could see how much he wanted to grab me, fuck me. But first—

"Let me look at you," he ordered in a throaty Irish growl. And he nudged my knees apart and moved between them, then stood there and just *looked.*

His gaze stroked all the way down my body, from the copper hair on my scalp all the way down to the soft copper hair between my thighs, each square millimeter of skin throbbing and aching in its wake. I'd never been looked at that way before, not with such utter devotion, such complete lust. He reached out with one hand and gently glided his palm over my breast, making me gasp. His touch was worshipful, as if he couldn't believe he finally had me. "You're the center of my fucking world, Beckett," he growled. "All that exists."

I tried to say that I felt the same, but I was choking up. I'd never thought anyone would feel that way about me. I grabbed his bicep and squeezed and nodded instead. He looked into my eyes and nodded back. He knew.

He slid a hand down between us, still slow and reverent. A thick finger parted my folds and pushed up inside me. He watched me, eyes hooded with lust, as he found my clit and brushed his thumb across it—

I groaned, mouth opening wide, and squeezed my thighs around his hand, twisting around his finger—

And that sent him over the edge. He couldn't wait any longer. He scooped both hands under my ass and lifted me again, marching me over to the padded table in the center of the room and laying me down on it on my back. He hooked his muscled arms under my knees and with one tug pulled me towards him, so that my groin was right at the edge. *Oh God, he's going to—Right here, on the table—*

He shoved down his scrub pants and boxer shorts. His cock sprang out, straining and ready, and he rolled on a condom. He stepped between my dangling legs and I gasped as the head brushed my wet folds....

And then he was in me. Fast at first, rushing into me, and I sucked in my breath and arched my back at the wonderful, silken friction of him. Then he slowed, but kept going, grabbing my hips and pinning me in place as he sank deeper and deeper, my eyes widening and my back arching as he filled me completely.

He leaned down and we kissed, open-mouthed and panting. His hands sought out mine and he pressed them down to the table above my head, his sculpted forearms like tree trunks. He knitted his fingers with mine, possessive but gentle. And then he began to move.

I groaned at how good it was, at the glorious hot stretch as he filled me, at the needful ache as he left me again. The moonlight coming through the window lit up his body, each hard slab of muscle edged in silver. He loomed over me: that broad chest and powerful back, narrowing down to that tight, powerful core and the hard ass that let him lunge into me again and again—

I caught my breath and bit my lip as the pleasure started to build, a swirling, violet hurricane that wound tighter and tighter, faster and faster. My fingers squeezed his in time with his thrusts, my hips beginning to rock and twist around him. He growled at how that felt and picked up the pace, moving mercilessly faster and faster, pounding at me until I had to squeeze my eyes tight shut, everything gone except the pleasure, coiled so tight and so hot inside me that I thought I'd explode. I began to cry out with each thrust, high little cries that didn't sound like me. I was panting and gasping, my hair sticking to my damp forehead. My legs scissored around him, heels climbing his back. God, I was out of control! And it felt *great.*

"Jesus, woman," he muttered. The more turned on he was, the stronger the Irish got in his voice and right now it was stronger than I'd ever heard it. "You're incredible. You drive me fucking mad."

Me? I did that to him? I was close, now, the climax thundering towards me.

I sensed him leaning down, felt the heat of his breath on my lips and then he was kissing me, hard, staccato little kisses on my panting lips that drove me absolutely crazy. Then his head moved lower and —*Oh Jesus!* He started doing the same thing to my nipples, catching each one with a quick little swipe of his tongue as his cock hammered into me faster and faster. His words came out as hot little rushes of air against the shining, sensitive flesh. "Beckett," he rasped, "I'm keeping you forever."

That did it. I cried out, my back arched and my head pressed into the softness of the padded table. My thighs crushed tight around his waist, but even that friction couldn't stop him: he kept slamming into me, each hard thrust lifting the pleasure higher. I squeezed his fingers so hard it must have hurt and came with a long, keening scream that they must have heard down in the Emergency Room. I spasmed and shuddered around him and then felt the heat of his own release. At last, I slumped back against the table, panting.

He leaned down over me, panting as well...and chuckling. He had a huge grin on his face and it was the most open, the most relaxed, I'd ever seen him. It was infectious: within seconds, I was giggling, too. And then he leaned even lower, wrapped his arms around me and kissed me.

When we'd dressed and turned the lights on, I insisted on clearing up the mess we'd made. The floor was littered with kidney bowls, instruments and boxes of drugs and, as we picked them up, I put them back in their proper places, lining everything up *just-so*.

"I swear," he muttered, "you enjoy the tidying more than the sex."

I was down on my hands and knees, trying to reach the last kidney bowl, so I whacked him playfully on the leg. The truth was, I was feeling a lot *less* obsessed with order. A little chaos had done me good. And I'd never look at an operating table the same way again. I took his offered hand and he hauled me to my feet, pulling me up as if I weighed nothing.

And then he just stood there, my hand clasped in his, staring down at me. "What?" I asked quietly.

He closed his eyes and sighed. When he opened them again, the pain I saw there made my chest ache. But it was different, now. He wasn't burying the pain any longer, hiding it away behind cocky arrogance. He was open.

He was ready.

"It was my fault," he said.

And he told me about the night he lost everything.

47

DOMINIC

WE SAT SIDE BY SIDE on the operating table and I stared at the shadow we cast on the wall, my big form next to her much smaller one. I spoke mechanically, trying to reduce everything to simple facts that wouldn't hurt. But each piece of memory was a razor-edged slice of that night that felt like it was cutting my throat. "We were living in Chicago. I was a resident at a hospital, Chrissy was a kindergarten teacher. Rachel was six, obsessed with ballet. I'd just finished my shift, called Chrissy to tell her I was on my way. But then...." The words seemed to thicken and stick to my tongue.

"A trauma came in," said Beckett.

I glanced across at her. She understood me. She understood how I was wired. "A trauma came in," I confirmed. I took a deep breath. "I could have let someone else take it. We weren't that busy. But it was a family. Kids. And...." My throat closed up.

"And you felt like it was your responsibility."

I closed my eyes and nodded. Kept them closed as I told her the next part. I could almost hear the buzz of the ER around me. "I didn't call Chrissy because I knew she'd be pissed. I kept thinking, *five more minutes*. But we couldn't get the mother breathing and one of the kids was bleeding into their chest. By the time I finally got everything sorted, I was an hour late." I swallowed, the glowing scarlet numbers of the ER clock clear in my memory. "Seven fifty-seven," I rasped. "That's what time it was when I ran out the door."

I still had my eyes closed. I felt her hand cover mine, so delicate and graceful next to my big, clumsy paw. It felt cool against the back of my hand, calming me. "When I got home, the house was dark," I said. I was still trying to break it down into the facts, but, as I lifted each one towards the surface, the pain welled up underneath, threatening to rush up and drown me. "I thought maybe Chrissy had taken Rachel out for dinner, but her car was there. I knock: no reply. I unlock the door and call for them. Nothing. Maybe the car wouldn't start and they got a cab. So I—"

I stopped and couldn't start again. It was like I'd hit a wall: my lips refused to form the next word. I could feel my feet sinking into the soft carpet Chrissy had chosen, could feel the wallpaper, smooth under my fingertips as I fumbled my way along the wall. I was *there*. And I couldn't bear to describe what I was feeling.

Then there was a pressure against my side. Beckett was leaning into me, pressing herself tightly against me from her hip all the way up to the top of her head, lending me her strength. And it worked.

"I was already halfway down the hall when it sunk in how dark it was. The light switch was back by the front door and I'm stubborn." I opened my eyes and glanced at her again, trying to lighten things. "You know how stubborn I am." I gave her a weak grin, but she just looked right back at me, caring but serious, determined to help. She wasn't going to let me sidetrack.

I nodded and carried on. "I wasn't going to walk back to the door, so I kept going, heading for the living room. But just as I get to the doorway, my foot hits something and I nearly trip. I think maybe Rachel's left her coat on the floor again, but it's too heavy. And then... and then a car passes by the house." I still had my eyes open, but I could see the scene in my head, could see the white light wash across the carpet and catch the edges of the dark shape. "And I could see it was a body. And I feel along the wall and find the light switch.... *and I can't fucking press it.*" The dark pain I'd been suppressing for years with women and booze and danger swarmed up my body, crushing my chest with its cold. My voice cracked. "I stand there and inside I'm screaming at myself: *get the light on.* But there's a part of me that—that already knows. That saw enough, from the headlights, that it knows who it is on the floor and what I'm going to find."

I swallowed and leaned forward, closing my eyes. "I press the light switch. And I'm staring down at my wife, Chrissy, flat out on the floor." When I drew in my breath, it shuddered. "Blood soaking the carpet around her. She's—" I swallowed again. "Cold."

Beckett's arms slid around my shoulders and she pressed her cheek to my shoulder. She was taking tiny, soft, scared little breaths, terrified for me then and for me now.

"*Now* I get myself moving, I run through the house, switching all the lights on, yelling Rachel's name. I check her bedroom, even check in the closet in case she's hiding there. Nothing. And I start to think, maybe she escaped, or maybe she was at a friend's house when it happened...." I trailed off.

This part was the hardest.

"I'm standing in the kitchen," I tell her. "I'm just about to call the cops when...I see my own reflection in the window. Outside, we had this little back yard and it's pitch black out there. And I realize I haven't checked there yet. And...." The pain had me, now: I was beneath its surface and it was consuming me. "And I...I *prayed.* I hadn't prayed since I was a kid, but I just stood there thinking *please. Please God, not her too. I can't live without them.*" I had to work hard to swallow. "And I hit the switch for the outside light and—she's lying there. In her pajamas. I run outside but she's cold, too. I gather her up in my arms and kneel there, crying, her blood soaking my shirt, until I finally manage to call the cops."

My shoulder felt hot and wet. I realized Beckett had her face pressed up against me there and that her silent tears were soaking through my scrubs. My eyes had gone wet, too.

"Two guys," I managed. "After jewelry and cash. You see—" I had to fight down the nausea and self-hate. "Chrissy opened the door for them because she thought they were me. They got there right when I should have got home."

Beckett lifted her head from my shoulder. I could feel her looking at me but couldn't bear to look at her: I felt too wretched. "Chrissy fought them," I said mechanically. "They killed her. Rachel ran downstairs when she heard her mother scream. Tried to escape out of the back door, but they caught her in the yard. Didn't want to leave any witnesses." I rubbed a hand across my face. "The cops caught them three blocks away. They did it all for a few hundred dollars in cash and a fifty dollar necklace."

I finally looked across at her. She knew, now. She understood why I was how I was.

"If I'd come home—" I started.

Her hand grabbed my chin, a mirror of what I always did to her. She stared up at me, so small next to me, but so fiercely determined. "It was *them*," she told me. "Those two guys. It was no one but them."

I glared at her. I'd been holding on too tightly, for too long, to let go of the guilt now.

But she glared right back at me and gave a little shake of her head. She wasn't giving up on me. And for the first time, I dared to believe that maybe, *maybe* she might be right. Maybe it wasn't my fault. The pain receded a little—it didn't disappear, but it shrank back until it wasn't drowning me. I inhaled... and it felt like the first full breath I'd taken since it happened.

I stared at Beckett. This incredible woman had conquered so much. Now, together, we'd conquered *this*. I wrapped my arms around her and pulled her into my chest. And then I kissed her, losing myself in her warm sweetness. I wasn't kidding myself that I was fixed. But for the first time, there was hope. A future for both of us: I had no idea where but as long as it involved her body pressed against mine in a big, warm bed. "Amy," I said softly—

The lights went out. The air conditioning whirred to a stop. Both of us blinked in surprise. "Are the power lines down again?" I asked.

"The power lines never got fixed," said Beckett, her voice rising in panic. "We've been on the emergency generator this whole time. *That must have failed.*" She looked up at me, her face deathly pale in the moonlight. "Oh Jesus, *the ventilators! Rebecca! There's no power!*"

Both of us scrambled for the door.

48

AMY

I T WAS *BLACK*. The moon kept going behind clouds and sometimes all we could see was the distant glow of a fire exit sign. It didn't help that the floor underfoot was slick with water from the firefighters' hoses. We each slipped and fell as we raced through the dark hallways, grabbing onto the other's hand to hold us up. I don't think we'd have found our way at all if the layout of the hospital hadn't been burned into my mind through years of working there.

No power meant no elevators so we pounded down four flights of stairs. We crashed into the ER and were greeted by an ear-splitting, discordant wail: every ventilator alarm going off at once. Bartell, Taylor and the nurses were running between patients, using their cell phones as flashlights.

Maggie emerged from the door to the basement, her hands held up in front of her to ward off our questions. "Generator's dead," she panted. "Either the fire damaged it or the water from the hoses."

"Can you fix it?!" demanded Bartell.

"Maybe," said Maggie, "But it'll take hours. We need to get another generator. The mining company will have one."

"How long for someone to drive over there, grab one and get back here?" asked Corrigan.

"In this snow?" Bartell shook his head. "Fifty minutes, an hour?"

"How long will the batteries in the ventilators last?" I asked breathlessly.

"Five minutes, tops," said Maggie. "*Shit!*" She sounded close to tears. I grabbed her hand and squeezed. I understood: keeping the hospital systems running was her job and she felt responsible. But no one could have prepared for this.

We all looked around at the patients. We had nine people on ventilators. Jesus, this was unbelievable: this was a US hospital, not some refugee camp, and these people were going to die because we couldn't give them something as basic as electricity. *How did this go so wrong?* My eyes fell on Rebecca and my chest went tight. I was the one who'd demanded we keep the ER open. She could have been evacuated to Colorado Springs. She might have made it—

"It's my fault," I whispered to myself.

Corrigan's hand grabbed mine. I looked up at his moonlit face and he pinned me with his gaze, then sternly shook his head. "We need to bag them," he said firmly. "Breathe for them until the new generator arrives."

"There's not enough people!" said Bartell.

I looked around desperately. He was right: we'd only had a skeleton staff and then the shooting had injured more people. Maggie couldn't help: she'd need to go and get the generator and she'd need someone to go with her to help move it. Out of habit, my mind went to Krista. She knew how to bag someone and she was reliable, so that was one patient taken care of—

My stomach lurched. Krista *was* one of the patients. She'd die along with Rebecca and the others. Even if we could somehow find enough people, the patients were too weak to survive a solid hour of manual ventilation. They needed ventilators. They needed *power.*

An idea came to me. A crazy, last-ditch idea, the sort of thing Corrigan would do. I grabbed his arm. "Get everyone you can find! Get them bagging patients!" I started to run.

Corrigan grabbed my arm. "Wait! Where are you going?" He

pulled me close, his eyes going from me to the darkened hospital. That fierce protective look in his eyes: *I don't want you out there alone.*

I gently pried his hand free. "You have to trust me. I have an idea. Send two people to get a generator, but leave Maggie free, I'll need her!"

Corrigan looked frantically around the ER. Patients. Nurses. A few cops. "Most of these people don't *know* how to bag a patient!"

"Then teach them!" And I ran for the basement.

49

DOMINIC

I T WAS TOTAL CHAOS. The ER was pitch-black save for a few cell phones. People were crying out in pain and calling for help, nurses were trying to run between them without running into each other and the frantic, high-pitched alarms of the ventilators made it impossible to think. The nurses were flustered and panicked. Bartell, even with all his years of experience, was sweating. All of them were used to the twenty-first century, where things like this just didn't happen.

But I wasn't. I'd worked in field hospitals, out under the stars in remote villages in the Congo, where the generators used to pack up all the time. All that time trying to bury my loss had been good for something. "*Alright!*" I bellowed.

People stopped and looked up, startled.

"*You!*" I yelled, pointing at Lloyd. "Do you and the other cops have flashlights in your cars?" He nodded. "Go get them, all of them, and hand them out. Then I want you to drive all the cars up to the doors —"—I pointed—"and shine your headlights in here. Go!"

He ran.

"Everybody else! If you're a cop, if you're a patient, if you're visiting family, if you can walk then I need you over here!"

They looked at each other uncertainly and then started trickling over, stumbling in the darkness. Eventually, I had two cops, one with an injured leg, a guy in his forties who'd been visiting his mother and a woman who'd just barely struggled out of bed, bandages wrapped around her head. I sent the uninjured cop and the visitor to go and get the generator. The others, I gave a crash course in manual ventilation. Before I'd even finished speaking, the first ventilator failed, its alarm changing to a long, continuous tone that faded away as the batteries ran flat. I rushed forward and switched the patient over to a bag, squeezing it in rhythm to force air into his lungs. But the other ventilators would start failing any minute. *Where the hell is Beckett? What's she doing?*

I took a deep breath. She'd said to trust her and I did. I just had to keep these people alive until she came back.

The next ventilator failed. Bartell jumped in and started bagging the patient. But as I counted the beat in my head, I was looking at the dwindling group of people. Two civilians, Lina, Adele, Taylor, Bartell and me. When Lloyd got back, that made eight. There were nine patients. One of them was going to die unless I could find one more volunteer. *Maggie?* Beckett had said she needed her. *Shit!* Who else could I get?

Another ventilator failed. Taylor started bagging. It was freezing in the ER, but I could feel the sweat running down my forehead. *How the hell are we going to choose who dies? The oldest? The weakest? Shit! Shit, shit shit!*

The room suddenly lit up as headlights stabbed in through the glass doors. Now at least we could see, a little. I looked around for anyone I'd missed....

"Adele!" I yelled. "Take over!"

She took over bagging my patient. I ran over to the man I'd seen hunched in the corner, his arms behind his back. I grabbed his shirt and hauled him to his feet. Seth blinked as the headlights lit up his face.

"You went to medical school, right?" I asked.

He eyed me doubtfully and then sullenly nodded and dropped

his eyes. The poor kid was being eaten up by guilt over what had happened.

I knew what that was like.

I saw Lloyd running past, handing out flashlights. "Hey! I need you to take the cuffs off this guy," I told him.

Lloyd saw who I was pointing at and blanched. "No! Are you kidding?"

"I need him!"

"He's in custody! He could run! He could get a weapon!"

I heard the continuous tone as another ventilator failed. Lina started bagging, counting in German under her breath. "Do it!" I snapped.

Lloyd uncuffed Seth, cursing under his breath.

"Now you can run," I told Seth. "You can go back to your dad. Or you can stay here and help us save lives." I heard another ventilator failing. "But you make a choice, right now, about what you want your life to be."

I didn't wait to see what happened, just grabbed Lloyd by the shoulder and ran with him back to the critical patients. I took my patient back from Adele and she took the one whose ventilator had just failed. But I could hear another one failing. And when I checked, it was Rebecca's....

Seth marched up out of the darkness and silently started bagging Rebecca. As he squeezed the bag, he locked eyes with Taylor. They held the gaze for a long moment before they looked away. He wasn't forgiven. Not even close.

But it was a start.

More and more of the ventilators failed. I only barely had time to talk Lloyd through what to do before he had to jump in, too. And then we were all occupied. The nine of us were all that was keeping nine people alive. We couldn't do it forever. Rebecca's fragile body couldn't take it - it needed the smooth, gentle rhythm of a ventilator.

Beckett, where are you?

50

AMY

I WAS PANTING, my lungs sucking down big, shuddering gasps of freezing air as I pounded down the stairs to the basement. *What if this doesn't work?* Rebecca and Krista and all the others were relying on me.

It was inky black in the stairwell. All I could see was the few steps in front of me, lit up by the bouncing, twitching cone of my cell phone's flashlight. Then I crashed through the door into the basement, coughing as the stink of burnt diesel hit me.

I sprinted through the parking garage to my car, jumped in and mashed the start button. *What if it doesn't start? What if I forgot to—*

The car came silently to life, headlights blindingly bright after all the darkness. I pushed the pedal to the floor and screeched up the ramp and into the open air. It had started snowing again and with no streetlights all I could see was darkness and whirling flakes. I didn't dare slow down: momentum was the only thing keeping the little car plowing through the bumper-deep snow. I had to guess where the street was and pray no pedestrians loomed out of the blizzard.

Come on, come on! In my mind, I could see Corrigan desperately trying to keep everyone alive. I couldn't see a thing. I had to drive by pure memory as I headed for the front of the hospital. *Right* at the

corner. About *that* far and *right* again and then *right* a final time about
here—

I misjudged it. I wound up driving at a patch of wall about six feet
to the right of the hospital's main doors. I wrenched the wheel and
felt the steering go light. The wheels slid on hard-packed snow and
the car pirouetted like an ice skater, heading straight for the concrete
wall at forty miles an hour. I wrenched the wheel the other way.
Please, please—

The car reluctantly straightened out and I got it heading towards
the doors. Two police cars were parked outside, shining their
headlights inside, and I shot between them. I stared at the sliding
glass doors, willing them to open. They were made to cope with
speeding gurneys so they should activate in time. But ten feet from
them, they were still firmly closed. Six feet. Four—

There's no power. Shit!

I screamed as the car crashed through the doors, safety glass
showering down all around me. But I was in. The car sped through
the ER, tires fighting for grip on the tiles. Everyone had looked round
at the crash of glass and most people had jumped aside but a few
patients were still standing right in my path, mouths open in shock. I
slammed my palm on the horn. *"Get out of the way!"* I yelled
desperately.

They scattered and I raced along the hallway. *Thank God this
thing is so small.* I clipped a supply trolley and it went flying, then
scraped a bed that was sticking out, but I kept my foot down, focused
on the frantic group of people gathered around the critical care
beds.

I screeched to a stop, groped for the button that released the
hood, and jumped out. Maggie, being Maggie, had figured out my
plan as soon as she saw my car. She grabbed the power cables from
the ventilators and started splicing them into the batteries that
powered my car.

I rushed over to the beds, staggering a little because my legs
suddenly didn't want to hold me up. I was still shaken from the skid, I
guess, and the exhaustion was hitting, too, but I had to help. Every

one of the ventilators was dark and silent and nine people were bagging patients in unison.

It was tempting to make straight for Rebecca but the guy bagging her, his back turned to me, looked like he knew what he was doing. I gently took over from a woman with a bandaged head and she slumped into a chair, relieved. As I squeezed the bag, my eyes met Corrigan's and the worry and affection in his gaze made all the exhaustion and shock melt away. He looked at me like I was the single reason he got up in the morning, the center of his whole world. Deep, tender care, that burning lust and a hint of caveman anger that made me feel warm and protected. *What did you think you were doing, running off like that?*

I held his gaze as we worked away, all nine of us in the same desperate rhythm. Everyone was tired, but no one was quitting. *Come on, come on—*

Suddenly, the ventilator next to me came to life, bathing my face in its glow. All of them lit up, the ER filling with the sound of slow, mechanical hissing. We staggered back from our patients, hands aching. Maggie straightened up from my car, grinning in relief.

"There should be enough power to keep them going for hours," I told the group, shocked at how tired I sounded. Then I blushed. "I, um... keep it fully charged."

Corrigan grabbed my waist and lifted me off my feet, crushing me against his chest. "Of course you do, Beckett," he told me. I could feel him ruefully shaking his head. "God, I love you."

A hot wave of emotion rippled down my body, hearing that, and I tightened my arms around his shoulders. God, I was ready to drop. I had no idea what time it was, only that it was late. Between the bank robbery and then Rebecca's surgery and then the hospital shooting and then Krista and the fire and then this, I hadn't stopped in about fourteen hours. Waking up in Corrigan's bed felt like a lifetime ago.

But now, finally, we could stop. I disentangled myself from Corrigan just long enough to join everyone else in high-fiving Maggie, and to check on Rebecca. The guy who'd been keeping her alive turned around—

Seth?! Colt's son?!

I twisted around and looked at Corrigan, but he just gave me a solemn nod. I bit my lip, then turned back to Seth. He wouldn't meet my eyes. I hesitated. After everything Seth's dad had done....

But Corrigan had trusted me, with my crazy plan. I had to trust his judgment too. I checked on Rebecca and her vitals looked strong. "You did great," I told Seth. And I meant it.

Seth nodded quickly. He still wouldn't meet my eyes, but I saw his shoulders drop in relief.

"Let's all just take a minute." Corrigan had raised his voice so that everyone in the ER could hear, that gorgeous Irish bass filling the room in a way mine never could. All of the volunteers nodded gratefully and stepped away from their patients, Seth included. I stayed where I was but let my head hang down and my eyes close. Corrigan was right: we deserved a moment's rest. We had plenty of time now to get a new generator back here to power the hospital. Everyone had made it through alive. We'd *won.*

Corrigan's big, warm hands closed on my shoulders and started massaging them. It was just about the best thing I'd felt in my life. I hadn't realized how much the hours of surgery had wrecked my back but under his strong fingers, my muscles turned from freezing, brittle concrete into warm taffy. I leaned back against his chest. A freezing wind was blowing through the ER from the smashed doors, chilling my front, but as long as I could snuggle back against him, I didn't care. "What do you say," he asked in a deep, Irish rasp, "to a cup of just-warm, six-hour-old coffee from the break room?"

"I would pay a thousand dollars for that, right now," I told him, my eyes still closed.

He leaned closer and his lips brushed the back of my neck. "I'll be right back," he told me. As his footsteps died away, the cold hit me. Thanks to me destroying the main doors, the ER was going from chilly to absolutely freezing: it was already so cold, I could see my breath. When Corrigan came back, I was going to cuddle into his chest and never move again.

I took a long, slow breath and let it out. The ER was strangely quiet, now that all the ventilator alarms had gone quiet. The volunteers had all moved with Corrigan down towards the break room and were swapping stories and laughing, high on adrenaline. I thought about joining them, but I didn't want to leave Rebecca. And, if I was honest, staying in this quiet little corner, away from everyone else, was comforting. I'd changed a lot, in the last few days, but I was still a dormouse at heart. Maybe when Corrigan got back, we'd go over there together. *Baby steps.*

I opened my eyes.

Colt was standing right in front of me.

51

AMY

HE HAD THAT vicious-looking hunting knife in his hand and he thrust it at me warningly, the point stopping an inch from my cheek. He needn't have bothered. As soon as I'd seen him, my throat had closed up. I couldn't have screamed for help if I'd wanted to.

I was suddenly aware of how isolated I was, down at this end of the ER. With the room almost totally dark, both of us blended right into the shadows unless you were a few feet away. No wonder he'd been able to slip in unobserved, especially with everyone occupied with bagging patients. And now he could shove the knife between my ribs and no one would even know. *Why did I stay here on my own? Why didn't I cluster with the people, like a normal person?* But if I had, he would have found someone else: Lina or Adele or Corrigan, and that thought scared me even more.

"Where's my son?" That voice: freezing, rusty metal clawing at my spine.

I didn't dare even jerk my head to show him. "He's over by the break room," I whispered. Then, "He saved this girl's life. He's a hero."

"He's *soft*." He said it as if there was no worse crime. "You're going to go and get him. And my pilot, you're going to get him, too. Bring them."

I nodded. Anything. Anything to get him out of here. The FBI would catch them eventually. I turned to go.

"*Wait.*" His voice was vicious and stinging, a whip soaked in whiskey.

I froze.

"Get your medical stuff. Need you to patch me up." He stepped a little closer and nodded downwards. I used the flashlight on my phone and caught my breath when I saw the blood soaking through his jeans.

I thought fast. If anyone saw he was here, it might turn into another firefight and more people would get hurt. The idea of being alone with him terrified me but... "I'll take you upstairs," I whispered. "Somewhere quiet, I can treat you there."

But he shook his head. "You can do it at our camp. You're coming with us."

My insides turned to ice. That happy, warm moment with Corrigan, our plans for the future...I felt it all being ripped away from me. I'd seen how little this man valued life. If I went with him, I was dead.

My plan to get him out of there without anyone knowing evaporated. I had to get help. I nodded to Colt that I'd do it. *As soon as I'm away from him, I'll get Corrigan and the cops....*

Then I froze inside as Colt put the knife to Rebecca's throat.

"You care about this one, don't you?" he said. "You tell anyone, I see a cop or that Irishman or *anyone,* she never wakes up."

I stared down at Rebecca's sleeping face. I'd stopped breathing. *Oh Jesus....* As soon as I'd treated him, he'd kill me.

But I had no choice. I nodded that I understood.

52

AMY

I DIDN'T WANT to see Corrigan. I was already so scared...if I saw him, it would be impossible to go through with this. And I had to, for Rebecca. So I sidled around the edge of the ER, staying in the shadows.

I found the pilot, bandages still covering his eyes. I had one of the cops uncuff him, telling him I needed to run a test, then led him off to a quiet spot. When I whispered Colt's plan in his ear, he went pale: God, he was as scared of Colt as I was. But he grimly nodded.

Seth was next. I sidled closer to the group of volunteers, trying to attract his attention without—

"*There* you are!"

My heart nearly stopped. Corrigan came up behind me, his warm chest against my back, and pressed a cup of coffee into my numb hand. "Drink that, you'll feel better."

I nodded silently and sipped some, not even tasting it. God, this was even harder than I'd thought. My whole body was screaming at me to tell him Colt was there. I didn't even have to say anything. All I had to do was turn around: as soon as he saw my face, he'd know something was wrong.

But then what? Rebecca would be dead. And if Corrigan ran in to try and save her, very probably he'd die, too.

Corrigan put his hands on my shoulders, trying to turn me around so he could kiss me....

I stepped away, stumbling out of his grip. "Got to go," I muttered. "Some stuff I need to take care of."

I could hear the confusion and hurt in his voice. "What...? Beckett?"

But at that second, the beep of a heart monitor stuttered and fell into a continuous tone. *Shit!* It was Earl: his heart had stopped. Corrigan and the other doctors rushed to help. Maggie gave a moan of horror and ran to Earl's side. I took a step forward to join them, then hung back. He had plenty of help... and this was my chance. No one was watching me.

I grabbed Seth. His eyes went wide as I whispered in his ear. I saw the emotions play over his face: shock, guilt, hurt. He glanced at Taylor, but she was occupied with Earl. He nodded and went to wait by the pilot.

I quickly ran to the supply closet and filled a bag. The floor was still red with Krista's blood and my stomach twisted: I was going off with the man who'd done this. But I had no choice.

I ran back through the ER. I'd almost made it to the safety of the darkness when Corrigan's voice brought me up short. "*Beckett!*"

I slowly turned around. I couldn't let him know.

Corrigan was in the middle of a flurry of activity. They were desperately trying to get Earl's heart going again and it killed me that I couldn't be in there with them, helping. From what I could see, Corrigan was putting pressure on a bleeder: he couldn't move. One of our repairs from earlier must have given way. "What's going on?" he demanded.

My mouth opened, but nothing came out. *This is the last time I'm ever going to see him. The very last time.* As soon as that thought hit, there was no chance of brazening my way through. I saw his face change: he could see something was horribly wrong. All I could do now was run, and get Colt out of there before he hurt Rebecca. But my feet wouldn't move.

"*Beckett,*" he said again. Then. "Amy?"

I silently shook my head. I didn't dare get close enough to kiss him because he might grab me and not let go. I mouthed *I love you.*

And then I ran. I grabbed the pilot and Seth as I passed them and we raced to Rebecca's bed. Colt put his knife away as we approached and nodded for us to follow him. In seconds, we were at the rear door. Outside, a pickup was waiting.

"I'm not coming," said Seth. "I want out."

Colt spun and stared at his son disbelievingly. Then he grabbed the front of his shirt and slammed him up against the wall, speaking in a low, dangerous voice I couldn't hear. At first, Seth twisted away, not wanting to listen. But then his face went pale and he stopped struggling. *What? What's he told him?*

Colt finally stepped back. Seth stared at him for a few seconds more, still aghast, then nodded. "I've got to get someone," he told his dad.

"Get in the damn pickup!" snapped Colt, pointing at the door.

But Seth squared his shoulders and lifted his chin. "No!"

Colt moved closer and the two of them faced off. But for the first time, Seth looked just as determined as his dad. "I'm not leaving without her," Seth said quietly. "I'll meet you at the camp."

They stared at each other. Seconds passed...and it was Colt who finally looked away. "Be quick," he told his son. Then he grabbed me and pulled me towards the door.

53

DOMINIC

"**P**RESSURE'S dropping," said Adele, her voice tight with panic. We had Taylor doing chest compressions to try to get Earl's heart going again. Maggie was frantically trying to wire up the defibrillator to Beckett's car so that it would charge. Lina was giving him a dose of epinephrine. And I'd got my fingers tight around the artery that had torn open. "Hang another two units," I ordered.

I looked desperately towards the darkness where I'd last seen Beckett. *What the hell is going on?* All I knew was, something was wrong. I needed to go after her, but if I took my hands away, Earl was dead for sure. *She wouldn't want that. She'd tell me not to.* But with every second that passed, I could feel her slipping away from me. It was Chicago, all over again. She was in danger and I was stuck here working—

I saw Bartell approaching with an armful of supplies. "I need you to take over!" I yelled. "I have to go!"

He looked at me in shock, then frowned. *Shit.* I didn't have time to argue with him, or explain—

Then he saw my expression and his face softened. "Go," he told me. He snapped on some gloves and took my place. "I got this."

I slapped him on the arm in thanks and ran. *Where the hell is she? I* ran through the darkened hallways, yelling her name. When she didn't answer, I got *really* scared.

Then I felt the wind. Since Beckett had smashed through the main doors, the temperature had dropped and dropped as freezing air surged in from outside. But now there seemed to be an actual current: the wind was blowing in through the front of the ER and out—

I jogged around a corner and saw the open rear door. Raced outside yelling Beckett's name....

It was snowing thick and fast. There was only one vehicle moving, a pickup speeding away from the hospital. And inside, twisting around to look back at me as they heard me yell...Colt and Beckett.

"No!" I called uselessly. I ran after them—

But it was too late. Their taillights disappeared into the blizzard... and they were gone.

54

AMY

FOUR MEN were waiting for us at the camp. They were all carrying guns and that was scary, but what was truly terrifying was the way they reacted when they saw Colt. They snapped to attention, but it wasn't with that look of fierce pride I'd seen in soldiers. And when they ran forward to meet us, it wasn't with the eagerness and smiles of cultists greeting their leader. They were meek and grim.

They were *scared.* Many of them were bigger than Colt, younger, with more muscle. But every man in that camp was terrified of him, of what he might do to them. That was the power Colt wielded. And now he had fifty million dollars to build his army. Soon, he'd have a thousand times the manpower.

And then it got worse.

Colt led me over to a van, its rear doors standing open. The man who'd been inside scrambled out and stood to attention. "All ready, sir," he said.

Inside the van, I could see a tangle of colored wires and then a solid wall of crates, filling almost all the space. I couldn't figure out what they were until Colt shone a flashlight inside. Then I saw the hazard warning symbol stamped on each one: *explosives.* The ones they'd stolen from the mining company. My mind shredded. Clearly, they were preparing to blow something up, but what? There were no government buildings in our tiny town. Were they going to drive into Denver and blow up an FBI office or something? *How can I warn them?*

"Get going," Colt told the man. "Once you get there, set the timer for thirty minutes and get back here. We'll be ready to go."

The man nodded, jumped in the van and sped off through the snow. A pickup followed close behind: to bring the man back, I realized. But where the hell were they going? The road they were on didn't lead to Denver, it climbed up to....

I slowly looked up. Through the falling snow, I could just catch glimpses of Mount Mercy as it towered over the town.

Everything reversed in my head. Corrigan, Earl and I... we'd all put *explosives* together with *far-right militia* and assumed they were going to blow up a building. But we'd been wrong all along. I knew now why Colt's gang hadn't bothered to wear masks. The phone lines had been down since before the robbery. No one outside the town knew his gang was even here. And now, no one ever would.

Colt was going to blow up the side of the mountain and bury the town under millions of tons of rock. Everyone who knew he'd been here would die. When the snow melted, the authorities would discover what looked like a terrible natural disaster: a small town swallowed up by a landslide that had been feared for hundreds of years. My mind reeled. *No one would even know the money was missing!* How long would it take to excavate the town, let alone dig down to the vault beneath the bank? Years? The authorities might not even bother, once it was clear there were no survivors. The government would assume its gold was still there under the debris and leave it be.

Colt would be free to build his army. No one would be looking for him, or keeping an eye on the CGF. Not until it was far too late.

I felt his gaze on me as I figured it out. I couldn't stop myself twisting around to stare at him in horror and he gazed back at me steadily, eyes utterly cold. I'd been right: he was going to kill me as soon as I'd patched him up. No way he'd leave a witness alive, after all that effort. But that thought was tiny, insignificant. I was one person. He was going to murder everyone in town. Rebecca. Krista. Adele. Lina. Corrigan. All the patients, all the townsfolk. Every one of them, wiped out.

And there was nothing I could do to stop him.

55

DOMINIC

THIS IS ALL *my fault.* As I stormed back into the ER, I was panting with fear and guilt. All Beckett had ever asked was to be left alone, to stay safely in her quiet, warm OR. Like an idiot I'd dragged her out of it, and now she was *out there,* somewhere in the freezing darkness, with a psycho who'd kill her in a heartbeat.

Bartell and the others had gotten Earl's heart going again. That was good, but I needed to find Beckett, *now.* I was going out of my mind and I had no idea where to even start looking.

Wait: *Seth.* Seth might know where his father was holed up. I frantically searched the darkened ER for him, then heard his voice coming from Exam One. I grabbed the curtain to wrench it aside, but froze when his words sank in.

"I know this is crazy." Seth's voice was a mirror of his dad's, deep, but mellow, full of emotion where Colt's was starkly bare. "I know I don't know you well. Hardly know you at all. I know you got no reason to trust me, after what my dad did." He took a deep breath, as if trying to keep his voice level, but I could hear the fear. "But you gotta come with me. *Right now.* Or you're going to die."

A soft moan of dread. *Taylor.* "Are they coming back here?"

"No. No, they're gone, for good, but—Look, Bethany, there's no time. We've got to go, *right now.*" The terror in his voice cut me to the bone. I recognized it because I felt it myself. He was worried about Taylor the way I was worried about Beckett. But why? Taylor was safe in the hospital.

I needed answers. I jerked the curtain aside. Seth was standing there with his hands on Taylor's shoulders, both of them looking up in shock as I appeared.

"Your dad has Beckett," I told Seth. "Where are they? And what the hell's going on? What's going to happen?"

Seth took a quick, ragged breath, grabbed Taylor's hand and pulled her towards the hallway. "I'll tell you," he said. "But after we're safe."

But Taylor snatched her hand back. "No! Tell us what's going on!" She looked around at the ER. "Is this place in danger?"

"Bethany, *please!* There's no time!" Seth was sweating, now, his face pale.

"No! Tell us!"

Seth hissed in a frustrated breath and ran his hands through his hair. For a second he was silent, his eyes flicking between us, judging our expressions. But we just stared back at him, resolute.

"My dad is going to bring down the side of the mountain," he said in a rush. "He's going to bury the town."

"*What?*" Even though there were several walls between me and it, I automatically looked up towards the mountain and the dark mass of rock poised over the town.

"I didn't know!" said Seth. "I *swear!* I only knew about the robbery and—I didn't think people would get hurt." He grabbed Taylor's hand again. "We've got to go, *now!*"

Taylor was still trying to take it in, her eyes huge and scared. "What? No! We've got to warn everyone! Evacuate the town!"

"There's no time! But if we go now, we can make it. Bethany, *please!*" Seth pulled her closer and, when she didn't start walking, he hooked a hand around her waist and dragged her along.

She shook her head and struggled out of his grip. "No! I'm not leaving everyone to die! There must be something we can do!"

Seth closed his eyes for a second and I could tell he was silently cursing. *This* is why he hadn't wanted to tell her.

There were tears in Taylor's eyes. "You were going to just get me out of town and—and not *tell* me and—"

"I just wanted to save you!" yelled Seth.

She shook her head. "I never would have forgiven you."

He stared back at her, his jaw set... and nodded. He could have lived with that... as long as she was safe.

Taylor bit her lip, blinked back tears and looked away. "There must be some safe place," she croaked. "If we got everyone out of town...."

"I keep telling you, there's no time!" said Seth. "If we marched everyone up the road towards Denver, way up into the hills, *maybe* we'd be safe there, but that would take hours."

I shook my head. "Most of the patients couldn't manage the journey. And even if they could, what then? They're in the hills in a blizzard with no shelter. The only way to save them is to stop your dad." I grabbed Seth's shoulders and made him look at me. "Can you tell me where he is?"

Seth nodded weakly. "In a camp in the hills. I was meant to meet him there." He gave me directions, then gave Bethany one last, pleading look.

She shook her head. "I'm staying here. The patients need me."

Seth gave a single, solemn nod. Then he put his hand on her cheek, pushing her hair back from her face. "Then I'm staying, too."

Taylor looked up at him, blinked back fresh tears, and I saw her melt.

And then I was off and running, thanking God I'd brought my pickup back from the forest. *I'm coming, Beckett. I'm coming.*

56

AMY

THE HELICOPTER was hidden in a clearing not far from the camp, camouflaged with branches and netting. As Colt's men loaded their guns and supplies, I carefully stripped the bandages away from the pilot's eyes. And then I did something that made my guts twist with guilt: I prayed that he'd been permanently blinded. If he couldn't fly, Colt was stuck here in town and he'd have to call off the plan....

The pilot gingerly opened his eyes. Blinked. Nodded. *Shit.*

"Not perfect," he muttered. "But I can get us out of here and set us down in Denver."

"Good enough," said Colt. "Let's load the gold. We can go as soon as Tucker and Reynolds get back from setting the bomb."

He stood and picked up a bag, grunting with the weight. And then he suddenly slumped forward, going down on one knee. When his men helped him up, there was a fresh scarlet stain on the snow.

"I need to operate on you," I told him.

"You can do it when we get there," he grunted. He tried to pick up the bag of gold again, but went pale and wavered, leaning on the pilot for support.

"You won't make it," I said. My heart was hammering. I wasn't lying, but just talking to him scared the hell out of me. I'd seen how unstable he was, how quickly he could turn to violence. It would be safer just to get in the helicopter with him: if he died on the way, I'd still be safely away from the landslide and maybe I could talk his men into letting me live. But everyone else would be dead. I had to convince him to delay things. I didn't have any plan beyond that: I just had to hope Corrigan was looking for me. "You've already lost too much blood. The exertion's making it worse. Another few minutes and your vitals will crash. I need to stop the bleeding *now.*"

Colt turned and gave me the full force of his glare. It was like falling into a pit so deep and dark you'd never be able to climb out of it. You found yourself searching desperately for some shred of compassion and there was absolutely none. All I was to him was a tool, something to fix his injuries so he could go on with his plan. And he was challenging me, willing me to back down, to say the surgery could wait,...

A week ago, I would have buckled, climbed into the helicopter with him and wept while everything I knew and loved was wiped off the face of the earth. Now... I took a deep breath and stared right back at him. "I need to stop the bleeding," I repeated. "*Now.*"

He held my gaze for another breathless second... then he pulled a radio from his belt and thumbed a button. "Change of plan," he said into the microphone. "Set the timer for an hour." Then he lay down in front of one of the pickups so that its headlights lit up his leg.

"*Here?!*" I shook my head. "Let me take you into town, we can find a building, a bed—"

"Here," Colt told me. "Or not at all."

I knelt beside him, heart hammering. The pilot climbed into the helicopter and started doing his pre-flight checks. The other two men took up positions around Colt, ready to kill me if I tried anything. The wind whipped the falling snow against my face and it was so cold, my hands were shaking. *This is insane.* I searched through the bag I'd brought and pulled out a needle.

"No needles," growled Colt.

"You need anesthetic."

"No! You think I'm letting you dose me with something? Knock me out?"

"This isn't a cowboy movie!" I snapped. The fear was making me lose it. "You can't just lie there and grit your teeth! If you thrash around, I could nick another artery and you could bleed out!"

Colt's lips drew back in a snarl. He pulled something from his belt, too fast to follow—

I went silent and meek in a heartbeat. The gun's barrel wavered and twitched an inch from my forehead. *Oh God, oh God*—

"Get to work," he said. "And you better hope you got steady hands."

57

DOMINIC

THE PICKUP slewed around the bend, wheels clawing for grip. The fresh snow, on top of the hard-packed, frozen stuff, combined to make the roads like ice. Driving this fast was insane, but I couldn't slow down. Any minute, I expected to hear the thunder of explosions that would mean the end for the town. Colt would be gone and Beckett with him. And once she'd outlived her usefulness, I knew what he'd do to her.

I skidded around the next corner. I was up in the hills, now, and climbing fast, a steep drop to my right. Another few minutes and I'd be at the camp.

As I came around the next bend, I turned the wheel... and nothing happened. The steering went light and the pickup just coasted on in a straight line... right towards the drop.

Shit! I hadn't put my safety belt on. I grabbed for it. Missed.

I bounced completely out of my seat as we went over the edge. The whole car dropped out from under me and then crashed up into me again, jolting my neck and slamming my teeth together so hard I felt one of them crack. We tobogganed down the hill doing sixty, bouncing off rocks. The brakes did nothing: the wheels were clogged with snow. I scrabbled again for my safety belt and prayed we didn't roll over.

The world outside was moving so fast, I could barely focus on it, but I glimpsed dark shapes rushing up in front of me that must be trees. *Fuck, fuck!* I wrenched the safety belt across me—too hard, it jerked to a stop and wouldn't move. I heard twigs snap and scrape as the car plunged into the forest. Ahead, what looked like a *really big* tree was coming up.

I closed my eyes. Forced myself to let the safety belt relax... then pulled it slowly across my chest and locked it in.

I expected a crunch but it was more of a bang, an explosion of metal slamming into wood. I heard glass shatter....

And then nothing.

58

AMY

I T WAS impossible.

Colt had rushed me out of the hospital in my scrubs and the bitter wind cut straight through the thin fabric, clawing away my body heat. My head throbbed and ached from the cold and my hands were numb and clumsy. Snow kept blowing into my eyes, blinding me, and the headlights weren't anything like the overhead lights in an operating theater. Half of the wound was in deep shadow and every time I glanced up, I was dazzled.

I'd cut away Colt's jeans and opened up the wound, but the more I saw, the worse it looked. The bullet that hit him must have hit something else first because it had dug into his leg in two separate pieces, lodging deep inside. Every time I tried to move the closer one, Colt cursed in pain and the gun barrel against my forehead twitched. I couldn't even see the other piece, yet.

I took a deep breath and shut everything out, drawing on all the focus the ER had taught me. I imagined Krista was still okay, joking and teasing and passing me my instruments as Brahms played in the background. I imagined Corrigan's warm hand on my back, chasing away the cold, telling me I could do it. And slowly, very slowly, I started to make progress, easing the bullet fragment millimeter by millimeter towards the surface. Finally, I had it where I could reach in and grab it with the forceps—

Colt gave a howl of pain and bucked, his leg jerking so hard his foot caught me in the ribs. There was a bang that seemed to split the forest in two and I felt searing pain down one side of my face. I fell backwards, winding up on my ass in the snow.

Colt lay there glaring at me, hissing between his teeth. I put my hand to my scalp and slowly explored.

I'd brushed a nerve with the forceps. Colt had jerked and the gun had gone off. If I hadn't been knocked to one side by him kicking me, the bullet would have killed me. As it was, it had missed me by a few inches, so close the muzzle flash had scorched my hair.

"Get back to it," grated Colt.

I struggled forward onto my knees. But when I looked down at his leg, my insides turned to ice water.

When his leg had moved, the muscles had spasmed and pulled the bullet fragment even deeper inside, undoing all my work. Worse, the bleeding had sped up. A stain was flowering around him in the snow, pale pink at the edges, vivid red closer in. Every inch it expanded was more precious blood gone.

"What's wrong?" Colt rasped.

I started working again, the barrel of the gun pressed against my temple. But I already knew it was useless. There was too much to fix and not enough time.

Colt was going to die. And as soon as he realized that, he'd kill me.

59

DOMINIC

I OPENED MY EYES. The first thing I saw was the gnarled trunk of a huge tree, lit by the flickering light of the pickup's one remaining headlight. It was closer than should have been possible.

The pickup had smashed into the tree so hard, the front of the car had almost wrapped around it. The tree trunk was about where the windshield wipers should have been. I would have slammed headfirst into it if the safety belt hadn't stopped me. I was dusted with broken glass and I had a broken tooth but otherwise, I was okay.

The damage was so bad, the doors were jammed shut so I had to climb out through a window. I looked up at the hill. The road was barely visible, high above me. The slope between me and it looked damn near vertical...and I was going to have to climb it on foot.

I started climbing. With each step, my feet sank knee-deep into the snow. My scrubs were soaked in seconds, snow clinging to me through the thin fabric and sending a deep chill into my bones. It was too steep to walk so I went on all fours, shoving my hands deep into the drifts to grab at the grass and tree roots beneath them. I wasn't wearing gloves and my hands went steadily numb. Then the pain started, a burning, prickling agony. Closing my fingers on a root felt like grabbing a hot pipe. And the road didn't seem to be getting any closer.

I gritted my teeth and pushed on, hauling myself up the hill a foot at a time. My legs screamed, the muscles forced beyond exhaustion. The pain in my hands turned white-hot and I knew frostbite must be close.

It took everything I had. By the time I finally hauled myself over the edge and rolled onto the road, I was heaving for breath and soaked with sweat. As I lay there, the vicious wind lashed my body, chilling me in an instant and leaving me shaking so hard, I wasn't sure I could stand. The moon had gone behind a cloud and, with no flashlight, it was almost totally black. Would I even be able to find the camp?

A deep tiredness hit me: hypothermia setting in. My body felt like lead and the frozen road I was lying on was like a feather mattress. All I wanted to do was go to sleep.

But then I thought of her. Of silky, copper hair and milky skin. Of the way she looked when she was scared. She was scared *right now.* She needed me.

I took a deep, ragged breath and pushed one hand into the road to lever me up, knowing how much it would hurt. I screamed loud enough to shake the trees, white fire blazing up my wrists and arms, but I was up onto my knees and the pain had chased away the tiredness. I got a foot under me and heaved myself up to standing, staggering a little.

Far off in the distance, I could see a glow that might be headlights. I turned towards it. And started to run.

60

AMY

"WHAT'S wrong?" asked Colt.

I shook my head, but there were too many clues, he was going to figure it out. The red stain had spread, its fingers almost brushing the trees. He must be feeling light-headed from blood loss, by now. And I knew he could see my tears, frozen into shining trails on my cheeks. Every time I tried to grab the bullet fragment, I just pushed it deeper, causing more bleeding that I had to frantically work to stop. There was just too much to do: I didn't have enough hands.

Colt grabbed the leg of one of his men as he walked past. "If I don't make it," he slurred, "kill her. Take the gold, blow the mountain and get out."

No. No no no. I worked frantically, no longer caring if I caused pain. Colt grunted and the gun barrel scraped painfully against my head, his finger tight on the trigger. But if I didn't save him, I was dead anyway. I could see the bullet fragment gleaming, in amongst the red and pink. Another minute and maybe—

"Take care of my son," Colt told his men.

And he died.

61

DOMINIC

A S I STAGGERED out of the trees, I saw Beckett on her knees next to Colt's motionless body. One of Colt's men pulled the gun from Colt's limp fingers.

He made the mistake of pointing it at the woman I loved.

I ran forward, bellowing in rage. The guy spun in shock and tried to bring the gun around, but it was too late. When my fist connected with his jaw, it felt like every nerve ending in my hand was being plunged into lava. But it worked. He went down and the gun went flying. But the other one swung his rifle towards me—

"*Wait!*" screamed Beckett. "I can still save him!"

We all turned to look at her. She was frantically scrabbling in a bag, pulling out a portable defibrillator. "I can save him," she repeated. She looked at me. "But I need his help!"

Colt's men looked at each other. There didn't seem to be a second-in-command. Colt was probably too distrusting to allow one. So with their leader gone, they didn't know what to do. At last, the man with the assault rifle waved me towards Beckett.

All I wanted to do was throw my arms around her and pull her close. But our only chance of making it out of this alive now hung on whether we could save Colt. I raced to Beckett's side. "How long has he been down?" I asked.

"Not long." She ripped open Colt's shirt and started fixing the defibrillator pads. "Get a shot of epi!"

Gritting my teeth, I managed to clamp my frozen fingers around the little bottle and fill a syringe.

"*Clear!*" yelled Beckett.

Colt's body jerked as the electricity slammed through him. As soon as he went limp, I gave him the whole dose of epinephrine. Beckett felt Colt's neck....

"Got a pulse," she said breathlessly. "We have to stop the bleeding, fast. I'm going to open up his leg while he's out and try to find the bleeders. There are two bullet fragments in there, too."

She grabbed a scalpel and started cutting. Colt's men cursed under their breath as she opened him up. But it was the only way to save him. Now that his heart was going again, the blood was pulsing out of him: we only had minutes.

But this was Beckett. Surgery was what she *did.*

Despite the cold and the pressure, she dropped into one of those Zen states of focus, the sort I knew I could never manage. Her hands were quick and precise, separating the tissue, finding the bleeders. My hands were still numb but I managed to clamp each one as she found it.

Every so often, she'd lean her shoulder to the left so that it pressed up against mine. Reassuring herself that I was still there. Neither of us had a hand free to touch and there was no time to kiss or even look at each other. But I pressed back against her each time she did it. *Yes. I'm here.* And she'd nod to herself and work on.

I passed her instruments as she needed them. Whenever my hands were free, I massaged the blood back into them. It hurt like hell, but they slowly began to come back to life. Beckett dug out the first bullet fragment, then the second. She sutured the final artery and we were done. She closed him up, bandaged the leg and we fell back on our asses in the snow, panting with relief. "He's okay," she told the men. "He'll live."

And then I grabbed her. I didn't care that we were still being held at gunpoint, didn't care about the cold air that gripping her waist made my throbbing hands scream in pain. Ever since she disappeared, I hadn't been able to breathe properly, hadn't been able to think about anything else. Now I finally had her in my arms, her softness crushed to my chest. We were still in danger but we were together and that was all I cared about. I kissed the top of her head as she nestled against me, then pushed her back, swept the hair back off her face and kissed her, hearing our joint moan of relief as our lips touched. God, she felt amazing, soft and warm in the middle of all this cold darkness. We kissed long and deep, and I felt her hot tears of relief against my cheeks.

Then the barrel of an assault rifle was thrust between us, pushing us apart. "Wake him up," one of the men told us.

Beckett shook her head. "He'll make it, but he needs to rest. He's lost too much blood—"

"*Wake him up!*" snapped the men. "I know you can give him something, adrenaline or shit like that."

Beckett and I looked at each other in horror. Beckett put her hands up to try to pacify the man. "Adrenaline could kill him," she explained. "He's too weak—"

The gun cocked. These guys were anxious and twitchy. They needed their leader back. Beckett swallowed and looked at me. *What do we do?*

I slowly nodded. We had to do it, or they'd kill us. But whether Colt woke up or not, we'd be useless to them afterwards and they'd kill us anyway. We needed a way out, quick.

The men watched Beckett closely as she filled a syringe of adrenaline. While their eyes were off me, I grabbed another syringe out of the bag and filled it with Haldol, a powerful tranquilizer, then held it in my palm so they couldn't see it.

Beckett raised her syringe. "Stand back," she told the men. "He'll come up fast."

They backed off and I backed off with them... a little too far, so that I was standing almost behind one of them. All their focus was on

Colt and making sure nothing happened to him. They weren't expecting us to attack them... I hoped. And the cockpit of the helicopter faced away from us, so the pilot wouldn't be able to see what was going on.

"One," counted Beckett, aiming the syringe. I heard one of the men hold his breath. "Two...."

I stabbed the syringe of Haldol into one guy's neck and pushed the plunger, then punched the other one as hard as I could in the face. They crumpled at the same time. Beckett gaped in shock... then threw down her syringe and ran into my arms. We hugged each other tight and I closed my eyes, breathing in her scent. I was never going to let her go again.

But then the darkness turned red as a bright light shone through my eyelids. I opened my eyes. A car was approaching, its headlights blazing through the trees.

Beckett cursed. "That's the guys who set the bomb coming back." She stared up at me. "We have to stop it!"

How? We didn't know anything about bombs. But if we didn't stop it, the whole town was going to be wiped out. *"Fuck,"* I muttered. "You know where it is?"

"Black van," she said instantly. "It's on a timer."

The headlights were coming closer. Once those guys got there and woke up their friends, it was all over. "Come on!" I grabbed her hand, then winced: I'd forgotten how much my hands hurt. "You drive!"

We jumped into the pickup—lucky for us, when they'd turned on the headlights to light Colt's operation, they'd left the keys in the ignition. Beckett carefully backed us up, then drove around the three unconscious men in the snow. Just as the other car arrived, we roared away towards the mountain.

62

AMY

THE ROAD to the mountain was slick with ice, but I pushed our speed up to fifty: we couldn't afford to go slow. I kept doing the math in my head: how long since the bomb was set? How much time did we have left? However I worked it out, the answer kept coming out as *not enough.*

Both of us were white-faced and grimly silent. Corrigan was nursing his hands in front of the heater and, from the look on his face, they were hurting even more as they thawed..

As we came over a rise, Corrigan suddenly said, "Stop!"

I glanced across at him, disbelieving, but he was stony-faced. *"Stop!"* he said again.

I hit the brakes and we skidded to a stop in the middle of the road.

"We'd be safe here," said Corrigan. "We're high enough above the town."

I looked down at the town. He was right.

"They had supplies back at the camp," Corrigan said. "Food, shelter. By now, those guys will have woken up, taken the gold and gone. We could survive there until the roads are clear."

I stared down at the town, then looked at him and shook my head, tears in my eyes.

He took my chin in his hand. "I *want* to save them," he told me, his voice strained. "I *need* to save you."

My stomach knotted. If we turned back now, I lost everyone and everything I knew. But I'd have him. *Oh Jesus, don't make me choose....* We stared into each other's eyes, both of us fighting the same battle. And the longer we hesitated, the less time we had....

"*Fuck it,*" I snapped. "We're doctors." I stamped hard on the gas and we shot forward. Corrigan's hand covered mine on the steering wheel and gently squeezed.

63

COLT

I SAT bolt upright, sucking in air like some kid waking up from a nightmare. Tucker, the guy who'd left to set the bomb, was standing over me with a syringe. The others were clustered behind him, looking terrified. "What happened?" I snapped.

"That Irish doctor showed up," said Tucker. "They got the jump on us and took off."

"They *got the jump on you?*" I snarled. He looked at his feet. Jesus, why was everyone except me so goddamn weak? "They're going to try to defuse the bomb. We gotta go after them."

I went to get up. Everyone rushed at me, pushing me back down to the snow. "Colt, you *died,*" said Tucker. "They had to bring you back! You need to rest." He looked at the others. "Let us get you into the chopper and let's *go!* Forget the mountain. We got the gold, we *won!*"

"It needs to be perfect!" I yelled. My voice shook the trees around us and he shrank back in fear. Why were they so worried about my health? My leg hurt like hell, but other than that I felt like a lion, every vein thrumming with life and power. "I'm not having the FBI on my back for another twenty years. Everyone's got to think the gold is still there, under the rubble. And no one can know we are here. That's the only way this works!"

"Colt, we gave you adrenaline," said Tucker, starting to lose his cool. "You're all fired up, but it'll pass. You can't get into a fight, you'll die."

I grabbed his gun right out of his hand and turned it on him. "Don't tell me what I can do!" I yelled. Everyone jumped back. I struggled to my feet, using a tree to support me when my bandaged leg refused to. The rage boiled up inside me, expanding with each booming crash of my heart. *These weak sons of bitches...* "Unload the gold!"

Their eyes bugged out. "What?!" asked Tucker.

"Unload the goddamn gold!" I yelled, the gun leveled right between his eyes. "You can take one bar each. That's adequate fucking compensation, if the money's all you care about. The rest of it stays here, with me. I'll build a new militia, with men I can trust!"

They cursed and pleaded and tried to talk me round, but I just kept the gun pointing right at their heads, my face stony. They slowly unloaded the heavy bags of gold, each man taking one shining bar for himself. Then they climbed aboard the chopper and the pilot started her up.

"Colt, *please!*" Tucker leaned out of the open door and yelled over the sound of the blades. "Even if you stop them, how are you going to make it out alone? The roads are still blocked."

"I won't be alone," I told him. I looked around. "Where's Seth?"

The men all shook their heads. "He never showed, Colt."

The rage rose higher, consuming me completely. *Traitor!* I slammed the door and stepped back. Watched as the chopper took off.

That bastard Irish doctor. He'd taken everything from me: my plan, my men, now my son.

I limped over to a pickup and started it up. I only needed one good leg to drive.

He'd taken everything from me. I was going to take everything from him.

64

AMY

WE'VE BEEN *driving too long.* We were on the mountain now, right under the cliff that overhung the town, but we hadn't seen any sign of the van. What if we'd missed it? It was black, if they'd hidden it in the trees beside the road we could have driven straight past it. And any second now it would explode and the whole side of the mountain would come down on us. *Should we turn back?* But what if the van was just around the next corner? I wanted to scream just to release the tension—

There!

They'd hadn't even tried to hide it. It was just parked by the side of the road, two wheels on the pavement. I skidded to a stop beside it and we jumped down into the thick snow. We each grabbed one of the rear doors and threw them open—

I'd seen the crates and the wires back at the camp. But now they were just background: the only thing that mattered was the digital clock.

It's hard to explain what it feels like, to see something counting down the time until you die. Death is always so distant you can push it out of your mind or so sudden you don't see it coming. This was mercilessly exact, each change in the crimson digits another of our final seconds gone. Corrigan and I both stared at it, transfixed.

We had one minute and thirty-two seconds left on this earth.

One minute and thirty-one seconds.

One minute thirty.

We stepped forward, then looked at each other helplessly. Corrigan's hands were doing the same as mine: grasping at thin air, aching with the need to do something, to stop it, but afraid to touch it.

"There's got to be a way to turn it off," said Corrigan. The stress made the Irish thick in his voice. "The people who set it, if they needed to change it...."

I nodded and tried to say *right,* but it came out as a weak croak. My eyes were going everywhere, searching for something marked *off, but* it was just a jumble of wires and circuits.

Whoever had made the thing had left their tools strewn over the bottom of the van. Corrigan grabbed a pair of wire cutters, turned them over and over in his hands as he thought... then handed them to me. I looked at him in horror. *Me?!*

"You have steadier hands," he told me.

I made the mistake of looking at the clock just as the numbers slipped from 1:00 to 0:59.

I've killed us. I had no idea which wire to cut, or if that would even stop it. We should have stopped and turned back when Corrigan said. Now it was too late: even if we started driving now, we still wouldn't make it out of the path of the landslide.

What am I doing here? The panic was rising up from my chest and taking control. I couldn't breathe, my lungs moving in painful fits and starts. *This is not my world. This is not what I do.* Why had I ever left my operating theater? If I'd just stayed there, in my safe little burrow....

Your life is meant to flash before your eyes, just before you die. I saw a different one, one where I'd stayed upstairs that day.

I'd never have met Corrigan. I wouldn't have been there when Rebecca had come in, and she would have died. Without her there, I wouldn't have pressed for the ER to stay open and we would have evacuated along with everyone else. We'd never have known about Colt or his plan. When the snow melted, we would have come back to find the town wiped out by what seemed like a natural disaster. Corrigan and I would have found new jobs and gone our separate ways.

We'd both be alive.

But we'd both be alone.

A big, warm hand came to rest between my shoulder blades. "I trust you," he said. And his voice was calm. He really did.

Twenty-three seconds.

I took a deep, shuddering breath and *focused*. I told myself that wires weren't so different to arteries, really. Feeding from a heart—the battery—to a brain—the clock—with nerves running from that to the muscles—the explosives.

Eleven seconds.

The weak point, the point where the brain could be cut off without throwing out a rogue signal, would be....

I heard Corrigan draw in his breath.

Would be.....

There. I lunged forward and snipped a canary-yellow wire before I changed my mind. When I looked at the clock, the display had gone dark. I'd never know how long we'd had left. I thought about asking Corrigan and then decided I didn't want to know.

And then it hit me that it was over. We'd won. I carefully laid the wire cutters down and then didn't so much hug Corrigan as fall into him, laying my head on the top of his pec. All of the exhaustion and emotion slammed down on me at once and if he hadn't wrapped me up in his arms I think I would have slid to the floor.

He let out a huge, shaky sigh and smoothed the hair on the back of my head with his palm. I snuggled into his chest and locked my arms so tight around his back that there was no danger, *none,* that anyone would ever separate us again. A bitterly cold wind was lashing the mountain and I could feel my ears and back and feet going numb. *We should really get inside.* But neither of us moved because that strip of flesh down our fronts, where we were pressed together, was so gloriously warm, neither of us was willing to sacrifice it. We rocked there silently for long minutes. Then he gently eased my head back, cupped my cheeks in his hands and kissed me.

It was slow at first, those hard lips gentler than I'd thought him capable of. For the first time, we weren't in the middle of a crisis and it changed everything. He explored me, teased me with little flicks of his tongue against my lips, the pleasure delicate and pink, but shot through with a wicked silver promise that made me press myself hard against him. His hands slid into my hair and our mouths opened, his lips seeking and demanding, drawing me out.

My hands grabbed at his biceps, then his shoulders, reassuring myself that this was real, that we'd done it, that he was *there*. And he ran his hands protectively down my back as if he wanted to cover all of me and keep me safe from the world. It was a kiss that was full of possibilities, of hope for the future.

Corrigan gently broke the kiss. "Come on," he said. "Let's get back to the hospital and—"

Colt stepped out of the darkness. He was limping badly, the bandages on his leg soaked with blood, and his face pale and damp with sweat. But his eyes were bright with vengeful fury and he was holding a gun.

Corrigan lunged forward, hands outstretched to grab the weapon.

And Colt raised his gun and shot me in the chest.

65

AMY

A T FIRST, just disbelief. *He can't have—No, I can't be—*
Then the pain. Searing and aching, throbbing with each
heartbeat. It hurt but, weirdly, it wasn't as bad as I'd imagined getting
shot would be. It was dull, somehow. *It must not be too serious. I'll be
okay.*

"*You fucker!*" yelled Corrigan and ran at Colt. Colt stood his
ground and tried to bring the gun around, but Corrigan was a human
battering ram, smacking into him and carrying him down to the
ground. Before they'd even landed, Corrigan was smashing his fist
into Colt's face with wild-eyed rage. Corrigan would win. Colt must
be close to passing out: how was he even on his feet?

Suddenly, my legs gave way. There was no warning, they just
collapsed under me as the muscles stopped working. The fall jolted
my chest, sending sharp waves of pain radiating outward, and I was
suddenly so weak that I couldn't even use my arms to break my fall. I
tried to scream, but even my lungs needed more energy than I could
give them.

Then I saw to my horror that Colt wasn't going limp under
Corrigan's punches. He was soaking them up, snarling up at the
Irishman. *How?* He still had hold of his gun and now he was trying to

force it down to point at Corrigan's head, the sinews in his forearms standing out like cords. *How is he—Oh God, they must have given him the adrenaline!* It would likely kill him, given his injuries. But until then, he was like some barbarian in a Berserker rage, his strength dialed up to eleven.

As I watched, the gun started to inch downwards towards Corrigan's head. Corrigan was grunting, wide-eyed with disbelief at Colt's strength. He had to stop punching and use both hands and even then, the gun kept moving.

I have to help him! I was lying on my side and I tried to worm my way towards them. And then the pain hit.

The shock had been tempering it. Now it blossomed out from the wound, a slow-motion explosion that felt like it was ripping me apart. I rolled onto my back, sobbing, and clasped my hands to my chest. When I felt the hot stickiness of blood, I felt sick. The pain kept coming, doubling and then trebling. It felt as if someone had shoved a red-hot spear of iron right through me and left it there, my body slow burning and blackening as the heat spread through me.

Colt was winning. His unnatural strength was forcing the gun down, a millimeter at the time. Its barrel was twitching and sometimes the twitch took it almost to Corrigan's forehead. *No!*

Through a haze of tears, I reached out towards him with one bloodied hand.

Corrigan's eyes caught the movement and he looked at me.

And then he got mad.

I thought he'd been angry before, when he ran at Colt. But this was different. Deeper. Darker. Vengeful.

The realization felt like my body had been slid into black, icy water. *He thinks I'm going to die.*

Corrigan roared, a wordless battle cry, and shoved Colt's arms and the gun they held to the ground. I heard a bone break. And then he slammed a fist across Colt's face and Colt lay still.

Corrigan hurled the gun off into the snow and ran to me, falling to his knees by my side. The rage was turning to fear, now, his face

pale with it. "Beckett?" He grabbed my hand. God, he was so warm...
or was I cold?

He put his hands on my wound. The pain seemed to be receding.
I felt my head loll and he took my chin in his hand and made me look
at him. "*No!*" He used *that* voice, but it was thick with emotion, the
Irish heavy in it. "No, you stay with me!"

I tried to speak, but it was so hard.... I tasted blood. There
suddenly seemed to be blood everywhere: leaking hotly into the
snow beneath me and pulsing from the wound under his hands. The
edges of my vision went dark.

"No!" There were tears in his eyes and my heart wrenched. Jesus,
for him this was Chrissy all over again. "You're going to be okay,
Beckett," he snapped, pressing on the wound. "You're going to be
okay!"

I put all the strength in my body into squeezing his hand. "I am," I
rasped with unshakable certainty. "You're going to save me."

66

DOMINIC

ER EYES CLOSED. *No. Jesus no....*

I scooped her up in my arms and for a second, I just knelt there. She felt so light, so fragile, like a bird shot out of the sky. How could he do this to her? How could anyone do this to *Beckett?*

Then I jumped to my feet. Her heart was still beating. There was still hope. I looked desperately around. I couldn't save her there. I had no equipment and no way to call for help. My only chance was to get her to the ER.

I carried her to the pickup and lay her on the back seat, then jumped into the driver's seat. We'd left the engine running. My foot twitched towards the gas—

I stopped as I saw Colt's body in the rear view mirror. *Fuck!*

I couldn't leave him there. If he woke, he was crazy enough to set off the bomb. We'd all die. But Beckett needed help *now*—

Cursing, I jumped out, picked up Colt's limp body and heaved him into the back of the pickup. Then I jumped back in and floored the gas.

I took the snow-covered road at sixty and didn't slow down when I hit town. But it still wasn't fast enough. I could see her growing paler each time I glanced in the mirror. I could feel the life slipping out of her. I tried talking to her, even yelling at her, but she wouldn't wake up. I pushed the gas even harder. *Come on!*

I screeched to a halt in front of the ER, scooped Beckett into my arms and ran inside through the empty doorway. Lloyd was sweeping up the broken glass and I nodded him towards my pickup. "Colt's in the back. Get some fucking handcuffs on him."

Lloyd nodded as if that was something he'd very much enjoy, and stalked outside.

I ran deeper into the ER. In the dark, no one had seen me, yet. "I need a gurney!" I yelled. "And I need help!" Taylor, Adele and Lina all clustered around me, asking what had happened, asking who it was. They couldn't see....

And then, mercy of mercies, the lights flickered on. Maggie must have wired up the replacement generator. Everyone blinked in the sudden glare and—

"*Oh Jesus, no!*" Taylor's voice was a weak rasp as she recognized Beckett. Adele and Lina went pale. We ran to the gurney Bartell had fetched and I laid Beckett on it.

For the first time, I could get a good look at the wound. The bullet had hit her dead-center, gone straight through her and come out of her back, doing God knows what damage on the way through.

Everyone was looking at me. "Tell us what you want," prompted Bartell.

God, they expected me to be a doctor. But I couldn't—Beckett wasn't a *patient,* she was one of us, she was *mine,* she wasn't meant to be—

"Corrigan!" snapped Bartell.

I nodded. Took a deep breath. *Ah, God....* And focused.

"Two units O-neg," I snapped. "Taylor, intubate, Adele, get me her vitals."

The air buzzed with numbers, all of them bad. I could see the blood on her lips: at least one lung had been damaged. "Rib spreader," I said. "We're going to have to—"

My throat contracted. I couldn't say *open her up.* Couldn't think of her that way. This was *Beckett,* she deserved to be above all this, out of harm's way.

The others helped me cut Beckett's clothes away. When I saw the ugly wound next to the gorgeous, pale skin I loved so much, I wanted to storm outside, find Colt and finish him.

I raised the scalpel... and froze. *Ah hell.* My stomach flipped over. I knew we needed to get into her chest. I knew that. But the thought of cutting into her—

Bartell's voice was urgent, but gentler than I'd thought him capable of. "Corrigan, I can do it." He reached for the scalpel.

"No!" I snatched it away, took a deep breath... and cut. Used the rib spreader to open her chest. And then I was staring at *her,* the essence of her, the stuff we rely on every day but never think about. Her blood. Her lungs.

Her softly beating heart.

I followed the bullet's path of destruction. The room swam behind wetness and I had to blink to see. It had come in at a steep angle, missing her heart, but tearing through one lung. It had nicked her spleen and kidney and left her bleeding from more places than I could count.

"Pressure's 90 over 60 and dropping," said Adele.

"She's going to need surgery," I said. "Call upstairs and—"

Everyone around the table went silent. *And call who?* Our only surgeon was on the table. Beckett was going to die unless....

"Put a mask on me," I ordered. "And I need clamps and sutures."

"But you're not a—" began Taylor

"It's the only chance she has," I told her.

Lina tied a mask over my mouth and helped me shove my arms into a surgical gown. Adele suctioned away blood, then handed me a clamp. I stared down at Beckett, my heart pounding in my chest. *How the hell does she do this?* To me, the maze of organs and blood vessels was chaos, just like the bustle of the ER was to her.

"Heart rate's 120," Adele told me, her voice tight.

I tried to focus. To forget that it was the woman I loved, to think about *systems* and *pressure* and which artery branched where. All the anatomy I'd learned in medical school slipped through my fingers like mist. *Fuck. I can't do this.*

I looked up for a second, towards her face. She looked peaceful. She could have been sleeping in my bed.

I was the only chance for her to wake up again.

I took a deep breath and pushed everything else out of my mind. And I went to work.

67

AMY

H E WAS the first thing I saw when I opened my eyes. Two deep, soulful pools of blue gazing down at me, his brow creased with worry. "You okay?" he asked immediately.

I tried to speak, but my throat ached, as if it was bruised from the inside. That started me coughing and that *really* hurt, like my whole chest was on fire. What the hell was wrong with me?

Then I remembered.

I managed a weak nod. Considering all that, I felt fine.

Corrigan's brow slowly uncreased and he gave me a big, wide grin.

I looked down at the sheet that covered my chest. "Was it bad?"

He shook his head. "Nah."

I kept staring at him. He huffed and looked away. When he looked back at me, I pinned him with a look. *Corrigan!*

"You've been out for a full day," he said. "I had to open your chest."

I looked down at myself in disbelief.

"I had my hands right inside you," he said. "In some cultures, that would make us married."

My heart flip-flopped. That didn't sound so bad. "Did you fix me?" I asked, shocked at how weak my voice was.

He acted mock-offended. "Are you doubting me?" Then he frowned. "I mean, I wasn't sure of a few things. Had to do some guessing. A kidney might be in backwards and I think I put your spleen where your liver should be—"—I lifted a hand as if to hit him —"*Yes!* Of course I fixed you!"

I bit my lip. Of course he fixed me. Just like I'd known he would. We looked at each other for a second and then he leaned down and gave me a very careful hug.

"Krista?"

"Recovering well. Everybody's doing well. Colt's in a cell at the police station. Phone lines are still down and the roads are still blocked. But look...."

He wheeled my bed around so that I was facing the window. It was noon and, above Mount Mercy, the snow clouds had parted. For the first time in days, we could see blue sky.

EPILOGUE

Two weeks later

"Mine's bigger," I said.

"But I have *two*," said Krista. We were standing in front of the mirrors in the locker room, our scrub tops lifted to our necks. "*And* two exit wounds." She counted off her scars, turning this way and that. "*One, two, three, four.*" She grinned proudly. "I look like I've been to war."

I shook my head and let my top fall back down. Both of us were still weak and not officially back at work yet, but we hadn't wanted to miss today. Today was the day Rebecca went home.

The blizzard had been over for two weeks, but the snow was so thick, it had taken the authorities two full days to get the road to Denver re-opened. When they did, Rebecca's parents had been the first people to arrive. They'd barely left her bedside since.

To reach the elevators, we had to cross the ER. The critical care beds had gone back upstairs and the doors I'd smashed through had been replaced. Outside, I could see Maggie supervising the unloading of the new generator from the back of a truck. Earl, who was technically still on sick leave, was out there with her in his civilian clothes, holding her hand. They were inseparable and I'd never seen them happier, although Earl grumbled to me that she'd made him cut back on the donuts to look after his heart.

We had our full complement of staff back and the ER was busier than ever. But the chaos didn't freak me out, anymore. I knew I'd always prefer the calm of the OR but everyone needs a little chaos in their lives.

The elevator doors slid open in front of me and I saw blue scrubs stretched over a broad, hard chest. I looked up into blue eyes that twinkled with mischief.

"Doctor Beckett," rumbled Corrigan.

"Doctor Corrigan," I said coolly.

We stood there staring at each other, not touching, but our eyes just eating each other up. It was a game we played. We'd be completely formal and professional whenever we saw each other, letting the tension build and build and then, when we couldn't take it anymore....

"Oh, please," muttered Krista, leaning between us to hit the button. "Get a room. And I don't mean the linen closet."

I flushed down to my roots. We'd have to be quieter, next time. But then I caught Corrigan's eyes and grinned.

Upstairs, we barely got through the door to Rebecca's room before Rebecca's mom threw her arms around me. "God bless you," she said into my neck. "Thank you."

I gently patted her back. This was nothing: when she'd first arrived and seen that her daughter was okay, she'd locked me in her arms and not let me escape for nearly a minute. I didn't mind at all. The poor woman had been worried out of her mind.

The family moved towards the door. Rebecca looked up at me with big eyes and a slightly shaky lower lip. "We're coming back, right?" she asked her mom. "We can all come back here. I want to learn how to ski."

"We'll try," said her mom. Her dad ruffled her hair. Rebecca kept her eyes on me, her lower lip getting shakier by the second. I knew exactly how she felt. After everything we'd been through, I was having trouble saying goodbye, too.

That's when Corrigan bent down and handed Rebecca a clumsily gift-wrapped package. When she tore off the paper, she found an aging, much-loved bunny rabbit. Rachel's rabbit.

"To remember us by," said Corrigan. He was grinning, but the emotion was thick in his voice. "He needs a good home."

Rebecca clutched the rabbit to her chest and nodded.

Corrigan straightened up and slipped an arm around my back. He found my hand and silently knitted his fingers with mine, squeezing them hard for a moment as we watched the family walk away. When they turned the corner, he drew in a deep breath and I saw the pain in his eyes fade and clear.

We came to the window that looked out over the town. The news trucks that had swarmed the hospital when the story broke were gradually disappearing, but the town was still full of reporters and the impact of being on the national news was still being felt. After seeing how pretty the town was, tourists were flooding the place. Corrigan and I had done what felt like a hundred interviews each, telling and retelling the story to reporters from both coasts and even a few international news stations.

We'd also both been debriefed by the FBI. Colt was in their custody and they'd picked up the rest of his gang in Denver. They'd been relying on the bomb to get away without a trace. Armed with all the eyewitness reports from Mount Mercy, the FBI had identified the men and tracked them down within days. The gold had been recovered and was on its way to a new, undisclosed hiding place. Colt was going to be in prison for the rest of his life and his men were looking at very long jail terms.

All except one. Both Corrigan and I had given the FBI long and heartfelt testimonies about how Seth had saved numerous lives and given us the information we needed to stop the bomb. He'd serve some time—he'd been involved in an armed robbery, after all—but with good behavior he'd be out in five years.

And Taylor had made it clear that she'd wait for him.

Corrigan and I had decided that we needed a break from the cold and I'd told him about always wanting to go somewhere *really* hot, where the sun would warm us right down to our bones. So in a month's time, when I was fully healed, we were flying off to the Caribbean to spend two weeks aboard a yacht called the *Fortune's Reward*, soaking up the sun and learning to scuba dive.

The question was what to do when we got back. There'd been one unexpected consequence of all the media coverage: that morning, both Corrigan and I had had job offers from a hospital in New York. They had one of the busiest ERs in the country and they were looking for a doctor and a surgeon who were good in a crisis.

Corrigan caught my eye in the window's reflection. "What do you think?" he asked gently.

I looked down at the town and took a deep breath. "I think," I said slowly, "I'm happy where I am." Bartell had asked if I'd be okay with being the first surgeon on the ER call list, instead of the last, and I'd accepted. Back in my burrow, but venturing down to the ER more. That was just the right balance of order and chaos. "But what about you?" I turned to look at him, suddenly worried. "You're used to moving around. You never stay anywhere."

He shook his head. "That wasn't moving around, that was running. And I've stopped running."

"But even before all that, you were used to cities. You were in Chicago. Mount Mercy is too quiet for you." My stomach was churning, now. I was imagining a future where he got bored and restless. I wouldn't want him to be unhappy, so I'd encourage him to leave, he wouldn't want to make me unhappy by dragging me to New York so he'd tell me to stay, we'd split up—

"*Beckett.*" He said it in *that* voice, the one that made my brain stop panicking and sit up and pay attention. The one that sent a wave of heat sliding down to my groin. When he saw I was listening, he continued. "This place *is* quiet." He put those big, warm hands on my cheeks. "But you know what?"

"What?"

He ran his thumbs over my cheekbones and then slid his hands back into my hair, knocking my surgical cap to the floor. "I've kind of got a taste for quiet."

And he leaned down and kissed me.

The End

Thank you for reading. If you enjoyed *Mount Mercy,* please consider leaving a review.

You may also like *Alaska Wild.*

Mason Boone. A former Navy SEAL who lives in isolation in the Alaskan mountains. He's rugged, untamed...and gorgeous. I'm an FBI agent; he's a fugitive on his way to prison. But when our plane crashes deep in the Alaskan wilderness, Mason becomes my only hope.

To survive the cold, the wild animals and the terrain, we'll need to stay close. But every time he touches me, I melt inside. He makes me feel protected like no man ever has and the way he looks at me, as if he just wants to push me up against a tree and rip my clothes off.... Could he be innocent of his crimes and can I help him escape the demons of his past? I'm a city girl but I'll need to learn to live as wild as him...because the other prisoner from our flight and his gang are out there...and they're hunting us.

Alaska Wild is out now, in ebook, paperback and audiobook.

You can find all my books at helenanewbury.com.

Printed in Great Britain
by Amazon

44908662R00182